DARK ILLUSION

DANA V. MOISON

DARK ILLUSION
Dana V. Moison

Amazon CreateSpace
September 26, 2015

Dedicated to my dear mother, with great love. You are a true model of inspiration.

DARK
ILLUSION

PROLOGUE

April 24, 1990

She could not take it anymore. The distorted figure looked at her from every angle, from every corner. She felt her throat constrict.

She had to do something.

She slammed her body up against the walls, spinning around in ecstasy, smashing the mirrors around her, feeling fresh cuts form on her skin and drops of blood begin to spill. The pain was cathartic.

She struck her head a third time. She could no longer stand up. She fell to the floor and her eyes closed. A sense of relief washed over her, a victorious smile spreading across her face. Now she was ready to open her eyes and enjoy the sweet darkness that encompassed her. No one would ridicule her anymore. No one could see her.

CHAPTER 1

What a cliché. The most beautiful woman he had ever seen was, in fact, a real-life supermodel.

Even as a young photographer, Andy Swain was rarely dazzled by the models posing in front of his camera lens. He did not perceive himself to be one who could be blinded by appearances, but this time his eyes were uncontrollably drawn, like a magnet.

How the mighty have fallen.

Andy accepted a glass of bubbly from one of the myriad waiters shifting through the crowd. Everyone who was anyone in the fashion industry was here. He looked away but his eyes kept returning to her, again and again.

She really is something, he thought to himself. Her body was shaped like an hourglass and her facial features were striking, as if drawn by a painter. She had an enviable agelessness to her, ironically enhanced by the few tiny lines that her smile had rendered. Her eyes, a glistening deep blue, combined with her lustrous dark hair, provided a stunning contrast to her porcelain skin.

Andy had heard other photographers swear that she was, indeed, the most beautiful woman on earth. "Great legends require great exaggerations," he would reply, wryly. Now, however, a few steps away from the global icon that was Gloria McIntyre, he realized how wrong he had been.

I'm lucky I don't have my hat. Otherwise I'd be forced to eat it.

She looked bored, as if she'd rather be someplace else. She wasn't speaking with anyone. Andy moved closer, emboldened by what he knew he had to say to her.

Eventually he approached her, but found himself suddenly lost for words.

"You are just . . ." Andy let his voice linger. That was not how he wanted to make his first move. He didn't want to gush over her like one of *those* guys. He never thought he would. He wasn't the kind of man who had trouble finding the right words around beautiful women.

Well, there's a first time for everything.

". . . I mean, you are a very impressive woman indeed. I wanted to–"

"Thanks," Gloria nonchalantly interrupted him. She had heard proclamations such as this many times before.

At first she didn't notice the young man standing in front of her, but when she glanced at him again, she could hardly take her eyes off of him. He was so handsome. His golden locks drooped over his olive green eyes, and his smile was absolutely captivating.

Maybe it's worth it to let him finish talking.

Gloria took a second look. If he was invited to this party, it must mean he was from the industry, she figured. But then she would have known him already.

So who is he? she wondered. Gloria liked to know exactly with what, or with whom, she was dealing.

"Gloria," she introduced herself curtly, although she knew it wasn't necessary.

"Andy Swain," he said, offering his hand.

His hand hung in the air. When Gloria saw he didn't intend to back down, she extended her hand to meet his.

"Your name sounds familiar."

"That would be my father, Andrew Swain, Sr. He founded A&A Swain, the legal firm."

So he was a lawyer, specializing in tedious small talk no doubt. And, yet, there was something about him, something appealing. She looked into his eyes.

"A&A? Are you working for your father then?"

Andy shook his head. "No, those are our initials, my father's and mine. He wanted me to become a lawyer, to join the firm and continue his legacy. But I chose to become a photographer. And still, the name remains. Perhaps he hopes I'll change my mind but . . ." Andy shrugged and grinned.

"You gave up being a high-priced lawyer for this?" she asked, looking around.

"Not exactly," he admitted with a self-deprecating smile. "Artistic photography is my real passion," he surprised her. Andy preferred to omit the fact that in order to afford his art practice, he needed to shoot models for a living.

"Ah, so that's why you came to a fashion website promo party," she teased. "Tell me, then, what do you see as art here?"

Gloria swept a graceful hand, indicating the grand space. The entire west wall was of glass and framed the Manhattan lights, some steady, some flickering, others in motion, all overlooking the Hudson River. But even that picturesque panorama failed to inject any excitement in the dull ambience of this party. It was the same party that spun over and over again, with the same framework, tasteless food, and meaningless, often spiteful conversations that never changed.

The only thing different was Andy.

He shrugged again and laughed. "I have to admit I pulled a lot of strings to get here."

"No doubt the effort paid off," a tiny smile crept to her lips, an odd phenomenon, as she rarely felt comfortable with strangers.

"It's not so bad. I got to meet you, didn't I?"

Gloria smiled distantly and looked away.

"I actually hoped for the chance to run into you," he added.

"Me? Why?" she asked, turning her head toward the skyline.

He may be too eager, but he sure deserves some points for being bold.

"I wanted to make you a proposal." She arched an eyebrow. "I meant a job offer."

Gloria was completely surprised – perhaps even a little bit insulted – that he had only come to discuss business matters with her. She had read him all wrong.

Worshiping models just ain't what it used to be.

"I'm sure you get dozens of offers every day," Andy continued, "but I have a feeling you might be interested in this one."

Interested in another of an endless series of photography sessions, one for a magazine cover or fashion company or makeup campaign? Hardly something special or intriguing. She rolled her eyes inwardly. Why did people always think their project was any different from anyone else's, she wondered.

Where's the art he was supposedly so passionate about?

Andy sensed he was losing her interest. He *had* to make her say yes.

He was talking but she wasn't listening. Her eyes, along with her thoughts, so it seemed, had focused on a distant spot on the horizon. But then the word "art" caught her attention.

". . . an artistic project designed to arouse worldly resonance."

She shifted her gaze back to him.

And . . . she's back! Andy smiled broadly, revealing a pair of perfect-looking dimples.

"I was hired to capture the true essence of beauty. Well, not beauty, but the idea of beauty, if you see what I mean. I'm talking about an artistic shoot, not just another campaign or commercial. And that takes a lot of work, starting with finding the ideal location, designing a magical background, and finding the perfect woman; because between you and me, there is no doubt that you are the fairer sex," he smiled. "That's why I need you. Now that I've seen and met you, I know that. If you don't agree to do this with me, I'll have to back out because I won't settle for anything less than perfect; it would defeat the whole purpose. And as far as I'm concerned, there is no one more suitable for this project than you."

It wasn't just a line, Gloria thought, looking at him. He appeared earnest, the artist in him revealing a glimpse of itself.

"I would think you'd be better off choosing someone younger. After all, most people equate youth with beauty." She cut right to the chase. She wanted to test his reaction.

"Superficial ones, yes. But that's not what I'm looking for. I want a timelessness, as in real, seemingly eternal beauty," Andy grinned. "Think of fine wine that reveals its quality over time; someone younger would lack that essential maturity." He paused and looked into her eyes. "In any case, I haven't seen any woman who's got the drop on you, young or not. Therefore, I implore you to agree. Because I won't do this without you."

The flattery helped. There was something about him that won her over, for now.

"It does sound intriguing."

He clasped his hands together. "Say you'll do it!"

"Well, I don't want to take the fall for ruining your project." That rarely seen smile slipped out again.

The truth was less altruistic, Gloria admitted to herself. Andy's offer enticed her competitive drive. She was well aware that, although still in demand, increasingly younger models were nipping at her heels, threatening to make people believe that she was yesterday's news. If she was going to retain that precarious perch at the top of the modeling world, she needed something to set her apart. Being crowned and marketed as the Ideal of Beauty might just do the trick. Then, no one could top her.

"I'd need to know more," she warned. "And we'd need to discuss all the details with my business manager before I commit."

"Great!" he called, as if it were a done deal, a big smile stretching across his face. "May I have your business card?"

* * *

Gloria sat with Arthur Cohen and her lawyer on one end of the table, while Andy and his lawyer occupied the other end. They were meeting to discuss the details of the contract.

Arthur Cohen was Gloria's personal manager. She did not have an agent; she didn't like them. Gloria was not one of those models who snapped up every offer available, and she was determined to participate in every decision affecting her professional route. She was easily as much a successful businesswoman as a successful model. Gloria always got what she wanted. Five minutes with her shattered the stereotype that where beauty existed, brains failed to follow.

Gloria glanced at Arthur's profile as he chatted with her lawyer. He really had changed her life. And although she no longer needed him to guide her through meetings like this, she was grateful to have him by her side. She had been seventeen when their paths first crossed. In desperation, she had taken a job waitressing at a coffee shop. Her third day on the job and she hated it already. But she couldn't afford to quit, not with her mother seriously ill and unable to work anymore. They had to move thousands of miles away from Gloria's hometown in order to provide her mother with the best medical treatment. The bills had been stacking up and there were no kind neighbors or friendly, familiar faces to rely on in times of need. Gloria just had to keep this job. It put food on the table and kept the electricity on in their tiny apartment at least.

Arthur had walked in that day, a change for him because his usual coffee spot had closed for renovations. He had taken a long look at the young waitress who served him and sensed that she was destined for great things. Was it fate, Gloria wondered? Regardless, she was still grateful that he had chosen her coffee shop over the others scattered along the block. The sun was shining on that warm spring day and Arthur had decided, uncharacteristically, to linger over his coffee at an outside table rather than getting it to go, as most Manhattanites did. The sun had indeed been shining down on her that day. Her life changed one-hundred-eighty-degrees as a result.

You've come a long way, baby. She bit her lip to keep from smiling.

Although modeling and the fashion industry were not Arthur's line of business, he had connections which he didn't hesitate to exploit on Gloria's behalf. Two of the top people in the industry were friends from his college days back when, as idealists, they all dreamed about changing the world and winning a Nobel Prize. That idealism hadn't lasted in the face of money's allure. Arthur urged his friends to meet her and wouldn't take no for an answer. Eventually, they gave in.

There had been no regrets.

Gloria broke into the modeling world and became a hot commodity in the industry overnight. Everyone wanted her. As far as the other models were concerned, ones that had been on the rise until she had come along, they hadn't stood a chance.

Gloria was grateful that she'd only been seventeen when Arthur "discovered" her. Nowhere was it truer than in modeling that time was the enemy, and timing was of the essence. Had she arrived on the scene on the heels of another model's big break, her career might have stalled. She might appear to be in control of her career to those looking in from the outside, but she knew very well that the industry was the one pulling all the strings. Only the handful of powerful people controlling this business had a real say in who would get to be Miss Congeniality, and not the public, even if they wanted to believe otherwise.

Gloria tilted her head slightly and pulled herself from her insightful memories back to the decorated meeting room. It wasn't time for reminiscing. She leaned over and listened.

After all of their business affairs had been settled, they moved on to discuss the details of the photo shoot. Andy had chosen to shoot in a magnificent forest in the southern peninsula of New Zealand, one he had discovered during his travels. He explained that the contrast between the wild scenery and Gloria, who looked like a delicate china doll, would create a breathtaking sight that would be absolutely mesmerizing. "In other words, perfect," he concluded with a grin.

Gloria felt excited to commence this new adventure. Unlike what she was used to, the crew would be pretty small. Besides Andy, Gloria, and Arthur, it would include a make-up artist, who was also the hair designer, an assistant photographer, and a general assistant whose job was to take care of all the logistics. It wasn't extravagant, but it was a solid plan. It seemed as though Andy had really thought this through. There was just one last thing to take care of.

Gloria picked up her pen. "Where do I sign?"

CHAPTER 2

"**O**h goody! I'm glad you woke up," a jubilant, feminine voice echoed in the background.

Julie did not know where she was or what was happening to her. Her eyes were blindfolded and her arms and legs were tightly chained to a chair. She could feel the blood draining from her joints, a sensation of excruciating pain. She ran a dry tongue over her parched lips, wondering how long she had been immured by her agony, and for how much longer would she have to suffer until she was rescued. *If* she would ever be rescued.

Half of the time Julie was unconscious and did not realize what was happening to her; and when she was conscious, the pain overwhelmed her so much that she felt like she would pass out any minute. She had cried and begged, but it just didn't stop.

She was trapped like a helpless animal, dreading her huntress.

"What's going on here?!" Julie yelled with every last bit of strength left in her. "How long have I been here? Why are you doing this to me?" she screamed in tears.

"You don't have to yell," the same female voice answered. "No one is going to hear you anyway. You've been here for two days, and no one has come to save you. But don't you worry, it will all be over soon."

Julie couldn't see the malicious smile on the woman's face when she said that.

Julie did not understand how she had gotten into this situation in the first place. The past week had seemed to be one of the best in her life. It had started with her coming back from the bachelorette party of the first one of her friends to get married. They had partied in Atlantic City, and Julie had even won two hundred dollars. Of course the very next day she had spent it all on a gorgeous dress that she had been wanting to buy for a long time. And then her mother had begun prying for present ideas for her upcoming birthday, which only further improved her mood.

Winter was in progress, but the frosty atmosphere had suddenly transformed into pleasant weather, and Julie felt like this had happened just for her. The highlight of the week had been when she met an important magazine editor who had told her that she had a really unique look and that she should give her a call if she were interested in modeling for the magazine. She had given Julie her business card. Julie had exclaimed in excitement that her lifelong dream was to be a model, and the editor, Kelly Danes was her name, had nodded and smiled. She'd only asked Julie not to tell anyone yet, because she did not want to be bothered by other girls craving the same incredible opportunity; it would be better if she told everyone only after everything was officially settled.

Julie had called Kelly the very next day, and they had agreed to meet at the editor's townhouse on the Upper East Side. Kelly had brought up the possibility of Julie having her portfolio photos taken, implying that she should dress up. Julie's enthusiasm grew with a burst of happiness when she thought about the new dress she had just bought, which would be perfect for the occasion. She really hoped she could impress Kelly.

That night, Julie had hailed for a cab rather than take the subway, like she usually did. She could not afford to be late to such an important meeting and ruin the great first impression she'd obviously left on Kelly. She had preferred not to take a chance and miss her train, or somehow not be able find her way from the subway station to Kelly's home. Anyway, she figured, although it got a bit warmer, the nights were significantly cooler; and she wasn't intending to show up on Kelly's doorstep with a frozen handshake while sniffing her nose. She wanted to look her absolute best.

The taxi had stopped in front of an impressive row of townhomes. Julie had made sure she was at the right address before paying the driver. The moment she had shut the car door behind her, she felt her heart pounding. By the time she had gotten to the door, it was racing. She had forced herself to take a deep breath and then pressed the doorbell. Kelly had answered the door right away and welcomed her in. She had explained that the studio was located in the basement floor and gestured with her hand toward a heavy looking door. Julie had automatically headed inside while Kelly locked the main door and then followed her downstairs.

The last thing Julie could remember was a violent blow to her head and her body plummeting down the stairs. She was still sprawled on the floor when she felt the texture of rough fabric, like a used kitchen towel, covering her face and a weird smell that quickly filled her nose. Then everything had turned black, just as it was doing once again, as Julie reluctantly gave in to the pain and slipped out of consciousness, yet another time . . .

When she finally regained awareness, God only knew after how long, she was awakened to a complete darkness that enfolded her eyes. She felt the ropes brush against her skin as she tried to move her hands. She was strapped to a chair, hazy and suffering terrible pain.

"What the hell is going on here?" Julie asked. "Kelly, is that you?" she called in helplessness.

"Patience, my dear," said Kelly's calm voice. "Soon it will all be as clear as day."

After several long minutes, Julie sensed how the coarse ropes binding her to the chair were being loosened, but she couldn't move. She was paralyzed with fear. She experienced a horrible, salty taste in her mouth. Had she been drugged? Julie moved her tongue over the corner of her cheek in an attempt to wipe out that poisonous flavor. Her eyes were still blindfolded, but she did not have enough strength to uncover them: she felt defenseless.

Kelly gripped her brutally and knocked her to the ground.

Julie felt every last bit of her bruised, naked flesh being dragged across the cold, rough floor and then tossed aside like a piece of meat.

"Oh Julie, you are so pretty!" Kelly cheered. "Let me just put on your new dress and some make-up, and then you can see for yourself that you are indeed . . . well . . . breathtaking!"

"What's going on here?" Julie asked again. She tried to scream, but her voice was already too hoarse from crying and yelling.

"Don't worry, sweetie, save your energy for later. You see, I just had to make a few minor adjustments before I could let you be photographed for my magazine. You probably understand that not just anyone can show up and instantly become a model. The secret all the breathtaking models keep is that the path to beauty is tied up with pain. *A lot of pain.*"

Julie felt her bare body being stuffed into a tight dress that pressed against her wounds, and then she was seated back on the chair. Cruel hands pulled her up mercilessly, without any consideration for the amount of pain she felt, so that she would sit up straight. Then the blindfold was removed from her eyes.

The entire room was lit, but it took a few minutes for her eyes to get used to the brightness before she could see clearly. Then she saw that all of the walls in the room were actually mirrors. She saw a woman with platinum shaded hair and carefully painted dark red lips, Kelly, standing proudly next to a woman sitting on a chair. She did not recognize the woman, but she was wearing her clothes. Julie stared at the eyes of the woman looking back at her and then she suddenly realized.

It was *her.*

She was overtaken by pure terror. *No, it's not possible!* Julie told herself and then stared again at her reflection. She shuddered when she saw herself in the mirror. Maybe this was all just a bad dream. This couldn't have happened to her. No, it had to be one of those horrible nightmares and she was going to wake up any minute now in her warm, comfortable bed, laughing at herself for having such a gruesome imagination.

But the nightmare didn't stop, and she was already awake.

"What the hell did you do to me?" Julie screamed, as the tears began pouring down her cheeks, burning her wounded skin.

"Look at you, all dressed up in your new dress. Julie, don't you think you look beautiful?"

Julie's entire body was peeling. Some of the wounds had begun to heal a little, but the ones on her face were still raw and painful. Her long chestnut hair, which she had been growing diligently ever since she was a child, had been chopped off and ripped out until her scalp was exposed, and the blood trickled down into her eyes, blending with her tears. It trailed through where her eyebrows once had been and were now torn out completely. Her nose seemed broken and twisted, covered with gore, and she had trouble breathing. Her mouth felt so parched and dry, yearning for some water, but all she could taste was that salty mix of blood and tears. She battled with herself not to throw up. It was an excruciating vision.

"What did you do to me?" Julie sobbed, staining her new dress with red tears. "Why did you do this to me?"

"It doesn't feel nice to be ugly, does it?" Kelly asked venomously. "When you're beautiful, you think you are above all, truly worth more than everybody else. Parading around like a queen no one can refuse. Oh, what vanity it takes to want to be a model! You trust your beauty to make life easier in an instant, without learning or working, without struggling for a livelihood, without doing anything but smiling and being perfect." Kelly's eyes narrowed at Julie.

"But it's not my fault that I am . . . was . . . beautiful," Julie reasoned.

"Maybe so," Kelly replied, "but you are the only one to blame for your pride. Don't you remember that your lifelong dream was to be no less than a model? For this you deserve the punishment you were given."

"But what about you?" Julie asked. "You're beautiful, too. Why aren't you punishing yourself?"

"Oh no, I'm not as beautiful as you are, well, *were*. In any case, I did not always look like this." As she spoke, Kelly remembered those godawful days. "You see, because of women like you, I've suffered all my life. I was never pretty enough. Girls like you always made fun of me." Deep in her heart she thought about one girl in particular, the one she had really wanted to see sitting on that chair. "I couldn't use my looks to get where I have gotten now. I wasn't arrogant enough to think that my beauty would open doors for me; rather, I relied on my devotion and talent and hard, very hard, work. And that is exactly your downfall," Kelly proclaimed in a firm voice. "If you don't understand yet," she added, "your sin is not beauty, but pride. You are not being punished for the way you look but for the way you allow yourself to behave." Kelly hurled the harsh words at her, leaving her speechless.

The last thing Julie saw was Kelly pointing a gun at her. She never heard her say, "It's so hard to be beautiful, don't ya think?"

* * *

The industrial garbage bag that concealed Julie's body waited impassively in the dark room where she had found her death. Kelly was too smart to try to dispose of the evidence in broad daylight.

It was morning now and she was on her way to work, but her mind drifted to other places. She wondered when the cops were going to find the body this time. Kelly wanted those who had more beauty and vanity than actual brains to know that they'd better watch out.

Kelly decided to take a quick detour through the offices of Ford Models on West 57th street near Central Park. As she drove past one of the most established modeling agencies in the city, she noticed a beautiful girl, about twenty years old, with golden locks and hazel eyes, gazing up at the building with an expression of amazement blended with hope. She pulled up next to her and rolled down the window.

"Hello, I'm the Editor in Chief of Inner Beauty magazine. We are currently looking for new models. Here's my business card. Give me a call, I think you have a bright future ahead of you."

CHAPTER 3

The NYPD was baffled by the mysterious series of murdered beautiful women all over Manhattan. Among the many young women who had been found lifeless, there was no common ground other than their stunning appearances, which had been brutally deformed. Nobody knew who could be responsible for these horrendous killings. There were no clues leading to the killer's identity.

Over the six years that Sharon had worked in the homicide squad of the Midtown South Precinct, she had faced dozens of different murder cases, but this was proving to be especially difficult. It was clear that they were dealing with a skilled criminal who did not leave any footprints behind. Sharon even wondered whether the killer had prior experience or perhaps connections to unsolved cases in other jurisdictions. She had contacted other squads and searched for similar cases in the police database, but no matches were found. It seemed as though the murderer had launched and groomed his ghastly career in New York City – and nowhere else.

Well, I guess even killers believe that The Big Apple is the place to be.

Working with police psychologists had enabled Sharon to assemble a vague profile of the killer. They were looking for a person who was very clever, a perfectionist, and probably behaved that way in his day-to-day life. As for the unsub's gender, both options were considered, though the fact that over ninety percent of serial killers were men was heavily taken into account. One possibility that seemed plausible was that the killer was a man who had suffered abuse and humiliation by a female figure and that the distortion of the faces likely symbolized a grand victory and revenge for his past. However, there were no signs of sexual assault, which was usually associated with male criminals, especially in light of the victims' striking beauty. But it could also relate to a sense of castration, Sharon reminded herself. Another profile, though less likely, suggested that the killer was a woman who was making amends with her own sense of inferiority by making other women, whom she deemed threatening, subordinate and uglier than her. Since statistically only a small percentage of serial killers were women, that lead did not seem very promising.

In any case, thus far there had been no evidence found which could confirm or refute any speculations, so they remained completely theoretical – not good when you're trying to solve a murder case. Sharon sighed inwardly: she was in desperate need of a lead.

The autopsy reports consistently showed that the injuries sustained on the bodies had been made during the forty-eight hours prior to their deaths, and that the joint damage indicated that they had been forcibly tied. Residual Chloroform and GHB, also known as a date rape drug, had been found in the victims' systems, though Sharon knew there was no evidence for sexual assault. It appeared that the killer wanted to make sure his victims couldn't fight back, which pointed out to a plausible physical disadvantage.

But how did they end up in this situation in the first place? Did the killer jump at them from behind? Or perhaps he slipped the drug into their drinks? So that could mean they met him willingly, and if so, then why? Different speculations came to Sharon's mind in an attempt to answer these questions. But she knew that there was no point trying to take a stab at all of these vague conjectures. She should be focused on actual facts. Only the problem was there weren't any. Time was breathing down her neck, and she definitely felt it.

Suddenly she heard the voice of her boss, Midtown South Precinct Captain, Rob Jackie.

"Davis, into my office, now." His icy voice dominated the room, imposing utter silence. A few officers, mostly Probies, glanced up in fear but then realized it wasn't their names being called.

Sharon crossed the hall in a speed that could have rivaled a marathoner, while gathering her long champagne blonde hair into a round bun at the top of her head. She stepped into the Captain's office and closed the door behind her.

"Is there something new?" she asked, pushing strands of golden hair away from her ocean green eyes.

"That's exactly what I intended to ask you, Davis, as the detective who is supposed to be in charge of this case," he answered rigidly.

Supposed to be in charge? It looked like her situation was getting worse by the minute.

He ignored her questioning expression. "It's been two months since the last murder. I would expect you to have found something by now. Anything," he sighed. "Do you have any leads?"

"Well . . ." Sharon tried to stall a little as she wondered what she could say that would distract her commander from the fact that she had no news for him. "We've put together two predominant profiles of the killer, and now I'm using them to find proof that confirms one of the descriptions. I'm planning on going through the files again; perhaps there's something we missed."

"We already did that," Rob grumbled. "Goddammit, Davis, we need to show some kind of progress, and you're not delivering. Do you want us to wait until it's too late and we have another body on our hands? You don't understand the kind of pressure I'm under. You know this is one of the most covered events in the last two and half years, which means if we don't solve it soon our asses will be on the line. I can't continue covering for you anymore." He stopped and took a deep breath. "If you think you can't handle it . . ."

"Rob, we both know I *can*. And you know nobody else could have gotten further with the slim evidence we have," she answered with confidence, though she didn't feel it. In the last year alone, four bodies had been found, and it was clear that the killer was gaining more confidence and experience. Each time a new body was discovered, Sharon felt the depth of her failure.

But she was never a quitter.

"Listen, I know it's a lot of drudge, but we need to go back in order to get to the bottom of this. There is no doubt that we are dealing with a professional; therefore, if there are any mistakes, they will be found in the first murder. We need to go back to square one. That's the only way to track this nutjob. We already know the guy's methods and his motives. All we need is one little mistake, and I am going to find it. I'll do whatever it takes. And that's a promise, Captain."

Sharon felt entranced by her brave speech. She had won Rob over and had managed to calm him yet again. She already saw the beginning of a smile forming on his lips and was waiting to hear his usual, "*Okay, Davis, counting on you, God knows why. Get moving.*"

But she did not hear those words. Rob's cell phone rang. He answered but did not say a single word throughout the duration of the call. Sharon noticed that the vein next to his forehead was beginning to stick out – a very bad sign. When he hung up, he said only one thing.

"We have another body."

CHAPTER 4

The sun had set and it was safe to leave. Kelly drove downtown with the remains of Julie safely stashed in the trunk of her Mercedes, concealed inside a black trash bag. While her eyes were searching for the perfect location to dump the body, her mind wandered almost three years back to Mandy Sheldon, her first victim.

They met when Mandy had come for a job interview at the bureau of Inner Beauty magazine, where Kelly worked as the Editor in Chief. It was instantly clear that Mandy's only talent was looking good behind the reception desk. She had waltzed into the office, beaming with the overconfidence of a stupid little girl who did not know her place. The stench of vanity was exuding from her. Kelly was infuriated by the audacity and assurance that Mandy had displayed in her ability to get a desirable position, and in such a prestigious workplace to boot, without even bothering to submit a resume. She just had to teach her a lesson.

Kelly had interrupted the interview and told Mandy that she'd noticed right away that Mandy had higher qualities than the role required. She had given Mandy her business card and told her to stay in touch. Of course Kelly hadn't actually thought about calling Mandy and had just planned on ridiculing her if she tried to approach her. That should teach her a lesson or two.

But as the hours went by, Kelly felt it was not enough. *The little imbecile must be punished.*

She had called Mandy that very same day and had offered her to model for next month's issue of Inner Beauty, which would be featuring young and promising new discoveries in the modeling world. Kelly might have even said that she was so impressed with Mandy that she wanted her to be on the cover. Any reasonable person would have doubted such an exaggerated offer, but Mandy's arrogance had triumphed over her reason, if she even had any, and she had immediately accepted it. After all, how could she have refused such an offer, when the alternative would have been working as a mere receptionist, away from the spotlight?

Kelly had set up a meeting with Mandy at her townhouse, allegedly for a photo shoot in her basement studio. She had convinced Mandy to keep everything a secret so she could surprise her family and friends when they saw her photo on the cover at the local news stands.

Actually, Kelly hadn't planned to take Mandy's life that night. She had only wanted to humiliate the young girl and crush her spirits, after which she would understand that she had no chance, ever, to model for her magazine – or any other for that matter. She had wanted to open this naive girl's eyes to the bitter truth, but they had refused to do so; therefore, they would remain closed forever.

Kelly remembered Mandy arriving at her house, dolled up from head to toe. How she had stepped inside, striding like a beauty queen, with her stiletto heels clicking on the hardwood floor. *Click-click-click*, to this day she could still hear clearly their hollow sound.

Mandy had oozed confidence and fake charm, admiring Kelly's home and complimenting her great taste. Kelly rolled her eyes inwardly: she couldn't care less what this little brat thought of her decorating skills.

Then Mandy had turned to Kelly and thanked her for making her dream come true. "I don't know what I would have done if I had to spend yet another year working a *desk job*," she'd spat out the last two words with disdain, oblivious to Kelly's tense expression. She had worked her butt off to become Editor in Chief. That was her dream. But to Mandy it was nothing more than a springboard for getting what she really wanted. "In fact," Mandy had continued, failing to notice her hostess growing hostility, "the real reason I applied for a job in Inner Beauty was to make connections in the fashion world and finally get my big break; I just never imagined it would happen so fast!" Her flawless grin had slapped Kelly right in the face. How could Mandy think that she could star on the cover of a famous magazine without any effort or audition, just like *that*? Kelly had felt her blood boiling and a storm raging inside of her. She had been so furious at this conceited girl for thinking that she deserved everything thanks to her looks alone.

Kelly had wanted to change it.

In a moment of unbridled fury, Kelly had erupted in rage and shoved Mandy with more force than she realized she possessed. Mandy's head had hit the coffee table and she lost consciousness. Kelly had panicked for a few long moments, not knowing what to do, but then it dawned on her that she had a golden opportunity. She could finally get back at all the beauties who had looked down on her for years and barely acknowledged her existence. She could finally get back at *her*. She was calling the shots now, and she would not be ignored, not by the likes of *her*, starting with Mandy Sheldon.

She dragged Mandy's weakened body down the stairs leading to the isolated basement, with her body taking a hard blow on each step it pounded down. She had continued dragging her across the dusty, wooden floor of the studio, the same place Mandy had believed so naively she would perpetuate her beauty and start her new life as a model.

That's "pretty" ironic, she'd joked with herself as her eyes focused on the defenseless girl.

Kelly had stopped once she stood in front of the only mirror in the studio, a huge mirror reaching all the way to the ceiling. She had begun to undress Mandy from her fancy clothes and roughly wiped the makeup off her face.

"What are you worth without all of this, huh?" Kelly had asked the unconscious Mandy while yanking out her hair. But that hadn't been enough. Her fingers had been tickling and wishing for more.

She had begun to slowly scratch Mandy's delicate face, and relished hearing the fainted girl's moans of pain. Every time Mandy opened her eyes, Kelly had pounded her again until she blacked out. Kelly hadn't known how she was going to get out of this trouble, or even if, but she didn't really care. She knew she couldn't let Mandy live, but she hadn't been sure that she would actually be able to kill her.

Perhaps the dark creature inside of her could.

When Mandy had opened her eyes, Kelly was standing in front of her with a gun. She had pointed the pistol at Mandy with trembling, hesitating hands. Kelly felt the darkness overtaking her yet again, but she couldn't fight it: "Do you want to live?" Kelly had asked, her voice merely breaking. She'd almost wanted Mandy to say yes.

Mandy had stared at her with a surprised, yet still terrified, look. She had opened her mouth, but then her eyes noticed her disfigured image in the mirror. She'd let out a shriek of pure fear. Instead of replying, she had begun to sob – tears of grief and bereavement for what was lost and could never be regained.

"I have nothing left! Nothing to live for, you've killed everything that I was," the stupid girl had replied.

"*Do you want to live?*" Kelly had screamed at her.

Mandy hesitated for a split second. Kelly hadn't given her another chance. She pulled the trigger.

Mandy had died almost instantly, but that hadn't stopped Kelly from talking to her lifeless body, which was still warm.

"It's your fault you're dead, not mine!" Kelly had slammed the words at her through tears of anger, shock, and fear, mixed with a little bit of elation. "I gave you a chance to live and you spat on it. You should have said yes. What kind of person waives their right to live?" she demanded. "If you had shown me that you had passion for anything else besides your phony cover, maybe I would have spared your life," she tried to justify herself, "but you are hollow from within, empty of all substance and, therefore, not worthy of taking one more breath on this earth." Kelly felt wickedness coursing through her veins and an evil smirk had appeared on her lips. "You got exactly what you deserved."

She had realized in that moment that she had unleashed a monster that had been lurking inside for nearly twenty years, and it would not surrender until the bitter end; there was no turning back. The fear and rage had morphed into total euphoria. It had been years since she had felt so alive, like she had on that seemingly far removed day in which her life had changed forever. She had tried to immerse herself in this heavenly feeling; but then the euphoria had begun to fade as panic and reason penetrated her mind and tainted her pure victory.

She had to pull things together. Get the body out of her house. Erase any connection between her and the heinous, but oh so sweet, act that had been done here. She had thought almost instinctively about calling her mother, but she had burned that bridge a long time ago.

When she was young, still an innocent girl, her mother used to help her sweep all of her mistakes under the carpet. But this had been no mistake. She wouldn't tell a living soul; the pleasure was all hers, a dark secret that would never be known.

Kelly had to act wisely and, just as important, quickly. She'd gone out and bought black trash bags, the biggest size available. Instinctively, she reached for her credit card but luckily had stopped herself in time and paid in cash. On the way back, she'd parked her car near the entrance and then sneaked back in, hoping that none of the neighbors had seen her. Kelly had shoved Mandy's body into the big trash bag and started scrubbing the floor clean of blood stains. She couldn't stand the sight of them. But first she had to get rid of the body.

Late at night, she had left her house and started driving, not knowing specifically where. Miles away from her home, on the other side of town, she had seen a large dumpster. She had stealthily dragged the bag from her car and had managed to lift it up just enough to heave it onto the bed of smelly black bags amassed within. She had left in haste immediately afterwards, before anyone could have noticed her, as if she had never been there. She'd started the car and had driven away from there as fast as she could. Her heart had been racing as fast as her Mercedes. After driving for a while, she'd calmed down; a malicious joy had begun to pull aside the veil of uncertainty that had cloaked her beforehand.

Mandy had indeed ended up exactly where she belonged – among garbage.

Had this tragic stumble actually been a revelation of her new destiny? The sense of remorse had faded and was replaced by a feeling of fulfillment. Kelly had quickly realized that if she intended to pursue this, she needed to change her tactic. Act more carefully. Make sure she did not leave any trace of evidence that could lead back to her. Maybe Mandy's death had been a crime of passion, but not anymore. From then on she had vowed to be cool and calculating, only acting with a strategic and precisely premeditated plan. Her composure, along with her roaring sensation of internal vengeance, had created the perfect killer: sophisticated, sharp, and ruthless.

Kelly always acted according to the rules she had set for herself, never deviated from the plan she had so carefully woven and, therefore, never got caught. She smirked with satisfaction but then a slight crease of concern formed between her eyes. Her Achilles' heel had been concealed in the first murder, in which she had not carefully calculated her steps. Now Kelly relished the panic she had created among all the beauties each time another victim was found; but the first time, when Mandy's body had been discovered, Kelly's blood had drained out of her heart all at once upon hearing the news.

Apparently, and not very shockingly, a human body weighs much more than the average garbage bag.

One of the garbage men had been curious to know what was inside of the big bag, which was suspiciously heavy, and had found the dead body of the former beauty. When the disfigured Jane Doe had turned out to be none other than the striking Mandy Sheldon, all the media channels had jumped on the story and had generated a media circus. Everyone had pressed the police to find the killer; after all, America's beauties could not be exposed to such danger, Kelly had thought resentfully. She had prayed that the cops would not find a fingerprint or a strand of platinum blonde colored hair that would lead to her. God had somehow heard her prayers and nothing had been found.

Sometimes Kelly wondered if things would have been blown up by the media to such grandiose proportions if the victims hadn't been so beautiful. The bitter truth was obvious.

Nowadays, Kelly eagerly waited for the disfigured bodies to be found. She already knew she would not get caught. That was her time of victory, despite the fact she wasn't able to share it with anyone else. But there was something more. Kelly enjoyed the media frenzy very much, but the real icing on the cake was far beyond the public's reach; that almost divine moment in which she relished the pure suffering and terror that spread on the former beauties faces as they looked at themselves for the first time in the mirror.

CHAPTER 5

After being stuck for twenty-two hours on the plane (of course, Gloria flew first class while Andy and Arthur settled for business class), they had arrived at the hotel (no less than five stars, needless to say) located in Christchurch, New Zealand. Gloria was a bit hazy from the flight and could not wait to take a long, rejuvenating bath.

"Gloria, meet me in my room in one hour?"

"Andy, it's better not to mix business and pleasure," she provoked him, although she wouldn't have minded making this one an exception.

"Don't worry, I can promise you that it's going to be strictly business," he answered warily.

"Impatient, huh? We just got here! Can't it wait until noon? I need time to recover." At her status, Gloria could afford this kind of behavior. If it had been someone else, she would have already been on her way back to New York. She knew very well that each minute spent was money down the drain.

"I wanted you to come over and try on the outfits for the photo shoot, but if you prefer not to wear anything, that's fine by me. This way we can really capture the true essence of beauty in its entire embodiment." Andy sent her a teasing smile.

"Tempting, but I think I'll keep my clothes on for the camera. I'll be there in an hour or two."

"One hour!" Andy called, though he knew he was fighting a losing battle.

Two hours later, Andy heard Gloria's knock on the door. She walked candidly into his room and lay on the edge of the bed, her short singlet revealing her shaped abs. Her hair emitted a sweet scent that filled the entire room.

"You're late," Andy said.

"Exactly as I told you earlier. I am very consistent that way," Gloria flashed a perfect smile.

Andy did not argue. He knew Gloria was not the type of person who was used to criticism. He ought to choose his battles and hold his tongue when necessary.

And this was one of those moments that he'd better shut up.

He watched her lying comfortably on his bed, gazing at the view out the window. After a few moments, she looked back at Andy and their eyes met. An awkward moment passed between them, and then Gloria rose at once and sat up straight, supposedly checking her reflection in the mirror. It was the first time he had seen her lower her eyes.

"So where are the costumes?" she finally asked in a formal tone, renouncing any tension between them.

"I'm way ahead of you," he smiled and spread out three ravishing dresses on the bed beside her.

Gloria tried them on, one by one. The first dress was a long, cherry-red strapless evening gown that made her look like a movie star. But not like one of those modern actresses, who appeared as though they were identical clones of each other; she looked as if she'd stepped right out of Hollywood's golden age, reminiscent of a dark-haired Grace Kelly.

The second one was a backless dress, in a shimmering light blue hue that accentuated the color of Gloria's eyes and made her look mermaidesque, like she was the ocean's incarnation on earth. But after she tried on the third dress, there was no doubt that it was the one. The nude color complemented Gloria's fair skin, and the glistening gemstones embraced her perfect silhouette and made her shine. The fabric was so fine that it seemed like an inseparable layer of her body and encircled her with a celestial aura. She was surrounded by light and magic, like a mythical goddess, possessing a powerful magnetism of beauty and allure.

"Wow!" Andy blurted. Gloria gave him a satisfied look. He felt as if he could gawk at her for hours, but at the same time he prayed she would change back into her jeans, so that he could maybe regain his focus on what they were here to do.

Too late, all he could think about was the vision of Gloria in that dress.

Before Gloria returned to her room, Andy stopped her. "Wait, there's something I need to talk to you about before we start the photo shoot."

"Why do I have to keep being stuck with you in this room?" she complained and immediately felt angry at herself. After all, she did want to spend time with him, and right now she was ruining any chance of that happening.

Change the situation immediately! she commanded herself.

". . . That is, when I can be stuck with you in a restaurant instead?" she added with her most charming smile. "I remember a great restaurant from my last visit to Christchurch, trust me. I'm exhausted, so we will talk about it tonight. I'll meet you in the hotel lobby at seven thirty." She left the room without waiting for an answer.

Andy was slightly confused, but after he realized what had just happened, he simply smiled. *Well, I'll be damned.*

All of Gloria's confidence wore off the second after she closed the door behind her. She just hoped she hadn't made a fool of herself.

* * *

While they were waiting for the main courses, Andy was thinking that Gloria was right, the restaurant really was great. It overlooked a peaceful, magical lake and had a warm and homey atmosphere, while still remaining very classy. They sat in the balcony where the whispers of nature blended with an old Sinatra song. The view was breathtaking.

Even what was around Gloria didn't look so bad.

He was surprised to discover that she was one of the most interesting people he had ever talked to, and he felt like they could continue talking all night long. Gloria told charming stories about her travels and proved to be genuinely cosmopolitan. She also shared with him insightful ideas that made her, at least in his eyes, the essence of sophistication. He wondered if having these feelings meant that he was crossing a certain line that could possibly affect his work later on, but he quickly realized he was not too eager to find out the answer.

Unlike the many women who envied Gloria's beauty, Andy believed it was actually a curse. After all, despite her being such a desirable woman, she was still single, he concluded. And it was as clear as day, even from the little time he had spent with her, that she could win anyone's heart easily.

Maybe even his.

He presumed that her tough exterior had come out of necessity due to her high status, yet he was able to see past it, and found that she was sensitive and witty as well. He simply enjoyed her company. It was a shame that the men she had dated in the past were so dazzled by her looks, that they had failed to notice her inner beauty.

The main courses arrived. Andy was sorry that now they would talk less and focus more on their food. He had a large lobster in a decadent cream sauce while Gloria had baked salmon and a green salad with no dressing on the side. The only thing they had in common was the bottle of Chardonnay.

"Wow, you sure went wild!" Andy taunted when he saw her so-called dinner. At least in this aspect she fitted the model stereotype.

"Yeah, maybe I should split it with you since you barely ordered anything for yourself," she replied with a grin.

After dinner, they glanced at the dessert menu, but ultimately Andy had to pass up the chocolate soufflé in light of his companion's hypercritical look. They were about to ask for the check when Gloria suddenly remembered that there was supposed to be a reason behind their dinner date.

"So . . . What did you want to talk to me about?" she asked.

"Haven't we talked enough already?" he answered a little bit confused as he winked at her.

"Andy, you wanted to talk to me about something important, remember?"

Andy had been having such a great time in the last couple of hours that he was secretly disappointed when he remembered that it wasn't a real date. He would have preferred not to ruin this delightful evening by talking about work and wanted to put off the discussion until tomorrow, but he knew Gloria would not let him do so.

"So . . ." Gloria leaned forward and looked into his eyes.

Andy hesitated but then continued. "I wanted to talk to you in more detail about the photo shoot. I haven't been completely honest with you."

Gloria remained silent but gave him a piercing glare in return.

"Or, rather, you can say that I just didn't tell you the whole story." Andy attempted to placate Gloria since he interpreted her silence as anger.

"What haven't you told me exactly?" she asked in a stoic way that did not betray her emotions at the moment.

"Well, this project is financed by Inner Beauty magazine. The Editor in Chief wants to devote an entire issue to the universal concept of beauty and its many manifestations across the world and over time. Your photo is supposed to be on the cover. Frankly, the editor insisted on only you and wasn't willing to settle for any other model, and I totally agree with her," he said, trying to flatter her.

Gloria, who had expected worse news, was not overly disappointed. She had never planned to break out of the boundaries of the commercial field, though it would have been nice to have seen her picture displayed in a gallery. She had actually been excited to take part in an artistic project and had made a note to herself to focus more on this field in the future, perhaps by posing for a portrait like the Mona Lisa she had adored so much.

The ultimate proof that modeling is not about looks, rather inspiration.

There was only one thing that bothered her. She had worked many times with Inner Beauty magazine in the past, but ever since the current Editor in Chief had taken over, the job offers had stopped coming. And even when she was finally mentioned, it was always next to some hideous photo of her taken by the paparazzi. A few years had passed since then, and now the very same editor was insisting that she be featured in the magazine? And on the cover no less?

Maybe she finally came to her senses, Gloria told herself. But still, this whole thing left her with a strange feeling. She had never met this editor, who had basically alienated her from the magazine, and now this same person was asking Gloria to be the star. It definitely made her wonder.

"She asked me not to tell you, at least not at first, that the project is for the magazine, since you get dozens of offers every day. She wanted to make sure that you accepted the offer," Andy interrupted her thoughts.

And she was probably right, Gloria figured. Chances were she would have declined the offer, but now, in front of Andy, she felt no regret.

"Well, it's not such a big deal. We can settle the score if you let me have a bite of that chocolate soufflé you wanted and don't tell anyone," she smiled flirtingly.

"No problem." Andy felt a huge relief. "But there is one more thing. Kelly Danes, the editor, is arriving in New Zealand after the photo shoot ends in about a week or so, and she's interested in meeting you. Apparently she has a vacation home here and she's invited us to stay with her."

CHAPTER 6

"So, Heather, what was the nature of the relationship between you and Julie?"

The latest body found had been identified as Julie Tyfer, though it looked nothing like the girl smiling in the photo. Like all the other victims, she had been incredibly beautiful, and Sharon would not have been surprised if she were a model. In light of the grim circumstances, Detective Davis had decided to focus first on Julie's friends and family while their memories were still fresh, before reviewing the other victims' cases yet again, as she had originally planned to do.

Julie's family resided in San Francisco, so they couldn't tell her anything specific about her circumstances in the last few days, the most crucial information. Sharon was hoping that a conversation with Julie's roommate, Heather, could shed some light on recent events.

"We've been roommates and best friends for almost two years." Heather sniffled and wiped her tears. "I met her the first week she moved to New York. Julie came here to pursue her dream of becoming a model." Heather paused and gazed at the photos of her friend's disfigured body. "I can't believe someone did this to her . . . that that's really Julie!" she burst into tears.

Sharon handed her a tissue. "It's very important that you try to recreate the last few days. As her roommate and best friend you probably were the closest person to her. Anything that comes to mind may help."

"We went with some friends to a bachelorette party in Atlantic City last weekend. Besides that nothing out of the ordinary has happened in the past week, although I did notice that Julie seemed happier. She was walking around smiling and even singing in the shower." Heather let out a small laugh through her tears.

"Do you think she'd met someone?"

"Julie used to go out on dates often. She was a very beautiful girl. But I'd never noticed anyone in particular. That's strange," she continued, "Julie usually told me everything, but this time I had a feeling that she was keeping something from me. When I asked her about it that very morning, she just laughed and said I was being paranoid, but still, that feeling nagged me."

"Do you think there was something, or someone, who had gotten her attention?"

"Yes," Heather nodded agreeably. "I'm sure something was keeping her mind busy, but I don't know what. I wish I could help you more," she sighed.

"That's okay," Sharon comforted her. "Sometimes, even what seems like the most trivial thing can be of help."

"I'm sorry, but I can't think of anything else."

As Sharon walked her out of the police station, Heather added, "It's probably nothing, but a few days ago, I saw

Julie put what appeared to be a business card in the drawer of her nightstand next to her bed. Perhaps it's nothing, but anyway, I'm supposed to sort out her things and send them to her parents tomorrow–"

"You may have helped me more than you realize," Sharon interrupted her excitedly. People tended to keep important things next to their bed; if that card had meant nothing, it probably would have been thrown away. This could turn out to be the lead that Sharon was so desperate to get.

"I'll escort you back to the apartment. I need to take a look at that piece of paper as soon as possible."

CHAPTER 7

"**K**elly Danes – Editor in Chief," was the name printed on the business card, which also carried the logo of what had been Sharon's favorite teen magazine during her adolescent years.

The possibility that this card had an actual connection to the murder case seemed quite farfetched, but if there was one lesson Sharon had never forgotten from her days at the academy, it was never to discount a possible lead in an investigation, because the missing piece of the puzzle could very well be hidden from the untrained eye; though Sharon assumed that even those who had written the academy text book would have questioned the validity of this so-called clue.

In any case, before she acted impetuously, she should try to learn from her mistakes by examining the previous cases, rather than being swept away by pursuing a wild theory that was based solely on a random business card. She didn't even know what she was looking for. Did she really believe that the Editor in Chief of Inner Beauty had something to do with the serial killings? There had to be a better explanation than *that*.

Sharon knew that Rob would probably think the same way. She could already hear him dismissing her. It was not surprising that a beautiful girl would have a business card from a fashion persona, and there was no proof that the card was even given to her by the actual editor. And, at the moment, Sharon could not approach the respected editor for clarification without implying that she was a person of interest – which would open up a whole new can of worms.

Sharon decided she should wait for the time being. There was no point in focusing on this new piece of information, whether it was relevant or not, until she retraced her steps from the first murder, as planned. Maybe then things would become clearer.

But she couldn't forsake this new lead all together; so in the meantime, she asked one of the rookies to provide her with every piece of information that existed about the renowned editor, ignoring the raised eyebrow in response. Sharon then started going through the old cases and conversation protocols, hoping, though without much faith, to find another lead.

"Well, I guess we have to start with you, Mandy. If there's any hope left, it's up to you," she said to the photo of the deceased and began reading the documents.

* * *

The successful magazine editor walked magnificently across the glossy marble floor toward the elevator. She confidently pressed the button and patiently waited until the down arrow in front of her flickered. The clicks of her heels were soon swallowed by the heavy doors. She was left alone, inside the designed compartment, waiting to be set free. After a few moments the doors opened for the second time, and the sound of her footsteps echoed throughout the underground parking lot. She slid elegantly into the seat of her Mercedes, inserted the key, and started driving.

It was rush hour and all routes were jammed. The thought that other people were probably staring jealously at her luxurious car caused her to grin. Kelly was always in a divine mood after one of her murders. It was as if she had gone on a pleasurable journey into the dark depths of her soul and regained the strength that she needed, at least enough to sustain her until the next time. It had been less than two days since she had said her final goodbye to Julie Tyfer, so the elevating effect had not yet faded.

The cars ahead of her crawled slowly through the heavy traffic, but it didn't bother her. Kelly remembered that she needed to stop on the way home to buy a new package of extra-large double layered trash bags to prevent leaks. She felt a slight tremor in her hands when the thought crossed her mind, not knowing for sure whether it had been due to excitement or fear. She tightened her grip on the steering wheel.

At times she was overtaken by the anxiety of someone finding out about her actions and preventing her from doing the only thing that filled her heart with happiness. She hurried to banish the apprehensive thoughts from her mind. No one was clever enough to track her down. She was too good for all those discouraged cops, who even after three years could not find the slightest clue to lead them to the identity of the infamous killer.

Kelly opened the window and exhaled a long breath, as if she were releasing along with it all of her self-doubts, leaving them behind in the cold New York air. Darkness fell and the dozens of surrounding cars seemed to Kelly like shining dots escorting her on the way back home. The traffic light changed, and Kelly pressed the gas pedal with full force.

From now on, no one could stop her.

* * *

Many hours had passed since sunset, and Sharon's eyes had become decisively tired. The light on her table lamp had dimmed, as if it were signaling her that it was time to stop. She finally broke down and decided to hurry back home so she could gain a few hours of sleep before the day dawned. She started putting the papers back in the file, but then her jaded eyes encountered a minor note from the interview protocol with Mandy Sheldon's sister. Two words caught her eyes and had immediately perked her back up – *Kelly Danes*.

Apparently, a few days before her disappearance, Mandy had called her sister and told her she had been discovered by a magazine editor, who had marked her as the next promising model when she'd gone for a job interview for a dull desk job. Mandy even had intended to frame the business card she had gotten from the editor as a souvenir of the glorious day that changed her life. She had asked her sister not to tell anyone just yet, because it was supposed to be a surprise. Later in her statement, the sister bemoaned the tragic loss of her baby sister, who did not get a chance to fulfill her life's wish.

Indeed, it's a rather strange coincidence, Sharon thought to herself. Julie Tyfer was also quite secretive in the days before she died, as her roommate Heather had declared. Perhaps she also had planned to surprise her loved ones with similar news? But still, all she had was some circumstantial, very weak evidence. Sharon started to think that perhaps the late hour was taking its toll and impairing her judgment. How could she even suspect someone so high up the ladder? Kelly Danes was a well-known public figure. Her work in Inner Beauty magazine had made her legendary. She mingled with haute couture designers as well as powerful politicians. She had a reputation for being tough – even fierce – but there were no complaints about assassinating models on the set, Sharon's sense of sarcasm interfered.

Kelly Danes was a handsome woman, no doubt, but maybe being constantly surrounded by gorgeous women as an inseparable part of her position had driven her over the edge? The odds were slim. Sharon released a soft yet frustrated groan. Perhaps her desperation to find something was getting the best of her, because she had actually decided to examine the vague idea instead of immediately rejecting it.

Maybe she wasn't as good as she used to be, if the only thing she had to hold on to was a crazy theory originating late in the night, just before dawn. It was clear to Sharon that with the given evidence, no one was going to take her seriously. But it didn't matter to her. The real question was if she should seriously consider this ridiculous lead now, or if she just needed to clear her desk, rest her head, and savor the few hours she had left before daylight would fill the office.

CHAPTER 8

The light of a new day broke through the luxurious curtains that covered the windows in Gloria's room. Warm rays penetrated through and fell like golden stripes around her bed. She felt as if she had awakened to a magical day, one that would be as magical as the previous night had been.

Before her eyes had adjusted to the morning light, a smile spread upon her face as her thoughts drifted back to last night with Andy. Gloria remembered their last moments together when he'd walked her to her room, before they had said goodnight.

She had relished his indecision whether to kiss her or not, probably wondering if it would come across as unprofessional rather than sincere. She was aware that she hadn't clarified her intentions, and that he had been a bit confused by her mixed signals. The truth was that Gloria herself was not yet sure which road to take. Despite the strong character that she'd had to develop at a young age, and that had further stiffened as her career soared, she was still afraid to get hurt.

But how much she'd missed having butterflies in her stomach.

Gloria longed to feel love again, true passion, a real piercing feeling without deception or hypocrisy.

Something to call her own, private and shielded from all the fame and glory that surrounded her. It had been a long time since she had felt that anything like this even had a chance in the reality she lived in, and it frightened her. But maybe here, thousands of miles away from home, she could succeed.

When her eyes had gotten used to the light and her blurry sight had become clear, she noticed the late hour flickering on the bedside clock's display. She had made breakfast plans with Andy before the beginning of the grueling day. Of course Arthur and the rest of the crew would be there as well. A slight crease of disappointment formed between her eyes but she quickly rushed to conceal it.

She had about ten minutes to create a fresh look, simple but still marvelous. Gloria knew she did not have to do much herself, since a whole team was waiting to make her (even more) beautiful for the exclusive photo shoot.

But only after twenty minutes Gloria finally felt she had achieved her goal and turned to the door. A feeble knock was heard. Who could it be at this time, she wondered? Gloria opened the door and found Andy, his flaxen hair slightly disheveled, holding in his hand a map that probably showed the way to the site of the photo shoot where they would be driving today.

"I knew you'd be late," he said in a deep, confident voice, but his timid smile gave him away.

The hotel breakfast was beyond belief. The buffets were filled with spectacular delicacies, and the waiters were ready to fulfill any request, in case something was missing – which was impossible.

Even before she entered the dining room, when the sweet smell of fresh pasties and cinnamon filled her nose, Gloria regretted taking this job. She could not afford to gain a single pound. As a model over thirty years old, the judgmental looks and criticism were turned her way now more than ever.

During the first years of her career, she had been so strict about her weight that Arthur had to hire a professional nutritionist out of concern for her health. In the last few years, after her status had been well established, she had allowed herself to enjoy the good things in life and indulged in something sweet from time to time, between projects; usually it was a rich chocolate dessert from a gourmet restaurant, but she also had a soft spot for simpler desserts from her childhood, like vanilla ice cream from Baskin Robbins.

Maybe just one tiny bite . . . A dangerous thought sneaked into her head.

No! she instantly ordered herself. It was well known that the first bite was never enough. It was better not to succumb to her craving.

"What's on your mind? You look like you're concentrating on something." Andy's voice interrupted her culinary thoughts, thank God.

"Nothing special, I'm just excited about today." Gloria lied through her teeth. After all, she was trying to charm him, not spook him with her weight complex.

"Yeah, me too." A perfect set of dimples framed his smile. "Want to know where we're going?"

* * *

The road leading to the forest was long, winding and filled with potholes, but was absolutely spectacular. Breathtaking mountains with snowy peaks and tiers of evergreen forests encompassed them from all sides. Their eyes were mesmerized by rare, vivid shades of blue and green, ones that existed only within the boundaries of nature. It was the kind of view most people only get to see on the National Geographic Channel.

Gloria was looking out the window, admiring the stunning view, when she felt Andy's leg touching hers. Though she typically travelled separately, she had joined the travel car with the rest of the crew, not because she wanted to mingle with the common folk, but simply because she enjoyed Andy's company. From the little that she knew of him, Gloria could almost certainly assume that he would not have abandoned his team at the prospect of a significant upgrade in his mode of transportation to the private rental jeep. He had an honest sense of loyalty, one that prevented him from putting himself first at the expense of others. Gloria admired that about him; therefore, she was also taking the opportunity to hopefully rebut her elitist image and was attempting to get in touch with her simpler side, which she knew was hidden inside of her, though possibly somewhere very deep.

The car careened around a sharp curve and their legs bumped slightly harder this time. Gloria felt a tingling sensation spreading from her knee to the rest of her body. She wanted to know how it would feel like to touch him again, but this time with intent, to run her fingers through his flaxen hair, stroke his chiseled face, fondle his muscly arms, lean her body against his wide chest. She knew that once they arrived at the shooting site they would have to act strictly professional, so timing became more crucial than ever. Maybe she just needed to take the reins and kiss him, even if the car was full of people whose names she hadn't even bothered to remember? *Not a chance in hell.* Gloria rejected the idea almost instantly, not just because she was a bit of a coward, but mostly because despite her age, she enjoyed secretly fantasizing about her knight in shining armor, just as a teenage girl would.

After two and a half hours the driver stopped to refuel one last time. The location of the photo shoot was pretty isolated and there were no gas stations nearby. The passengers had a twenty minute break before continuing on their long and bumpy journey.

Gloria sneaked into the minimarket at the station and went to the one place that always made her feel better, the chocolate bar section. She stood in front of the rows of shelves, noticing the usual chocolate bars like Kit Kat and Snickers, along with some unknown brands that were probably familiar only to local eyes.

This section always made her feel calm, because as a child, when she was sad, her mother used to take her grocery shopping and would always let her choose a chocolate bar to sweeten her sorrow. The trick never failed. A few years later, her mother became unwell and their sweet trips to the grocery store ceased, but Gloria kept returning by herself to those familiar shelves, where she could always find comfort – even if she hadn't bought a single candy bar in the last decade.

"Need some change?" she heard Andy's voice behind her. "If I were you, I would go for the Twix."

Gloria frowned. "Do you really think that just a few hours before I'm going to be photographed in the tightest dress on earth, for which I've spent countless hours at the gym, I would actually buy a chocolate bar?"

Andy must have lost his mind, she inevitably concluded.

"Then why are you standing here?" he asked confusedly.

Gloria stared at him but then began laughing, forgetting about maintaining the self-restraint she had so carefully adopted. The reason why she was poised in front of rows and rows of candy bars was obvious only to her. Standing and staring at shelves filled with sweet treats for minutes on end, without buying a single one, just made sense to her; in other people's eyes it came across as a bit odd, to say the least.

Soon enough Andy joined Gloria in laughter. They just stood there, indifferent to the curious glances turned at them, bursting into laughter. When their eyes met, the laughter vanished without a trace and was replaced by silence. They looked at each other, smiling and somewhat embarrassed.

There was only one way out of this situation. Andy leaned over and kissed her. For the first time. In a convenience store. Of a gas station. It was just as magical as it would have been anywhere else.

Gloria glanced behind her as she walked back to the car. *The chocolate shelves never let you down.*

CHAPTER 9

Even after two days of hard thinking, which seemed like forever, Sharon was having a hard time letting go of the idea that just maybe, somehow, the successful magazine editor had something to do with the horrifying series of murders. Suspecting Kelly as the killer seemed quite ridiculous, even for Sharon, but she had a gut feeling that there was a connection, at least if not directly, then indirectly. Of course the shortage of actual physical evidence was a huge setback, but she knew she had to find a way to figure out what was linking the two worlds that seemed so opposing: the ideal illusion of the beauty industry versus the ugly reality she had to deal with on a daily basis.

Sharon picked up the editor's business card and twiddled it. She knew that right now she could not put forth even the slightest suspicion about Kelly. Her unsuccessful record thus far in trying to solve this series of crimes did not give her the right to offer Rob such an unsubstantiated suggestion. She just might find herself being thrown off the case. In spite of this, Sharon knew that if she ignored her hunch, it would weigh on her conscience. She had to make a decision and fast. She took a deep breath and dialed.

"Hello?"

"Hello, this is Sharon Davis speaking, New York police department."

"Is this about that fine I neglected to pay?" Kelly giggled, but her heartbeat accelerated.

"Not really, I'm a homicide detective." Sharon stopped before she continued in an attempt to gauge Kelly's reaction. All she could hear was silence.

"Yes . . ." Kelly could barely overcome the dryness that engulfed her throat.

"I was hoping that you might be able to help us. It's about the series of murders that you may have heard of, The Sleeping Beauties."

"And how can *I* help exactly?" Kelly tried to feign surprise in her voice.

"It's possible that you have a connection to some of the victims." Sharon stopped and waited for a response.

Oh no, the bitter end had come. The hand that held the phone was not so steady anymore. Kelly wasn't sure how she should act. Any word could give her away. But she would not let the pressure get to her. Now, more than ever, Kelly needed to stay in control.

She pressed the receiver closer to her ear and listened.

"They were beautiful girls who may have had a connection to the modeling world. One of them even showed up for a job interview at your magazine and left with your business card."

Bloody Mandy Sheldon, Kelly resented her on the inside. Her pulse began to stabilize. It was merely a coincidence. The cops needed her help due to her position, not because of some kind of suspicion. Otherwise, they would not have settled for just a phone call.

"Perhaps you remember something of the sort?"

"Well, in my field of work I am in touch with many young women, all beautiful. Handing out my business card is really nothing special," Kelly calmly replied.

"True, but it's not every day that one of those girls gets murdered," Sharon commented.

"No doubt," Kelly tried to appear cooperative. "Remind me of the name of the poor girl and I will try to recall any detail about her that might be of help to you." Kelly hated the feminine voice on the other end of the line; she did not speak to her with the respect she deserved.

"Mandy Sheldon," the familiar name rang in Kelly's ear.

When speaking, Sharon emphasized each syllable in the name of the deceased.

"Truthfully, I don't remember anything specific, but I wouldn't be surprised if I had liked her and had given her my business card." Kelly tried to sound casual in order to put the detective's mind at ease, but in reality she was yearning to end this overbearing conversation.

"In what circumstances, exactly, do you give your card to these young ladies?" Sharon was curious. Something didn't add up. This had been the hottest story dominating the media outlets. It didn't make sense that a public figure such as Kelly would not remember a person whose picture had appeared all over the papers and news channels for weeks, especially when she had met this young woman just a short time before her death. Sharon had no doubt that Kelly *had* to remember Mandy.

After all, she had had an unforgettable appearance.

I could never forget her name.

"Usually I give my card to girls I want to connect with agencies that work with the magazine. After that, my job is done. After all, I'm not a fairy godmother who can make them into stars overnight," explained Kelly.

That's not what Mandy told her sister, Sharon thought. She had no doubt that there was more at play than what was meeting the eye. Kelly was revealing a lot less than she knew, but why was she doing this? At this stage Sharon decided not to correct Kelly's mistake. This conversation had reached a dead end anyway. She needed to calculate her next steps carefully.

However, Sharon's passion tended to take precedence over her common sense.

"Miss Danes," Sharon knew very well that the rest of the sentence would not go quietly. "We would really appreciate it if you could come down to the station and give us your statement. It would be highly appreciated by the New York Police Department."

"*Excuse me?*" Kelly's composure broke for the first time in the conversation. "Are you accusing me of something?"

"Of course not," Sharon forced herself to let the lie flow from her lips. "Like I said, it would be a gesture of good faith that might help us move forward with the investigation." Although there was nothing insulting or hostile in her words, Sharon knew that her tone of voice was sending an entirely different message.

"Do you even understand who you are dealing with?" Kelly snapped. "I'm not some mobster you can twirl around your little finger so you can try and impress your boss. Do you think I have time to help you do your *dirty work*?"

That was the final straw that broke the proud detective's back.

"Well, if you don't come willingly to help us with our 'dirty work' . . ." The anger erupted from her throat, "it would give me great pleasure to officially bring you in for interrogation."

"That's absurd. Given my personal acquaintance with the commissioner, I doubt I'll ever step foot in your office."

"Your *highness*," Sharon enunciated venomously, "an official invitation will arrive by tomorrow. I'll be happy to see you then!" She hung up without waiting for a response.

Sharon knew that she had crossed the line and was going to get hell from Rob. There was no way he was going to authorize her to summon Miss *Kelly Danes* for questioning and damage the editor's reputation without any substantiating evidence. Sharon knew she was in trouble, but she didn't care. She now had no doubt this woman was connected to the murders, one way or another.

Sharon felt like she was back on the horse, having finally found the lead she had been seeking for so long, even if to everyone else it looked like she had lost her mind.

* * *

Anyone who had been in the vicinity of Kelly Danes' townhouse moments after her conversation with Detective Davis would have heard the screams of rage coming out from her home.

Who the hell does she think she is? And to even suspect a dignified woman such as myself? Kelly could not stand the degradation that had been oozing from the detective's tone of voice, but worse, she could not stand the fact that someone had succeeded in linking her to her sweet, sinful secret.

How could it be that a miserable cop, who was just trying to cover her own ass, had succeeded in connecting her with her own monstrosity? Kelly figured that right now it only appeared to be purely circumstantial, otherwise the detective would have already arrested her, but if, God forbid, another slip were revealed, there could be severe consequences.

She had to nip this in the bud. Kelly opened her phone book and looked for the police commissioner's number.

CHAPTER 10

"**D**avis, are you out of your *mind*?" Rob's enraged voice jarred on Sharon's ears.

She knew she was doomed.

"What were you thinking, confronting a respected woman like Kelly Danes as a murder suspect? And making it seem as if it were being backed up by the department? Why should I have to catch hell from the commissioner and look like an idiot just because I was not aware that my head detective has gone nuts?!" Rob did not even wait for a response. "This is the first time the commissioner has actually called me by the right name, and he did it to imply, not so subtlety, that if I keep making the wrong decisions I will be transferred to the traffic division!"

"Rob, I really am sorry that you were in the line of fire because of me."

"It was more like a firing squad," he ranted. "It's hard for me to believe that you don't understand how your actions can get us all in trouble. So congratulations, you've proved you have balls, but for what?"

Sharon could not bear the disappointed look on Rob's face. She began to have doubts about her audacious decision to go after Kelly. She had never imagined that her actions might cause the whole department to look bad.

But damn it, she knew she was right. She felt it in her bones.

"Listen, you've known me for a long time. I know that sometimes I'm a little bit hasty, and I tend to forget that I'm not a bounty hunter who answers to no one. But have I ever performed in a way that has hurt the progress of an investigation?"

She managed to silence him, but only for a moment.

"Davis, we both know that you're good at what you do. That's not the problem here." He took a deep breath. "This case might be too much for one investigator. Maybe I should add someone to balance you, like Bryant."

Rob knew she wouldn't accept this suggestion amicably, to say the least.

"*What*?" Her cheeks turned red. "Mark Bryant is a chauvinistic idiot who has managed to get ahead only because he is his father's son. We both know he is useless and that's why he has never been in charge of a case on his own. And now you want to assign him to *me*?"

Rob knew that Sharon was right, but he had to mediate between the pressures from above and what was going on in the field. And, unfortunately, the sexist idiot's father had been the deputy commissioner for years. But that wasn't something he was about to share with a subordinate.

"If you don't want this case to be reassigned to someone else . . ." Rob stressed slowly, "you'll have to learn to restrain yourself. You can't just do whatever you want. From now on you need to answer to me and get my approval for every single move you plan to make. And no more shenanigans."

Anyone else would have heard in those words a warning or a reprimand, but Sharon identified the final lifeline her boss had tossed her.

"Thanks, Rob," she said quietly, almost whispering.

"And that means that your special interest in the editor, who is also the commissioner's friend, ends now."

"That's impossible," Sharon stated.

"For God's sake, I'm an inch away from the point where this case is taken off my hands, and that means your hands as well. We both know there's no way Kelly Danes is a legitimate murder suspect, so just look for another way to find the information that you thought you could get from her."

As highly as he valued Sharon, Rob found it extremely difficult to understand how she could have connected the respectable editor to the heinous series of murders.

Sharon couldn't give up so easily; she decided to present her findings to Rob. She couldn't keep on doing this alone.

"Okay, but first, I want to explain to you why we *should* keep investigating Miss Danes."

"I didn't think otherwise. Be in my office in two minutes on the dot."

The truth was he had already begun to wonder what this whole thing was about. Sharon was too professional to make false accusations. He was intrigued.

CHAPTER 11

This woman absolutely intrigued him.

Andy was sitting in the passenger seat with the road map spread across his knees, just in case the GPS system stopped working due to reception difficulties in the remote area. They were getting closer to their destination, and Andy had moved to the front of the car in order to direct the driver exactly where he wanted to go. Now he had to look at the road and concentrate on the route, though he would have preferred returning to the back seat, where Gloria sat, her laughter echoing in the background.

A smile crept to his face as he remembered their first kiss in the gas station's minimart. He still wondered why Gloria had lingered in front of the chocolate bars without buying anything, but he was glad she had. In any case, he thought to himself, she could not have found anything sweeter than the taste of her lips.

The famous model remained an enigma in his eyes. Andy had always been attracted to mysterious women, but Gloria was in a league of her own. For years she had been, due to her profession, flaunted in public, but hadn't actually revealed anything. The media, like a hungry vulture, had tried sinking its claws into her, but she refused to surrender.

He had noticed that even now, when they were so far away from all the commotion, somewhere in the wilds of New Zealand, she did not let her guard down. Force of habit, he guessed. He, too, would probably have longed for his privacy if he were confronted by the flash of paparazzi cameras every time he left his front door.

Andy held a renewed appreciation for Gloria for having to endure his presence. She was constantly surrounded by photographers, whether at work, where they demanded her to pose for them, or outside of work, where she was chased by them relentlessly as they hoped to catch a photo worthy of the next tabloid cover. One might say they belonged to two different camps, photographers and the photographed – at times against their will.

He toyed with the idea that they were a modern version of Romeo and Juliet, but hoped their story would have a different ending. He had a feeling that something good had the potential to grow between them, even if it were just for a few short days until reality hit them when they get back to civilization.

But why was he getting ahead of himself? Before worrying that their affair might end, he first needed to make sure it actually started. Andy had no idea if Gloria felt the same way. They hadn't had a chance to be alone after that magical moment at the minimart, and he surely didn't intend to have the *relationship talk* in front of the whole crew. It wouldn't be very professional of him.

Andy had to clear his mind. He decided that for now, it would be better to focus solely on work – which was an immensely difficult mission considering the fact that he was being paid to shoot Gloria.

Whoever said that the life of a model photographer was easy?

CHAPTER 12

After listening to Sharon's persuasive arguments regarding her special interest in the editor, Kelly Danes, Rob could not reject her inquiry. Chances were that Miss Danes wasn't the infamous serial killer they were after, but it would be careless not to investigate. Nevertheless, he forbade Sharon from contacting Kelly again, at least not until she presented him with something more concrete that justified confrontation. He could not face the commissioner empty handed again.

In any case, he thought, it was a good thing that Sharon hadn't gone too far and actually blamed Kelly Danes for murder. That was the last thing he needed right now.

* * *

Kelly had barely dodged the bullet that had been shot directly at her. The graze of the slug on her neck was a painful reminder. Luckily, the blood had clotted and she was out of danger, for now.

She had almost fallen into an abyss because of an insignificant investigator trying to prove herself to her boss. Who was this *Sharon Davis*, and why was she so determined to take her down? She could hear it in the detective's voice, when they had spoken on the phone.

Kelly had not missed the doubt, the suspicion, and the desire to blame her for something, no matter what it was. It seemed as though she had unknowingly made herself an enemy.

Nonetheless, the odds were in her favor. She had the power, the connections, and all the means necessary to crush her rival, but still she was afraid to act. The determination and tenacity Kelly recognized in the detective could not be tossed away so easily, not even with all the money and the connections she had.

For the first time in almost three years, ever since that first unripe act of murder, she was worried. Kelly understood that she had to be extra careful and take a step back.

How she hated Detective Davis for it.

Maybe she should run far away from here; she still hadn't fulfilled her destiny.

On the other hand, Kelly thought, maybe she was looking at this all wrong. It was clear that the low class detective would not stop trying to discover whatever it was that she thought Kelly was hiding, and the harder Kelly resisted, the less chance the cop would give up. In fact, she might even try to persuade others that she was right.

Or even worse, she might actually succeed.

How did the old saying go? *Keep your friends close and your enemies closer...*

CHAPTER 13

Luckily for Gloria, when they arrived at the shooting site, it was pouring rain, and there was no choice but to delay the photo shoot until the next day. Great, she had gained another day off with Andy. Ever since their hot kiss at the gas station, they hadn't gotten a chance to be alone, though they had been sitting just inches away from one another most of the time during the ride to the remote destination.

Gloria knew very well the power of the right timing. It was clear to her that if she and Andy didn't clarify matters and make important decisions regarding what had happened between them just hours ago, what was burning inside of her would fade in a mist of doubt and become a sweet, yet unfulfilled, memory. She did not want another memory. Not this time.

Gloria pined for something that she hadn't had for so long and had not even realized was missed. Going by her estimation, the spark between them had twenty-four hours left before disappearing forever. This extra day together was her and Andy's last chance to ignite the fire. And here, by a miraculous coincidence, or perhaps even fate, they were trapped in a cozy lodge while the rain was closing in on them.

Aphrodite had left them no escape.

Andy sat alone in his room. Arthur kept Gloria busy with reviewing the dozens of job offers that she had received for the coming days when they returned from New Zealand, so Andy was left with nothing to do other than further dive into the plans for the photo shoot. He acknowledged the great value of this project; this would actually be the first time his work would receive international coverage. He was so thankful to Kelly Danes for this opportunity and the free hand she had given him in producing the photo shoot. And he was glad that soon enough he could thank her in person.

He looked out from his window onto the drops of rain that blurred the peaceful scenery surrounding the inn. This rain could be a blessing in disguise, he thought. This way Andy gained precious hours of preparation time. He took a deep breath and then exhaled, watching his warm breath condensing upon touching the cool glass window. Who was he kidding? He was as ready as one could possibly be. He had spent hours planning every little detail and he couldn't wait to start shooting. So why was he not terribly disappointed after having to reschedule the photo shoot for tomorrow? Andy asked himself and immediately knew the answer. *Gloria*. Maybe this rain is in fact a blessing in disguise, Andy decided, because it gives me the opportunity to settle things with Gloria before the shooting starts. Before we would have to act as professionals and she might get the wrong impression, like that I am not absolutely fascinated by her and would like to get to know her better. So I have to make my intentions clear beforehand; the question is how to follow through.

Gloria was trying to plan what exactly she would say to Andy and how to tell him about her feelings. The businesswoman in her emerged even in the territory of the girl in love. Gloria could not avoid being prudent here as well, but for some reason she could not organize her thoughts and pave a path that would lead her to her goal. Eventually she decided to take the road that she had chosen only a few rare times throughout her life: the one that headed into the unknown. Simply knock on Andy's door and damn it, whatever happens, happens.

When she approached Andy's room her steps were not so determined. Gloria stopped in front of the door, wondering if she should back down. Let *him* pursue *her*.

Isn't that the least an international supermodel could ask for?

She was afraid he would never knock on her door. That their story would be over before it had even begun. Could it be that I am too intimidating, Gloria asked herself? Is Andy too afraid to make a move because it won't be professional of him? Or maybe he thinks that I am just toying with him and not really interested? Gloria knew this job meant a great deal to Andy and that he wouldn't dare risk it unless he had a damn good reason. Could it be that she just wasn't a good enough reason? A crease of concern formed between her eyes. In that case, she should probably wait for him to lead the way.

But Gloria had never left her future up to fate, and she definitely would not start doing it now. Especially after she already had gone through her midlife crisis, which in her case, of course, had started at the age of twenty-five.

Gloria ordered herself to pick up her hand and execute the elementary action of knocking on the door, an action she never had trouble executing before. So why was it so difficult right now? Her hand already had risen up. Her heart started pounding. An oppressive heat took over her entire body. Her clenched fingers made their way to the door but never got a chance to reach their destination.

Andy opened the door before she ever knocked.

"I was just on my way to see you," Andy explained. He looked just as confused as Gloria was, as if he, too, had been sitting in his room for the past hour, running all kinds of scenarios through his head. A smile of relief spread across Gloria's face, which made Andy feel even more confused. But then, as he was processing the image before his eyes, he began to smile.

Andy realized he wasn't the only fool in love.

CHAPTER 14

Even if she'd had a hundred opportunities, Sharon would have never guessed who was on the other end of the line.

"Hello," she answered nonchalantly, not really paying attention, as she was tied up with the case.

"Hello, Detective Davis, this is Kelly Danes speaking."

Sharon almost dropped the receiver. There was no doubt Kelly had managed to get her full attention.

"Hello, Miss Danes." Sharon, still completely surprised, was trying to choose her words carefully so she wouldn't get in trouble again. "I hadn't expected to hear from you."

And I was forbidden from ever contacting you again.

"Indeed, I know our last conversation did not end on a positive note . . ." Kelly said.

Sharon was already intrigued.

". . . And yet, I've decided that if you believe that I can somehow help with finding the person who murdered all those poor girls, then it is my duty to do so."

Sharon had not expected this. She was very good at reading others, and the last time they'd talked she hadn't noticed that Kelly was eager to help.

Can the leopard change its spots?

"Miss Danes, you've managed to surprise me." Sharon decided not to disclose her reservations or the questions building up inside of her. She had to figure out what was going on here. "We would be happy to have your assistance about anything you can remember regarding the case."

Kelly was smiling from the other side of the line. Detective Davis had just let the fox guard the henhouse.

"I'll do my best to answer your questions, Detective Davis, but I honestly don't think I remember much."

No worries, there's plenty of information between the lines, Sharon thought. "Great. Let's schedule a meeting as soon as possible."

"My schedule is free tomorrow afternoon. You can stop by my office if you'd like." Kelly preferred to stay on home turf.

Ordinarily, Sharon would have never agreed to meet with a potential witness – let alone a possible suspect – outside the police station, especially when she was still questioning their motives. But this time it worked perfectly. That way no one, not even Rob, would find out about her renewed contact with Kelly.

"Done. What's the address?"

CHAPTER 15

The very next day, Sharon left the office early, saying she had a dental appointment. Rob had no choice but to assent in a silent frown, if only because Sharon had never missed a day of work. In fact, she used to stay at work long hours after punching her card. This was exactly why he was wondering if she really was on her way to the dentist, or maybe the state of her pearly whites wasn't really that bad.

The roads of Manhattan were swamped with cars, the yellow taxis the city was known for standing out among them. Traffic was heavier than usual, and Sharon was relieved that she wasn't driving. The address Kelly had given her was only a couple of blocks away from the subway station and Sharon was glad to walk them by foot. Those ten minutes were like a vacation for her, filled with different colors, sounds, and flavors.

I really need to get out more, she determined.

She arrived at an impressively polished office building. The Inner Beauty logo was displayed above the entrance, along with some other well-known symbols.

To her surprise, when she entered the big corner office, Kelly greeted her warmly.

"Would you like something to drink? Coffee, tea, water?" she asked in a sweet tone.

"Strong coffee. Thanks." Sharon chose to play along with Kelly as long as she couldn't be sure if it was all an act or not. In any case, it had been nearly two hours since her last cup of coffee, which was unheard of.

They chatted while Kelly's assistant served their drinks, and then, to Kelly's request, left and closed the office door behind her.

"Well, as I made clear in our conversation yesterday, I'm here to help." Kelly smiled but seethed inwardly over the lie that came out of her mouth, and even more over the fake kindness she had to maintain for now. "I will do my best to answer all of your questions, Detective Davis."

"Alright, let's start with the first victim, Mandy Sheldon."

Kelly couldn't bear to hear that hideous name even one more time, but of course she didn't say anything.

"As I'd mentioned in our previous talk," Sharon continued, also trying to avoid that awkwardness after they'd both lost their tempers, "The deceased's sister said Mandy got your business card just days before she was found dead."

Kelly had prepared herself for this moment. She knew that she had to change her version of things. This was the one spot where she might slip.

"Indeed, after our conversation, I did try to remember the poor girl. I even asked my secretary to print her photo. Still, it's been three years."

Sharon nodded understandingly. She wondered what had led to this gracious cooperation. Perhaps Kelly really was a model citizen? There was no doubt that Miss Danes was a respectable and influential woman – far from the lonesome killer stereotype. Sharon almost began to question herself and understand Rob's logic, who at times found her theories scattered and bizarre.

But damn it, something didn't feel right.

"And I was able to remember her. Gorgeous girl. A real sweetheart. She originally came in for a job interview as a receptionist, were you aware of that?" Kelly asked with faux naivety.

"Of course." Sharon tried to project confidence in her answers. "Mandy had told her sister every little detail," she added in the hope that Kelly would take the bait.

Oh, Mandy, you have been dead for three years and still make things so complicated!

"Anyway," Kelly continued, "as soon as I saw her, I realized she had great potential and that she could have become an asset for the magazine," Kelly tried to emphasize the fact that she had lost out from the girl's death. "You see, when models are discovered by the magazine, they sign an exclusivity contract. They can shoot commercials and campaigns, because we want them to get famous as well, but in regards to interviews, covers, and juicy scoops, we get first exclusivity," Kelly explained, hoping she managed to distract the simple cop, who obviously knew very little about how things worked in the fashion industry.

"And that was all to your relationship with Mandy?" Sharon stayed focused. She wanted to see if Kelly would lie to her again.

"Pretty much." Kelly chose her words carefully. She didn't know what and how much the detective knew, so she tried not to get tangled in her own answers. Kelly wanted to leave herself an escape route, an option to claim she had been misunderstood.

"I would love to hear about the *minor* details as well," Sharon forced a smile. She began to lose her patience. So far Kelly hadn't told her anything new.

Kelly felt her heart beating strongly. She was as excited as an actress reciting her lines in front of an audience for the first time, afraid she might not portray well enough the part that she had taken upon herself.

"Certainly, as I mentioned, I am here to help," she tried to gain some time. Kelly was not yet sure which tactic to use. Eventually she decided. "Actually, I'm a bit confused. It's been a long time, and I'm not sure what exactly you expect to hear. It's not like I was her best friend."

No, just the fairy godmother who had promised to make all of her dreams come true.

"It's hard for me to think of anything else worth mentioning. Just ask what you want to know." Kelly hoped with all her heart that it would end there.

"Alright, so how exactly does this whole model discovery thing work? Did you have to register Mandy with an agency or update her name in your records?"

Damn it, this cop isn't stupid.

"Actually we didn't get that far along in this process since . . . well, you know what happened."

Yes, just too bad you didn't even bother to remember the girl you promised the moon to, who suddenly got murdered.

"And it didn't seem suspicious to you that someone who had gotten an opportunity like that never contacted you?"

"Well, I'm a very busy woman, so if someone is foolish enough to pass up a once-in-a-lifetime opportunity, I'm not going to chase after them."

Sharon could feel the hidden contempt in Kelly's words.

"Didn't you have her number? You just offered her a *'once-in-a-lifetime opportunity'* and moved on? Your assistant didn't take her information?" she wondered. The detective in her had to dig deeper.

Something just doesn't add up.

"As I was saying, pursuing aspiring models is not a part of my daily agenda. I saw potential in the girl, presented her with an offer that's hard to refuse, and told her to get my card from my secretary." Kelly tried to tie up any lose ends that she may have left. "And that's it. The ball was in her court."

"So you're saying that Mandy's case was like any other of a girl who you've offered to make into a model?" Sharon was just waiting for Kelly to make a mistake.

"Well . . . yes." Kelly yearned to get out of the mess she'd made.

"And do those cases tend to repeat themselves much?"

Actually, Kelly had never offered any girl the fast track to fame, besides those gullible buffoons who had fallen victim to her exploits. There was no chance in hell she would help those vain, lucky girls reach any further than the local dumpster.

"Not very often, but it definitely wasn't the only time I'd given my card to someone who showed promise," she said nonchalantly.

"Can you give me any names?" The conversation had slowly evolved from a friendly dialogue into a line of questioning.

Shit! Kelly was outraged but tried not to disclose her feelings in front of the detective. "I'm sorry but my brain is so busy concentrating on other topics: the preparations for the March issue are in full force. I even needed some time to be able to recall Mandy." The smile on her face could not conceal her discomfort.

"Don't worry," Sharon answered with the same artificial sweetness that Kelly had greeted her with when she'd entered her office. "The names are probably updated in your records, right?"

Why do you keep prying, you stupid cop? Leave me alone!

"They have to be somewhere . . ." Kelly was mad at herself for not having been properly prepared for these questions. She had underestimated her rival. "But how is this connected to your case?"

"You're right. We got a little off topic." Sharon preferred to dismiss the matter for now and not provoke an attack. For the time being she should try to extract as much information as she possibly could. After all, she was certain that there were no names in the system.

If beforehand Sharon had still been debating, now she had no doubt at all that this woman was hiding something.

"Okay, back to Mandy."

Marvelous . . . Kelly nodded and held the coffee mug close to her lips.

"So, basically, you offered to make her the next 'it girl,' am I right?" Sharon abandoned the subtle tactic she had used earlier. She understood that she had to hit where it hurt.

Kelly took a long sip of her coffee.

"The next 'it girl'? That's a bit farfetched, if you ask me."

"That's what Mandy had told her sister."

Kelly's face flushed, but she quickly recovered. "Well, it makes sense that she had presented it that way.

It seems like a classic case of exaggeration. The girl was probably trying to make her sister proud."

Even though Kelly's explanation made sense, Sharon couldn't trust her.

"Still, it doesn't make sense that Mandy had imagined the whole thing. Is it possible that you'd given her the impression that she was special? That she was headed toward a bright future?"

Oh, Mandy, why couldn't you keep your stupid mouth shut?

Kelly picked up the printed photo of Mandy lying on the table and pretended to focus on her image.

"Well, she was a real beauty," Kelly tried to talk about her with warm affection. "I might have said she had the potential to become a star, but, for sure, I did not make any extravagant promises."

Sharon nodded and took a sip of her coffee. "Miss Danes, do you watch the news?" she asked casually.

"Obviously," she smirked. "In my line of work I have to stay informed and aware of changes at all times, from fashion to politics." Kelly pulled out her usual response to these kinds of questions, and immediately regretted it. She understood where this question was leading.

"What I'm having trouble understanding is how you *didn't* recognize Mandy's face being smeared all over the television stations reporting her murder, when you had offered her a modeling career just a few days before it happened!?"

That was more of a statement than a question. The answer was obvious.

It wasn't possible.

Kelly knew she was in trouble. She fell right into the detective's trap. She had no choice but to remain silent. Tiny frown lines appeared between her eyebrows as she tried to think of a way out. Eventually she came up with a slight solution, the only solution, for explaining her bizarre behavior.

After a few minutes had passed in dreadful silence, Kelly said, "You got me."

The surprised detective didn't know what to expect.

"I did remember Mandy Sheldon. Of course I remembered her. It's not every day that I offer a dream career to a girl who gets murdered."

Maybe finally some light can be shed, Sharon hoped.

"As you may remember, our first conversation did not go over well. I sensed hostility and disrespect from you; therefore, I wasn't too eager to try and help you. Honestly, I also felt as if I had nothing to offer the police."

Sharon preferred not to respond and instead just kept listening.

"However, after our talk, when I had a chance to relax and think it through, I realized that maybe I could help in a way I might not be aware of. After all, I am not a professional detective and I don't know much about these affairs."

The subtle flattery interlaced in her words did not elude Sharon.

". . . I thought that if I could contribute in any way, I should." Kelly tried to portray herself as an honest citizen. "And still, I felt embarrassed for having said that I didn't know the girl in question, when in fact I did." She was avoiding the word lie. "So I was trying to think of a way I could answer your questions without embarrassing myself completely."

For the first time since their conversation had

begun, Kelly felt that there might be a chance the suspecting cop believed her.

Sharon found herself in a quandary. She was certain this woman was not the angel she portrayed herself to be. On the other hand, Kelly was a respected and well-connected businesswoman that in one phone call to the police commissioner had buried the entire story, and yet she chose to recant her account and initiate this meeting.

Sharon decided to continue, slow and steady.

"I can understand how our first conversation may have formed the basis for a lack of cooperation, and I appreciate the fact that despite that, we are here today."

Kelly nodded in agreement; her facial expression seemed calmer now.

"Just one last thing," Sharon added.

"Yes, Detective?" *Aren't we done yet?*

"In regards to the last victim, Julie Tyfer."

"Yes?"

Sharon pulled out a photo of the deceased and placed it in front of Kelly.

"Apparently Julie also had received your business card, only a few days before she was killed. Do you remember her?"

Kelly knew there was no escape. She couldn't deny this. For once she would have to answer sincerely.

"Sure. Lovely girl," she forced a smile.

"How did you meet?"

"I was on my way to a business meeting when I noticed her passing by. Julie smiled at me. Usually I don't just hand out my card, but she had a certain grace. I immediately suspected she wasn't from New York," Kelly grinned. "No self-respecting New Yorker would smile at a stranger."

Soon enough I'll even convince myself I was smitten by her.

"I was surprised I hadn't heard from her, but then . . . this whole tragedy repeated itself."

"A nasty *déjà vu* to have to go through twice, huh?" Sharon's forthrightness stood in complete contrast to Kelly's refined language.

"Without a shadow of a doubt . . ."

"Okay, I guess I got all the information I needed." *Not even close . . .* "Is there anything you would like to add?"

"I think I told you everything I know, but I will keep your card just in case." *Sayonara baby!*

"So we're done here. Thank you for your cooperation, Miss Danes. Have a pleasant day."

CHAPTER 16

"Come on, you don't want to be late on the first day, do you?"

"And I won't. I'm a professional."

"Don't think I'm a man of little faith, but I have yet to see your famed punctuality."

"Perhaps you don't deserve it . . ." The dawn had yet to break and already she'd begun taunting him.

"Why would you think that?" He decided to play along.

"Maybe because you tend to forget you're still a rookie in this business."

"Or maybe that's because you're a supermodel and you don't have to bother being nice to people anymore?"

"Ah, is that what you think of me? That's the reason this whole 'us' thing isn't going to work."

"Right now neither one of us is working . . . and that means the whole schedule is being delayed!"

"Like all men, changing the subject the minute the conversation gets a bit more serious . . ."

"Does this conversation really seem serious to you?"

"Perhaps. Maybe this is the most serious conversation I've ever had with a man."

"I really hope you're trying to baffle me as usual."

"And what if I'm not? Will you feel sorry for me?"

"Yes."

"Why?"

"Because you are a beautiful, smart, rich, and famous woman who likes to abuse the men in her life."

Gloria smiled. "Why do you say that? Arthur seems pretty happy to me!"

"You're right. I was kidding. After all, we've agreed it's not a serious conversation, right?"

"Andy!"

"Gloria . . ."

"Maybe you are like all the other men. It serves you right that I'm abusing you," she said with a playful pout.

"Finally, the cat is out of the bag!"

"Andy!"

"Gloria . . ."

"Why are you so mean to me?" she whined.

"Me? In the last five minutes you have already insulted me three times!"

"Oh, really? I forgive you then . . ."

"I forgive you, too."

"But I didn't apologize!" she exclaimed.

"That didn't stop you from forgiving me," he countered.

"But that was because you were actually wrong!"

"I'm so confused that maybe I could have been. That's what happens when I don't get my morning cup of coffee," Andy admitted.

A triumphant expression spread across her face.

"But . . ." Andy mustered all of his strength for the final act. "That has nothing to do with the fact that you are still late!"

"I'm not late! We're supposed to leave at six thirty. I have two whole minutes left!"

"But you're not even dressed yet!"

"Sure I am."

"Gloria, I don't think it's a good idea for you to come downstairs wearing my shirt. Only my shirt . . ."

"Why? It's big enough to cover everything."

"You're absolutely right. Let's go."

"I still have about thirty seconds left, don't I?"

At the speed of light, typical of a runway model who has to change into countless different outfits during one fashion show, Gloria took off Andy's shirt. For the split second her body flashed before his eyes, Andy forgot entirely where he was. When he had regained his senses, Gloria had already changed back into the clothes she'd been wearing the night before.

They had met on the pretense of discussing the schedule for tomorrow, but it had merely been an excuse. They'd sipped some wine, perhaps a bit more than they should have, knowing in their hearts that one thing would lead to another. They'd talked and laughed, and then came that moment, when their eyes locked and their intentions were clear without the need for words. They'd only had a few hours until morning arrived and Andy couldn't bear the thought of spending one more night without her.

Every crevice of her body was his. He had caressed her body slowly, moving his fingers, along every bend and curve; the warmth of her body made the tips of his fingers tingle. Andy had felt like a boy gazing upon a woman for the first time, insatiably mesmerized by her delicate features. His lips had traced her body, relishing everything in their path. She tasted like a mixture of salty and sweet, and his taste buds had craved for more. Once he had reached her breasts, he stopped and pressed his head into her chest, which was moving up and down like the tide, and listened to her heart. His breathing mixed with hers into a swirl of intoxication, his breath covered her skin in a steamy cloak. They were enveloped by warmth and infatuation.

Andy had leaned over Gloria, swallowing in his gaze her dazzling beauty, ravishing it with his eyes. She was as captivating as the picturesque scenery that had surrounded them. *Mesmerizing like blue and Green,* he had determined while staring at her, thinking back on the curvy road that had gotten them here, focusing on the curves revealed before him now. He had whispered sweet words into her ear while his hands remained busy fondling her. He could feel the warmth expanding between her thighs and had felt his body reacting to her unspoken demand. Then he had spread her legs and penetrated her. At that very moment his lips had become one with her lips, his hands had become one with her hands, and they'd both become one.

"Okay, now we really are late," Gloria interrupted the marvel that had taken over his mind and rushed toward the door.

"Wait, hold on," Andy took her hand and twirled Gloria back to him for a long, soft kiss.

"Five more minutes won't change much," he smiled.

CHAPTER 17

Detective Davis left the grand office building, heading straight into the bitter cold of New York City. As the icy wind engulfed her, she curled into her woolen scarf so that only her turquoise-colored eyes remained visible peeping out. The smirking umbrella vendors were the only remaining evidence of the rain that had assaulted the city just moments ago. Sharon barely noticed any puddles. *A harmless drizzle*, she thought to herself, looking at all the agitated tourists who didn't know what to do with their newly purchased umbrellas.

It took her a few minutes to grow accustomed to the frosty air. If she hadn't been right in the middle of solving a murder case, she would have walked home. Central Park was only a few steps away, but Sharon had to settle for a quick glance. Her picnic would have to be postponed for another time.

The slightest drops of rain on her shoulder caused Sharon to quicken her pace toward the subway. She spotted the yellow letters on the black sign pointing to the stairs leading underground, but then her eyes lit up as she spotted a Dunkin' Donuts. Sharon veered off course and walked in, indulging in the heavenly smell.

"You're just in time," said the guy behind the counter as he brought out a tray of fresh doughnuts. He was about seventeen years old.

"Great, I'll take two. Actually make it four; I'll eat them while they're still warm." Sharon figured she wouldn't have time for dinner later.

The surprised boy raised an eyebrow. She did not look like the kind of person who could consume so much dough.

"It's okay, I'm a cop; we're used to it. It comes with the territory," she smiled.

The boy smiled back.

"And also coffee, the largest cup you've got."

Luckily there weren't many people on the train, so Sharon quickly found an empty seat. She settled in her place and prepared to enjoy her feast. She had finished her coffee while she'd been waiting for the train, but now she was regretting her indulgence. Sharon bit into the hot, crispy dough, savoring the sweet taste that spread through her mouth.

I never realized how much happiness lies within a doughnut.

But the universe never gave her a break. The vibrating cell phone in her pant pocket made her jump in her seat. The old lady sitting next to Sharon frowned at her.

"Sorry," she mumbled as she finished the last bite of her doughnut. "Hello?"

"Hi, Davis, it's Rob. I called to check how it went at the dentist's office."

"Ha? Ah, yeah, it went great," she said, struggling to swallow the last of the doughnut.

"What did the doctor say?"

"That I should visit more often." Sharon ran her tongue over her teeth in an attempt to wipe off the stubborn, sticky crumbs. If she was lying about going to the dentist, she should at least make sure her teeth were clean.

"That's it? No root canals?"

"Not this time, but I did get a recommendation for a new toothpaste."

"So you're not going to tell me what you were really up to?"

"What do you mean?" Sharon asked.

"I wasn't born yesterday, you know."

"Rob, I'm offended. Do you really think I would lie to you?"

"Only white lies, like your teeth," he teased. "I'm assuming it had something to do with Kelly Danes?"

Sharon froze.

"Well, maybe it's better if I didn't know. As long as it ends here. See you tomorrow morning?"

"I'll be there with bells on."

"Good. I hope, at least, that this crazy idea of yours, the one that Kelly Danes has something to do with all of this, is out of your system. Good night, Davis. Don't forget to brush your teeth before you go to bed," she could hear Rob laughing before he hung up.

The train stopped, and the name of Sharon's station was announced. She stood up at once, making sure her bag of doughnuts wasn't forgotten on the bench, and walked toward the electronic doors. Frankly, Sharon could not seem to get past that "crazy idea" of hers. Her talk with Kelly had only made her more suspicious.

I don't trust that woman.

It may have appeared that the conversation Kelly initiated had been a gesture of good will, but the more Sharon thought about it, the more she realized something was off. Kelly may have answered her questions in a way that would have set the mind of most investigators at ease, but Sharon found it hard to believe any word coming out of that woman's mouth. She couldn't put her finger on it, but it was there, living, breathing, and kicking.

Kelly's brief disclosure of contempt toward Mandy had not escaped Sharon, even if it had been concealed behind a curtain of beautiful words. Of course Sharon didn't plan to accuse the distinguished businesswoman of murder just because she clearly hadn't liked one of the victims, but she could not let it go either. Sharon had to do something. But what was the next step? Another talk with Kelly wouldn't be helpful, she concluded. This was a very smart woman and, therefore, she was dangerous. If Sharon didn't play her cards right, she could lose it all; and she couldn't afford that.

This woman, without a doubt, was hiding something. Sharon could feel it. She did not know what exactly, but it was her job to find out, *at all costs*.

CHAPTER 18

Could it be that the young man had managed to thaw the ice queen's heart?

The crew members were laughing between themselves. As matter of fact, she was not at all as horrible as they had expected someone of her status to be. They even liked her. As for him, it was impossible not to love him. He had immediately won their admiration and loyalty.

It was clear from the start that the poor fellow was smitten. They just hoped she would be smart enough to give him a fighting chance. But that very morning, as Gloria and Andy had been seen walking down the stairs together, trying not to look at each other, they'd realized something had happened between them. The secretive smiles they had snuck to each other a moment before they joined Kristin, Ben, and Jonny, had left no doubt.

A split second after they sat down at the table, Arthur showed up, a coffee mug in his hand.

"What took you so long? It's like you actually want to miss another day's work and spend it at the inn," he fondly chided them. "And you don't want that, do you?"

The actual answer was quite obvious for everyone seated at that table, except for Arthur. Like a blinded father, he could not see that his little girl was in love. Gloria spotted the looks between the staff employees.

Goodbye, discretion.

Arthur placed the mug in front of Gloria. "Lukewarm, weak latte, with skim milk and no sugar, just the way you like it," he smiled at her. "Don't worry, guys. Your coffee will be here any minute." Arthur calmed the rest of the group, who were craving their morning coffee.

"I have no idea how you can drink that stuff," Andy wondered. "I'm not even sure it's really coffee."

Gloria gave him a sidelong glance. "So what would you call it, exactly?"

"I wouldn't call it by any name. I would just pour it down the sink."

Everyone around the table snickered, except Gloria, who seemed deeply offended.

"I'm sorry, I didn't mean it," Andy apologized, suddenly regretting his choice of words. "I just prefer the barbarian version of steamy, black coffee. Hard core."

A hint of a smile was seen at the corners of her lips, but she wasn't completely satisfied.

"Okay, fine. Tomorrow I will try, um, *coffee à la Gloria*. I promise," he sighed.

Gloria grinned from ear to ear. Andy leaned over to kiss her, but then he noticed the looks on his colleagues' faces, and especially Arthur's. He improvised and reached his hand for the jar of sugar on Gloria's right side.

"And what exactly are you going to sweeten?" Gloria teased him, being that her mug was the only one on the table.

At that exact moment, Tom, the owner, placed on the table a large pitcher of steaming coffee.

"It never hurts to be prepared," Andy answered triumphantly. The attractive dimples that cornered his smile only enhanced his victorious expression.

Gloria could no longer hold back, nor did she want to. She leaned over to Andy and kissed him passionately, ignoring everyone around them and their stunned looks. The ice queen was gone; all that remained was a couple in love.

CHAPTER 19

Sharon sat at her windowsill, peering out at the magnificent view of Manhattan, holding in her hand a warm mug of homemade macchiato. She loved snuggling up in her blanket with a cup of piping hot coffee, straight from the espresso machine, when it was cold and rainy outside.

Like everything else in New York, even the cold was intense. Sharon placed a hand on the transparent window and felt the frost. The idea that the thin glass was all that separated her from the outside made Sharon appreciate even more the hours of rest she spent in her cozy apartment.

Sharon's gaze landed on a large raindrop slowly dribbling down the glass pane, while her thoughts were running relentlessly. Sitting on the ledge of the windowsill overlooking the big world always calmed her and put her mind at ease. It helped her to contemplate things and consider options she wouldn't have come up with in the pressure chamber where she worked.

The view of the grand and tireless city felt near yet far away at the same time. Sharon almost never took advantage of the fact that she was living in a cultural center that was known worldwide as a tourist magnet.

A bitter sense of disappointment nipped through her heart when she realized all those tourists had probably gotten to know the city better than her, a longtime resident. When, for instance, was the last time she had gone to a Broadway show? Or had visited one of the dozens of museums the city had to offer? Or even had enjoyed some window shopping on Fifth Avenue? It seemed as though the only attraction she visited on a regular basis was Starbucks.

Sharon had trouble recalling the last time she'd gone out to a good restaurant. It was probably months ago. She usually ordered huge amounts of Chinese takeout and fed on the leftovers for the rest of the week – and it was never a problem. But now, when she had a few moments to herself, she began to feel the self-pity rising from the oblivion within her.

The view seen from the window merged with her reflection in the clear glass. She stared at her distorted image but then quickly shifted her gaze and focused on a distant spot in the horizon. Sharon never paid too much attention to her looks, although people found her to be beautiful. In spite of that, she hadn't gone on a date in months, and the last time she had, it had been with a guy from work, a narcotics officer, so there was no one to balance the madness. Needless to say it had turned out to be catastrophic.

Sharon accepted the fact she was a workaholic. She knew she should join a support group. Quit her job. Fly to Paris without giving notice. Or perhaps, God forbid, take a sick day and spend it in Manhattan. Sharon promised herself she would do each and every one of those things.

Right after she cracked this case.

She took another sip of the hot beverage and felt it coursing through her body, as if it too were searching for the answer she had been longing for. Sharon didn't have an actual reason to treat Kelly Danes as a suspect, but her intuition would not let her give up. Even the meeting that Kelly had initiated, on the grounds of allegedly assisting, implied a cover-up attempt. Sharon felt as if she had reached a dead end. She had to get results and fast, or else Rob might assign Bryant to the case – and then the killer's identity would remain a mystery forever.

Sharon had already read all the documents that her Probie had managed to find regarding Kelly Danes. She had hoped, for his sake, that he hadn't missed anything; he did not want to find himself on her bad side. Even her good side was pretty rough around the edges.

Sharon browsed through the documents a second time and still couldn't find anything that caught her attention, mainly because most of the information included things like fashion reviews found in gossip columns discussing the outfits Kelly wore to various charity benefits, and basic information such as her former addresses, marital status, and copies of her tax returns.

Yeah, Sharon, that's where you'll find the answer. Maybe you should arrest her because she filed her taxes late?

Sharon groaned in desperation. She realized that she couldn't find whatever it was that she was looking for in the police reports, and, as always, she had to take a risk or she could forget about this case, because it would be assigned to someone else. Sharon took the last sip of her coffee and placed the mug on the coffee table;

then she reached for the phone. She knew what she had to do.

When Sharon dialed Rob's number she desperately hoped he would not shut her down, but she knew that even if he did, it wouldn't stop her.

"Hello?"

"Hey, it's Davis."

"Goddammit, can't it wait until tomorrow?"

"No, I'm going to Arizona."

"What the hell are you talking about? Do I need to remind you that there is a serial killer on the loose?"

"That's exactly why I'm going."

"I don't understand."

"I'm going to meet Kelly's parents."

CHAPTER 20

"There's no way in hell that you're going anywhere!"

"Rob, I've never been so sure of something in my life. I have to go."

"And who's going to pay for that exactly?"

"I will, with my salary. I'd hoped that the department would, but if that's what it takes, I'll pay for it out of my own pocket."

"You do realize that you're crazy, right?"

"Yes."

"This is your answer? *Yes?* No explanation or even an apology?"

"Okay, Rob, I'm sorry for being crazy. But I'm still going."

"I don't understand. Didn't we agree that you wouldn't get involved with Kelly Danes anymore? Or shall I remind you of my talk with the commissioner? I am telling you flat out: *You are not going anywhere.*"

* * *

"Detective Davis, would you like something to drink? I made fresh lemonade."

"That sounds great, Mrs. Danes. Thank you."

"Mrs. Danes?" A smile formed on her face. "Please, call me Miranda."

Sharon took another homemade cookie from the stacked tray. Table manners were definitely not her strong suit, nor was controlling her gluttony. Kelly's mother retuned to the living room as Sharon was trying to find a napkin to wipe the cookie crumbs off her lips. It wasn't very professional to lead a conversation with a mouth full of chocolate chip oatmeal cookies, no matter how delicious they may be.

Miranda watched Sharon with delight. "It's been so long since someone has enjoyed my cooking. After Kelly left it was just me and Harold, my husband, but he passed away a couple of years ago from a heart attack."

"What a waste," Sharon blurted, lacking every bit of tact.

Miranda stared at her with a confused look that conveyed a shortage of understanding.

"I meant, it's a shame that no one has had the chance to enjoy your delicious food." She hoped the compliment would compensate for her bluntness. How many times had she told herself not to fire out every single thought that went through her mind?

"That's nice of you, dear. I would love for you to stay for dinner. As always, I've made too much food. A force of habit, I suppose."

Sharon desperately wanted to accept Miranda's invitation, not just because the alternative was a tuna sandwich and a pack of Pringles that she'd bought at the airport, but because she recognized loneliness in Miranda's eyes, the longing for company. It was clear that her daughter did not visit often.

"We'll see when we're done," Sharon tried to avoid a direct answer. "I hope our talk won't make you miss dinner," she added with a smile.

Miranda smiled back. She was warm and folksy, a typical small town woman, lacking the suspiciousness that typically characterized city people. She may not have been the intellectual type, but she sure had a huge heart.

Kind of the antithesis of Kelly.

* * *

"Rob, I'm not asking for your permission. I am telling you that I'm going, and I don't care if you don't like it because the commissioner has you by the *balls*."

Anyone else would have gotten an immediate suspension, or at least a harsh reprimand. Rob, however, was used to Sharon's ruggedness, so he let it slide.

"Well, no wonder he has me by the balls when you're getting me in trouble all the time. Damn it, Davis, you are the only one in this division I can trust with my eyes closed. Don't play tricks on me now."

That last sentence, half a warning and half a compliment, touched Sharon.

"Do you really think *I* would play a trick on you? Why do you think I called you in the first place?"

"Okay. Then explain to me what's so interesting about Kelly Danes' parents?"

* * *

"My Kelly has always worked hard. Even in elementary school she used to sit for hours in her room, making sure she had done all of her homework, even the optional assignments. She was an exceptional student," Miranda smiled proudly.

Sharon thought one thing: Kelly hadn't had any friends.

"Well, it's not surprising, then, that she's gotten so far in life," Sharon replied. She couldn't treat Kelly as a suspect or question Miranda's answers. She had told Miranda that Kelly had known two of the victims from the notorious murders; therefore, it was necessary to confirm that she was not in any danger. Sharon had explained that she'd been sent here, on account of Kelly's good relationship with the police commissioner, to make sure there was no risk to her life. She'd said just about enough to let Miranda connect the dots herself. Needless to say, the unsettled mother was determined to help in any way to protect her daughter.

"Yes, perhaps even too far," she mumbled without thinking. Sharon could hear the sadness in her voice. It was obvious Miranda missed her daughter.

"Sounds like Kelly's success in school made some people jealous."

"Maybe in elementary school, but by high school nobody cared."

"So Kelly was excluded because she was more mature for her age?"

"I don't think that's why. Kelly was always alone. She never fit in. She was a nice, quiet girl, so nobody picked on her."

The girl Sharon envisioned did not resemble even one bit the woman that she had gotten to know. She almost felt sorry for her.

"Was there another reason?" Sharon could not help asking.

"Kelly was very insecure and kept to herself. I don't think she even tried to make friends."

"Not even one?"

Miranda paused for a brief moment. It seemed as if she was hesitating about something, not certain if she was disclosing too much.

"Maybe one friend," she finally said. Her eyes fixated on a framed photo of a mousy looking girl.

"Who is that?" Sharon asked. She hadn't realized that Kelly had siblings.

"It's Kelly."

Detective Davis was stunned. The graceless character gazing out of the frame was nothing like the woman Sharon had met the other day. The look in her eyes was dreadful and timid, so different from the belligerent Kelly she knew.

A true case of "The Ugly Duckling"...

"She looks so different now," Sharon could not conceal her astonishment.

"Yes, I know. My daughter put quite a lot of effort in creating a *new* Kelly. I'm not sure I have come to terms with it yet, but after what the poor girl went through ..."

"Excuse me?"

Miranda's eyes revealed that she had said too much.

* * *

"Listen, Rob, this woman knows something. I can feel it in my bones. I have to find out what she is trying to hide!"

"And you think *her mother* will tell *you* about her daughter's deepest, darkest secrets?"

"I have no idea, but there's nothing else for me to do. I can't just sit on my ass and wallow in the fact that this case is going nowhere."

"You really believe that the mother of a magazine editor living thousands of miles away can help us in a murder case?"

"Come on, you know it's not like it sounds."

"It's exactly like it sounds."

"You've got me there, but we both know that you'll end up agreeing with me anyway, so can we just skip to that part of the conversation? I need to start packing."

"One night."

"Huh?"

"That's all that I can scrape from the budget. You have less than forty-eight hours to find out whatever it is that you're looking for. After that you come straight back here."

"You won't regret it," she assured him.

"I already am," Rob sighed.

If you can't beat 'em, join 'em.

* * *

"It's nothing. Forget I said anything." Miranda shifted her gaze away from Sharon.

"Miranda, any information concerning your daughter could help us keep her safe. There's no way of knowing how the mind of a serial killer works." Sharon hoped that planting a seed of horror in the mind of the worried mother would lead to something.

"I'm sure *that* has nothing to do with Kelly's life today," Miranda asserted. "It happened twenty years ago, so it's really not relevant."

Sharon quickly did the math. *1990*.

"What exactly happened?"

"I'm sorry, but I'm not interested in discussing it. And I don't think my Kelly would want me to talk about it. If you think it's important, you can always ask her."

Only if I want Rob's balls to be removed permanently.

"No, there's no need for that. But I would love to see some more photos of Kelly. After all, she *is* the editor of my favorite magazine growing up," Sharon smiled.

Miranda took the bait.

CHAPTER 21

The flash of Andy's camera was merging with the fragile sunlight of the new day. Even though the photos from yesterday had come out well, to a great extent due to Gloria's professionalism, Andy claimed that the daylight was too bright; therefore, they should start shooting at sunrise. Due to his meticulousness, or some would even say compulsiveness, everybody had to wake up before the clock struck four.

Andy was adjusting the camera lens while Gloria demonstrated a variety of poses, at times approaching the camera and sometimes pulling away, displaying flamboyant postures in some of them and choosing to express subtlety in others. Her sheer tiredness and lack of sleep were not apparent, neither in Gloria's demeanor nor her appearance. Minutes after she'd woken up, Gloria's "small beauty army" had surrounded the model and made her absolutely stunning; but, just in case, she was still thankful for Photoshop.

Perhaps due to the criticism she was exposed to as a model, or maybe because she was simply a perfectionist, Gloria was not entirely pleased with herself. She had found peace with whom she was (that wasn't so hard), but she could not stand her shortcomings. She might have to live with them, but she did not have to like them.

Arthur watched Gloria and Andy working together in perfect synchrony. *They are a good team,* he noted to himself. Usually Gloria would pick on the slightest things, but now she was letting Andy take the lead. And it wasn't just for the camera; recently even Arthur had noticed that Gloria had let most of the little things go, those things that used to bother her so much in the past, and he credited this to Andy. As one of the few people who knew Gloria well, from every line on her hand to every slight wrinkle on her face (though he'd never drawn her attention to them, of course), Arthur knew how much Gloria tended to be hard on herself and felt relieved knowing that outside of him she had Andy by her side.

Arthur studied Gloria's delicate movements while Andy's camera lens perpetuated every graceful moment of her image, gazing at the view that encircled her. Gloria may have starred in dozens of campaigns, but this was definitely the highlight of her career, he thought, wholeheartedly. She had reached the very top.

Arthur wanted to cherish this moment of seeing Gloria at the peak of her beauty and maturity, despite the standard norms of the modelling field, which dictated that she was running out of time. He did not understand why exactly these thoughts were popping into his mind right now, but when he looked at her again, Arthur felt a subtle dampness starting to form in the corners of his eyes. Maybe he didn't have to worry so much about his little star anymore. He flashed a big smile, and Gloria noticed him and grinned back, right before she turned her head back to the camera.

* * *

Andy just loved the way the translucent fabric of Gloria's dress fluttered in the light breeze; it made her look remarkably heavenly. He remembered when they had been sitting together in his hotel room, debating which outfit to pick for the photo shoot. It already seemed like so long ago. It was hard to believe that it had been only a few short days, considering how far they'd come since then.

His heart still skipped a beat when he thought about the first time he had seen her, at that dull party, drawing all eyes toward her like a human magnet of beauty. He couldn't believe he had kissed the most beautiful woman in the world in the candy aisle of a gas station minimart, and he still asked himself if their passionate night together had been a dream or reality.

Could he really be in love? The smile that appeared on his face every time he touched Gloria, saw her, or merely thought of her, stated that he was. The last time he had been so enchanted by a girl had been when he was a seventeen-year-old boy falling in love for the first time; but it had been a childish, naive love that had ended as quickly as it had begun. This time it was different. It was *real*. He felt it deep down in his soul. He had hoped that this was not unrequited love, that he wasn't acting like a stupid boy, being misled by his idol and eventually ending up hurt. Andy knew Gloria had many admires, that she lived the kind of life other people could not even dream about, and he wished to be a worthy candidate for her heart. When he had held her close, had kissed her neck and listened to her ever-accelerating breathing, he had dared to believe that he just might be.

Andy then reflected on the moment he had accepted Kelly Danes' prestigious job offer, how excited he had been about what was yet to come: the national exposure that would launch his career, the ridiculously high salary, traveling to New Zealand and revisiting its breathtaking scenery. He had never imagined that, ultimately, what would make him feel most on top of the world would be . . . a girl!

There is no doubt women have an inexplicable mystical pull over humanity, he concluded.

CHAPTER 22

On her way back from Miranda's house, Sharon still could not entirely grasp the tremendous transformation Kelly's looks had undergone.

Surely there had been a great deal of plastic surgeries involved – a quantity that indicated self-loathing rather than the desire to be fashionable. Sharon couldn't shake off the image of that small, mousy girl with her sheepish eyes staring back at her from the photos. The tragic image had been seared into her mind, not because it was extremely ugly or repulsive, but since it seemed as if every feature in Kelly's face had been screaming for help. Her desperation managed to penetrate the photos.

Who the hell made you feel like that?

Sharon knew it was already too late; that poor girl did not exist anymore. From her ashes had risen a new woman, one who was forceful and dangerous. Sharon began to wonder how things would have turned out if . . .

She had gotten carried away in a sea of thoughts again; she had to clear her mind. She needed to forget about those old photos, they were not relevant to the case right now. But there was one more thing that bothered her: the image of a beautiful girl who could be seen in one of the pictures and somehow seemed vaguely familiar. Sharon tried to focus and think where she recognized her from. Was she an employee in Kelly's office? Or perhaps related to one of the victims? She just couldn't seem to recall.

Sharon pulled over in front of the roadside motel where she intended to spend the night. What interested her now was 1990. She had to figure out what had happened then, that had caused Kelly to transform herself from head to toe.

She opened the squeaky door marked 18. The room was small and dense, overtaken by a compelling odor of air freshener. The cheap, faded wallpaper had begun to peel off, revealing a crumbling wall and a cobweb that had maintained a status of honor – it seemed as though no one dared to come near it.

Sharon took one look at the shabby armchair, which surely had seen better days, and sat down on the bed instead. *At least they have to change the sheets*, she figured. She pulled the laptop out of her bag, along with a box of Pringles, immediately regretting for having to politely decline Miranda's invitation for dinner. The lamp on the nightstand emitted a feeble, yellow light, like a dying man trying to take his last breath. On top of one of the two shelves in the room, next to the dusty Bible, there was a half-eaten Cheetos bag, left by the previous tenant, if not the one before.

Who, for God's sake, leaves half a bag of Cheetos on a shelf in a hotel room?

At that point Sharon realized that she was getting distracted. She had to focus. She brushed off the Pringles crumbs that had fallen onto her clothes, opened her laptop, and prayed for a wireless connection. She didn't even dare to blink as she stared at the screen.

Hallelujah!

She connected, but just barely; Sharon hoped that whoever's Wi-Fi network she'd joined would stay online long enough for her to find what she needed. She tried crossing Kelly's name with the year 1990, but nothing came up. Even adding the name of her hometown, Winslow, didn't surface any unusual incidents in relation to Kelly Danes. All she found were a few articles and a couple of interviews with the successful magazine editor. Not a single clue that would lead to a dark Pandora's Box.

Kelly Danes, is your influence so great that you even got Google on your side?

The Wi-Fi connection failed, and Sharon tried to open the search window again. She began to fear of the possibility of having to spend long hours in dense archives, though even then the odds that someone would have written about the doings of a small town girl in a New York newspaper were slim; unless it had been something really terrible. And if that were the case, she would have already seen it on her computer screen.

The apprehension that this whole trip might have been in vain began to nibble at her consciousness. Sharon couldn't bear the thought of disappointing Rob, or herself for that matter. She desperately needed something that would revive the case, which currently seemed as if it had reached a dead end.

It's just so unfair.

Sharon decided to call Miranda and try to glean one more piece of information out of her, though she was not very optimistic that she could.

"Hello, Mrs. Danes?"

"You know, it's pretty funny when you call me that."

"Still too formal for you?" Sharon chuckled.

"No, not because of that. It's just that my last name is Whitesporte."

CHAPTER 23

Kelly was sitting in her luxurious corner office, overlooking the panorama of the most powerful city in the world. She felt like a queen ruling over her subordinates with an iron fist, manipulating the commoners as if they were helpless puppets at her mercy. In a way, it was true. Kelly decided who deserved to live, and, far more important, who deserved to die. She held the fate of those buffoons in her hands and crushed it with pleasure.

Kelly admired the black bud that had sprouted within her, which had begun to blossom, only reaching its full glory in that special moment when the scaffold landed. What a shame that no one could appreciate her hard work. But there was no choice; it was a mission she had to execute on her own. Any other option would lead to her downfall. That was why it was her duty to neutralize anyone who might stand in her way.

So far she did well. Kelly had made the snooping detective believe that she was a model citizen who had unfortunately found herself caught in a problematic situation. She was so proud of the creativity and resourcefulness she had demonstrated. She could not stand aside while someone questioned her innocence. She always had to be in control.

Kelly was appalled when she remembered the vulgar tone and impudent attitude that had characterized her opponent. Under different circumstances, she would have thrown that boorish cop out of her office on the spot; instead, she had served her coffee and patiently answered each and every one of her irritating questions. Luckily, Kelly emitted a long sigh, this chapter was behind her now, signed and sealed by her victory. The cop hadn't made contact since then. It may have been only three days, but it seemed like Detective Davis would not be bothering her anymore. Kelly was free once more, and she craved to feel yet again the power to condemn lives. She spotted suitable candidates everywhere – beautiful, vain, who ought to be taught a lesson – but Kelly knew that she had to stay low and not succumb to her urges, no matter how strong they might be.

Those killing moments, delightful as they might have been, were just a small part of a larger picture. They had prepared her for her true calling, a mission she had set for herself years ago. Soon she would be able to fulfill her heart's most secret desire: the oh-so-sweet revenge.

The nightmares about that bloody day had followed her for many nights. But in her dreams, that same marvelous moment she aspired for also appeared. Now it seemed closer than ever. The mere thought of it made her hands tremble with excitement and her fingers tingle with anticipation. Kelly burst into an insane, uncontrollable laughter, and was glad that there was no one in the office to witness her bizarre behavior. She forced herself to thrust her manicured, polished nails deep into her arms so she would calm down, creating for herself some sort of personal straight jacket.

Kelly took a deep breath and ignored the involuntary tears that flooded her eyes. She saw them as a sign of weakness, the rock bottom she had sworn never to hit again. Her body was moving back and forth, as if it was trying to break through from her incarcerating grip. Kelly suddenly realized that it was rather disturbing that no one around her had noticed that she was not mentally stable. And, despite that, she had successfully managed to establish herself as tops in her field, becoming one of the most influential pillars of strength in the city. After all, she had the power to decide which articles would be included in a supposedly innocent magazine, which, in essence, functioned as a bible for millions of impressionable young girls across the country.

What kind of idiots live in this country, that I have a free hand in sculpting their children's minds . . .

Of course it wasn't completely their fault. Kelly had played her part perfectly. A model citizen, a successful businesswoman, a role model . . . How glad she was that she hadn't listened to the old Kelly, that miserable nobody who wouldn't even have dared to dream of standing where the new Kelly paced so naturally.

Unlike the old Kelly, nowadays she fought for whatever she wanted, without any fears or hesitations, even if it meant trampling everything in her path. She was determined, strong, and had a spark of brilliance that the plebeians might interpret as madness, but she knew what she was worth. Nothing would stand in her way.

She had suffered through horrible injustices in the past and now it was time to correct them – starting with Gloria McIntyre's existence on this planet. Kelly had all the means necessary to crush her completely.

Kelly proudly recalled the step-by-step plan she had devised. The way she had used her connections in the advertising world to track down an aspiring, young photographer, one who would be willing to do anything she said in order to win the amazing "opportunity" she had offered him. How she had guided, telling him exactly how to present his proposal to the conceited princess so she would accept it, while making it clear to him that if the model refused, everything he dreamed of would slip through his fingers. She had been smart enough to ensure that he had plenty of talent and charm, too, so her plan would not fall apart due to the fact that he was merely an insignificant pawn. The way she had directed him to determine the right timing to reveal the "truth" about the desired project, without understanding that everything he said was a downright lie, thus making him an accomplice without even knowing it. How she had rented an impressive mansion on the other side of the world, just to make certain that her highness would agree to meet with her. And, finally, the fact that she had, once and for all, managed to isolate and capture in her net the bitch who had destroyed her life.

How, at long last, she would eliminate the supermodel.

CHAPTER 24

After Sharon had thanked Miranda and hung up the phone, she slumped down onto the bed and chortled to herself. Finally, she had found the missing piece of the puzzle. That had been the elusive reason why she couldn't find a shred of information about the renowned editor's past: Kelly had changed her last name.

In the course of their conversation, Miranda had told Sharon that years ago, after settling down in New York, Kelly had notified her that she was changing her last name to something "catchier," as she had phrased it.

Sharon's fingers tingled as they brushed against the keyboard. Now she could find what she had been looking for all this time. That key component, the one that would help her crack this case and accuse Kelly Danes-Whitesporte of murder. Or accessory murder. Or something. As long as it got her somewhere in this investigation.

Sharon didn't know what exactly she would find out. For a moment she was worried that this lead would slip out of her hands, or maybe that it was never really there, but her intuitions screamed at her from within and signaled her to trust her instincts. Sharon started typing Kelly's original name on the search window.

KELLY WH . . .

The browser closed; the internet had been disconnected. Sharon tried to reconnect, but no luck. For the first time in a long time she wanted to burst into tears. This couldn't happen now! Not when she was so close. Sharon tried over and over again to get the connection back, moving to different sides of the room and searching for other available networks, but it was clear that it was a lost cause. It was late at night and the user of the computer she had zeroed in on must have turned it off. She was stuck. She picked up her cell phone for the second time that night and called Rob, ignoring the late hour and the time difference to boot, hoping that he might still answer.

Shit, it went to voicemail.

"Hey, Rob. It's Sharon . . . Call me as soon as you get this message . . . Kelly's real last name is Whitesporte . . . Something happened to her in 1990, here in Arizona . . . Her mother refused to talk about it . . . You have to find out what the hell it was, it's just I'm out of the Wi-Fi connec–"

The recording time ended. *That's just how it goes when you have no idea what to say,* Sharon scolded herself. She hoped Rob would get the message in time. She couldn't wait to be back in New York and have the department's advanced search engines at her disposal, or at least a decent internet connection. Some of the airports offered wireless connections, so maybe she'd get lucky. That was her only chance of finding out about Kelly before going back to New York. Her flight was leaving first thing in the morning, and never in her life had she been happier to start a day so early.

* * *

On the same night that Sharon celebrated her biggest breakthrough, Kelly's worst nightmare came to life. Kelly came back home, still feeling euphoric from the little celebration in her office. She pressed the button on her answering machine, not really expecting any messages, but to her surprise, there actually was one. Perhaps the most frightening message she could have gotten.

"Hi, honey, it's Mom. We haven't talked in *so long* and I miss you. I know I'm not supposed to call, but I have a feeling I may have done something wrong. A Detective Davis came over to meet me, in order to make sure that no one might be trying to harm you, you know, because of that serial murder story. She told me that you knew some of the victims and that you might be in danger! Why didn't you tell me anything? Why did you stop calling? Well, anyhow, that's not the point. I . . . I'm really sorry, but I almost told her . . . you know what . . . But I stopped myself just in time! I didn't tell her anything. I'm really sorry, honey, but don't worry. I don't think she noticed, and she respected my request not to talk about it."

Kelly tried to choke back her anger and listen to the rest of the message.

". . . In any case, she was really nice! We were looking at old photos and nibbled on some of those homemade oatmeal cookies you like so much."

I hate oatmeal cookies.

". . . You know what, if you'd like, I'll make two batches for you first thing in the morning and send them to you! I hope you're not mad. Please, call me back, or at least write . . . I just haven't heard from you in so long. Love you!"

Kelly began coughing violently. The coughs took over her entire body, becoming worse and worse. She collapsed on the glaring floor of her lavish home. Tiny beads of perspiration began covering her skin. For a few long minutes, Kelly felt as if she were suffocating; she was gasping for air. Gradually, her breathing began to adjust and the coughing stopped, but the heat was still emanating from her body, slowly, like a dying ember.

Kelly barely got up and then staggered toward the bathroom. She pulled a towel off of the shining towel rack that matched the other items embellishing the decorated space. She wetted it and ran it across her face and then over the rest of her sweltering body. The immediate coolness soothed her. On her way to the master bedroom, Kelly took off her clothes, leaving them scattered throughout the hall, until she remained completely naked. She fell onto her bed, curled up in a fetal position, with her face turned toward the ceiling, her eyes gazing at it with a blank look. Shortly after, they began to tear up. Was this the beginning of her great downfall? Was it possible that she had been too complacent, believing wholeheartedly that all the pieces would fall into place and complete the perfect vision that she had built in her mind?

"You stupid hillbilly!!!" she roared toward the ceiling.

The spacious room replied with her echoing cry.

Why did you do this to me, Mom? Why are you sticking your nose where it doesn't belong?

The tears had already dried on her cheeks; there were no new ones to replace them.

*I can't believe that stupid cop has done this to me. Who does she think she is, going behind my back to see **my mother**?*

All of a sudden a frightening thought penetrated her mind.

She couldn't have done this on her own. Someone authorized her to do this. Unless she has a death wish . . .

Kelly didn't know which was worse, knowing that she was doomed because of a detective who wasn't worth the slime that stuck to her shoes, or the fact that she hadn't tricked her as well as she'd thought. Kelly was closer than ever to giving up her dream and devoting herself to the loss, but then her inherent survival instinct kicked in. She was not going to give up.

If she wants war, she will get war. Sharon Davis has no idea what she's gotten herself into.

Kelly got up swiftly, a complete contrast to the way she had arrived in bed. She marched lightly toward her closet, got dressed quickly, and went down to the basement. She passed all the mirrors surrounding the room without looking at them even once. Kelly typed in the access code to the high-tech safe she had installed there: The date of that awful day in 1990; a day she would never forget. She took out stacks and stacks of green bills and one single gun.

If there was anything Kelly was addicted to, it was revenge.

CHAPTER 25

The flight back to New York lasted just a few hours, but seemed to Sharon like an eternity.

She hadn't been able to get hold of Rob before the flight, presumably because of the time difference, and she had been sentenced to spend the next five and a half hours without any possibility of making contact with the outside world. Even though she'd had very few hours of sleep the night before, different thoughts and scenarios were racing through her mind. She felt as if time were passing insufferably slow, minute by minute. Her only comfort was that she had a window seat.

Sharon gazed down at the lights of the city waking up below her during takeoff and a tiny smile crept to the corners of her lips. She remembered her last visit to Arizona, at the age of fourteen, during a family vacation. That summer it had been her younger brother's turn to choose the destination. Like any adventurous ten-year-old boy, Sean had chosen the Grand Canyon. Sharon had not been thrilled, to say the least. Even back then, she had already adopted the sarcasm and rough edges that had become an integral part of her personality as an adult, and his choice hadn't suited her. She had felt frustrated and cheated; she couldn't believe that her annoying parents were dragging her to spend a whole week in the middle of nowhere Arizona, along with her equally annoying brother, away from all of her friends. On top of that, during the exact same week as the family trip, Jeremy Crane, the most popular boy in school, had thrown a pool party at his house, and she had been devastated when she realized she was going to miss it. In hindsight, it had only been an above ground swimming pool in the backyard of an average house in Brooklyn, but in young Sharon's eyes it had been no less glamorous than the Oscars. Of course, her parents hadn't agreed to cancel a family tradition. Instead, they'd promised her that she would have fun on the trip, even if she didn't believe it. Eventually the prophecy fulfilled itself, but Sharon had never dared to admit it to her parents; after all, she'd had a stiff reputation to maintain.

Sharon resolved to tell them the truth this weekend, even if it was twelve years later. *You were right, Mom and Dad, I did have fun on that trip.* And they had the ultimate proof: a photo from that trip, the one with the Grand Canyon stretching behind Sharon in all of its glory, her blonde hair glinting beneath the bright July sun while she was smiling at the camera. Her parents had framed the special photo, which had captured their moody teenage daughter cracking a smile, at long last, and had hung it on the wall along the stairs, where all the family photos were proudly displayed.

It suddenly hit her that she hadn't visited her parents' house in a long time. Besides the occasional trip out to some shady crime scene, she hadn't stepped outside the borders of Manhattan much. It was unbelievable how long it had been since she had spent real quality time with her family. She had met her parents a few weeks ago for dinner, but it had been shortened because something came up at work. She hadn't seen her brother, now a student at Stanford University, for a few months, not since Christmas. She couldn't recall if he had a girlfriend or not, and that made her pretty sad, because they had been very close when they were younger.

This job was taking a toll not just on her, but also on the people closest to her, she sadly realized. Ever since she'd taken on this case, she hadn't really had time to have a life of her own. She had dedicated her everything to finding this damned murderer, or murderess, a possibility which seemed realistic now more than ever.

The countless hours she had spent reading the case files, which she could now recite by heart; the long nights lying awake in her bed, unable to fall asleep, in an attempt to figure out what the hell was she missing; the power struggles with her boss, followed by the way in which she had jeopardized her position; and, most of all, the deep sense of defeat each time a new victim was found. All of these had made it clear to her that this was much more than just a job. More than just a case.

It was personal.

Her left foot started tapping rapidly against the floor of the plane. The sudden rush of emotions tingled inside of her to the extent that Sharon felt as if she needed to run a marathon to get rid of them, but the red seatbelt sign was still on.

Can't you just give me a break?

Sharon wasn't sure who she was complaining to, but the thought vanished from her mind as quickly as it had appeared, because at that exact moment a strange force held her leg and prevented it from moving.

To her surprise, she found on her lap the hand of the man sitting next to her.

In any other situation he would have ended up flattened on the ground, groaning in agony, but Sharon assumed this would not be acceptable on an airplane.

"Calm down," he smiled. It seemed as if he were saying it more for her sake than for his.

His grin, warm and friendly, managed to soften all of her defense mechanisms. For a moment, she forgot how to strike back.

"I wish there were someone to tell me that every day . . ." she admitted, surprised by her own candidness.

"I'm Chris," he introduced himself, still smiling.

"Sharon," she smiled back.

The flight attendant passed with the beverage cart.

"I would like some orange juice please, and the lady will have . . ." he purposely spoke in a pompous, official tone.

Sharon smiled, "Water, that's all. Thanks."

After the flight attendant had served them their drinks and moved on to the next row, he turned to her.

"What are you so nervous about, Sharon?" His interest seemed sincere.

Sharon focused on a distant spot out the window. "Believe me, you don't want to know, and I wouldn't even know where to begin."

She turned and looked at him. He seemed to be in his late twenties and had dark hair that complemented his blue eyes. Not that Sharon noticed.

"Let's start with something easier. Are you just visiting or . . . ?"

"I was born and raised in New York," she answered proudly.

"My deepest condolences," he teased.

"Thanks, I could use it."

"How come?"

"I got seated next to a wiseass on the plane."

"Wow! I'm dealing with a pro. So I guess we're even?"

"Seriously? If anything, it's two to one, in my favor."

"Sounds about right," he chuckled.

They smiled at each other. It had been so long since Sharon had a conversation that wasn't related somehow to a murder case. It was nice.

"So, Sharon, what were you doing in Arizona?"

"Work stuff . . . By your response I'm guessing you're not from New York."

"Not originally. I recently moved to New York for a job, but I can't really say I've adapted to the big city life."

"New York isn't your cup of tea?" Her lips curled into a smile.

"Actually, from the little that I've seen, it looks cool. But the last few months I've been so busy getting situated with my new job that I haven't really gotten many chances to experience the city," he admitted. "Honestly, though, what bothers me the most is the people."

"Oh, really?" she asked playfully. *Am I flirting with him?*

"They're all such egoistical pricks. Everyone in the office hates me because I'm the new guy. They haven't even given me a chance to prove what an asshole I really am!"

Sharon laughed out loud. The bald man in the seat in front of her turned his head back and gave her a disapproving glare. But she was still smiling.

"Though it could be that I just haven't gotten to Know New York properly . . ."

Sharon immediately sensed where he was going with this, but she wasn't entirely convinced that he was actually hitting on her.

". . . Maybe if a cool New Yorker decided to prove me wrong . . ."

Sharon froze. She had no idea how to react. She could barely crack a smile.

"So, what do you say?" He kept smiling, but it was obvious that he was nervous, too.

She looked into his eyes for a few seconds before answering. "Okay, sure. Why the hell not?" Sharon decided to jump at the opportunity, even if in a few days she would end up cancelling because of work.

"Great! Here's my card. Call me when you get some time off work."

"In that case, we will never see each other again. It's better if you take my card."

CHAPTER 26

"Information. How may I help you?"

"Hello, operator, may I get the address corresponding to a phone number, please?"

Kelly held in her hand the business card of Detective Davis. She knew exactly what to do.

"Of course, could you please tell me the number?"

* * *

Sharon had finally reached the top of the staircase, which this time seemed to be longer than ever. In just a few minutes she would reach her warm bed and, most important, the telephone. She had forgotten to charge her cell phone before the flight, and now it was turned off and lifeless. She was eager to hear what Rob had found out, whether there had been any breakthroughs in the past few hours, or, perhaps, she had once again jumped to conclusions too quickly.

In the last minute she had before arriving at her apartment door, Sharon let her thoughts drift to other things: that cute guy she'd met on the plane, her gruesome tiredness and aching muscles, and how much she longed for a warm bubble bath. She knew the latter was most likely not going to happen and she would probably have to settle for a quick shower before diving back into the case. But since she still had a few more seconds to fantasize, she threw in a good glass of wine as well. The only thing her imagination and reality had in common was the Chinese takeout she was about to order from her favorite restaurant, conveniently located just a few blocks away from her home. She was starving.

Sharon reached her doorstep and began rummaging through her big, messy bag for her keys. What a surprise, she couldn't find them. She started to fear that she had lost them, or perhaps even packed them in her suitcase. In that moment she felt the exhaustion and post-flight nerves more than ever. She grasped the doorknob and made a wish:

Please, God, could you give me some slack, just this once?

When Sharon turned the door knob, the greatest miracle happened. The door pushed open.

Thanks!

Sharon entered the dark apartment, dragging her suitcase behind her, and closed the door. And then, in a split second, it hit her: something wasn't right. She *never* forgot to lock the door when she left.

She immediately dropped everything and reached down to her left side, where her holster always remained close to her. But it wasn't there.

Damn those stupid rules that forbid boarding a flight with a visible weapon!

Her Glock was at the bottom of the messy bag that had gotten her in this mess in the first place.

Sharon pulled back slowly, feeling relieved that she hadn't turned on the light yet, which gave her a certain advantage. She was so close to the door when . . .

"If you move one more inch I'll blow your head off."

Sharon knew that voice too well. Before she realized what exactly was going on, the room lit up and Kelly's image stood before her, pointing a gun.

A swirl of emotions rushed through her. Fear, due to the threat that had appeared without warning; confusion, in light of the fact that Kelly had broken into her home; frustration, that she hadn't detected the danger in time; but everything, oddly enough, was diluted by the feeling of satisfaction that came from knowing that she had been right all along. She knew there had been something suspicious about this woman, and this confirmed everything.

"Move!" Kelly ordered her and pointed at a chair that had been placed in the center of the room. "And no sudden movements or else . . ."

Sharon had no choice but to do as Kelly said. She tried to quickly think of a way to get out of this situation, but nothing came to mind. Kelly was the one holding all the cards.

"And look what I found," she flaunted the pair of handcuffs that Sharon kept in her nightstand. "Not much fun when someone goes snooping through your business, huh?"

Sharon gave her a piercing look, but did not say a word.

"What happened? Cat got your tongue?"

Sharon remained silent without taking her eyes off of Kelly.

"You didn't seem to have a problem talking to *my mom*. So why are you so quiet *with me* all of a sudden?"

"I guess your mom is nicer than you."

"Oh, finally, I'm just delighted to hear your voice! And I would watch my mouth if I were you; I don't think you can afford to be rude." She moved toward Sharon, threatening her with the pistol to make her hold still, and then shackled her hands behind the chair with the handcuffs. Sharon's attempts to break free from them hurt her wrists.

"Do you like being cuffed, or do you prefer playing the good cop in bed, too?" Kelly caressed Sharon's face and looked straight into her eyes: "You're so pretty. If I didn't already know you're a cop, I'd have bet you were a model." The gentle stroke turned into an aggressive grip as Kelly sunk her claws deep into Sharon's skin.

"Leave me alone!" Sharon yelled as she turned her head away to evade the harsh grasp.

Kelly pulled back, still pointing the gun at Sharon. "What a coincidence. That's exactly what I wanted to tell you," her tone rose as she spoke. "Why were you digging so deep, Sharon?"

Where the hell did I slip up?

"Why, for God's sake, is your apartment filled with files about me?" Kelly continued in an escalating eruption. "Why, in heaven's name, did you fly all the way to Arizona just to meet my mom?" Her wrath took over completely. Tears of anger washed into her eyes.

Sharon thought she'd noticed a slight tremor in the firm hands clutching the gun.

"Looks like I was right," Sharon answered defiantly. Even with her life in danger she could not refrain from speaking her mind.

Kelly was ready to kill her on the spot.

"Perhaps . . ." she replied. "Let's see if your little investigation was worth the price you are about to pay," Kelly smirked.

"Do you really want to dig yourself into an even deeper hole by killing a cop?" Sharon tried to approach Kelly's voice of reason.

"There's nothing I can do. You went too far. You know too much."

"I guess you really have no boundaries, if you're willing to kill an innocent person. But that's exactly what you did to all those poor girls."

"*Poor* girls?" Kelly snapped. "Believe me, they had it coming. Every single one of them deserved to die. If I could, I would kill them all over again, with pleasure." A smile formed on her dark red lips.

Sharon caught a glimpse of the madness in Kelly's eyes. Not that she needed further proof. She had to find a way to stall. That might be her only chance.

"So why did they have it coming?"

Kelly's moment of glory had come. So far, she hadn't been appreciated for her sacred work disposing of those vain, hollow sinners from this world. She'd had to keep her sweet secret hidden from everyone; but now she was facing a golden opportunity. The stupid cop would understand the mistake she had made before her inevitable death.

"Sharon, are you familiar with the seven deadly sins?" she asked in an odd serenity.

"Sure, but what's that got to do with it?"

"Name them," Kelly commanded.

Sharon raised an eyebrow. "Okay . . . Wrath, envy, lust, sloth, gluttony, pride, and greed."

"Do you know what the punishment is for committing such a sin?"

"Death, if I'm not mistaken. But if that were really the case, then most of the world's population would have been gone by now," she answered wryly.

"Do you know which one is considered to be the deadliest sin of all?" Kelly continued, ignoring Sharon's witticisms.

"I don't know. Wrath? Pride? Envy? I never got around to really pondering it . . ."

"*H-u-b-r-i-s*," Kelly enunciated, with each syllable slowly rolling off her tongue, like a whispering snake.

"Ah, Okay . . ." Sharon began to understand what Kelly was getting at.

"Do you have any clue why it is the worst of all sins?"

"Why don't you tell me, Kelly?"

"With pleasure," she released a wicked grin. "Oh, the primordial sin of pride. That unstoppable desire to be more than everyone else, wanting the entire world to orbit your existence, like you're the sun itself. Thinking you are the acme of perfection." Kelly's tone of speech was borderline theatrical. "Unlike the other sins, the arrogant person fails to recognize their own faults and refuses to acknowledge the truth." She was entranced by her own words. "They are blind to themselves and to reality. Therefore, one whose sin is pride is like a dying patient with an incurable disease, their only possible resolution is death," she concluded.

"But doesn't it mean that the sinner would bring about their own self-destruction?" Sharon tried to reason with her.

"In today's world, a world that's cultivating an entire culture that worships Hubris, it seems like there's a need for some *'divine intervention.'*"

Damn it, this woman thinks she's God!

Sharon could almost see the entire picture, but she needed Kelly to complete the final brush strokes.

"So these girls you murdered . . ."

"Were braggarts; narcissistic, hollow shells of human beings. There was no way to help them. Personally, I see it more as a mercy killing than an actual murder."

Sharon sighed in despair. *I only wish that mercy could have been one of your virtues.*

Kelly began to detail the entire saga to Sharon, everything she had done in the last two years. The meeting with Mandy and the desire to teach her a lesson. The eruption of rage that had led to her death. The satisfaction she had felt from her illicit act and the urge to never stop. The way in which her actions had become more calculated and controlled, but just as pleasurable. That sense of purpose that accompanied each and every one of her killings. And, finally, exactly how she had taken the life of each girl and then brilliantly covered her tracks.

"So that's it? You're going to kill beautiful, arrogant women until you get arrested?" Sharon hadn't expected the truth to be so bland.

"No. You could say that until now I was just practicing for the real battle."

"What do you mean?"

"I think it's best that I don't tell you. You know, considering the fact that you're a cop and all . . ."

"But you're going to kill me no matter what, right? So at least before I die tell me what I couldn't figure out myself." Sharon wouldn't stop short of getting to the truth.

"Hmm . . . You make a valid point. But don't be too harsh on yourself; no one can compete with me. You certainly challenged me, though."

"Thanks . . ." Sharon felt the taste of the bitter end in her mouth. Her own bitter end.

"Do you know Gloria McIntyre?" Kelly asked.

"The model? Of course."

"I want her dead."

"Why?"

"Slow, painful, inevitable death," Kelly went on, as if she hadn't heard Sharon's question. She closed her eyes for a brief moment. Sharon became vigilant and prepared to make a move.

But almost instantly, Kelly opened her eyes wide, her hands still aiming the gun straight at Sharon's heart.

". . . And that's exactly what I'm about to do."

"And how exactly are you going to do that? I'm sure she's surrounded by dozens of bodyguards. Why the hell would she let you go anywhere near her?"

"Because I'm the Editor in Chief of a famous fashion magazine? I meet with models on a daily basis."

The awful truth hit Sharon. Kelly really had thought of every little detail.

"But why her? I can understand how a supermodel might appear to be more conceited than the average beauty, but still, why are you risking everything just because of her?"

Kelly's gaze wondered elsewhere, somewhere far away from the tiny apartment in Downtown Manhattan, but immediately turned back to Sharon, who also had forgotten for a moment where she was while trying to connect the dots and tie them up together, like she had always done during those long nights she'd spent at her cluttered desk.

"That's a long story and our time is almost up. I still have a lot to do ahead of me."

"Do you really think that no one will figure out you killed me? Do you think my boss doesn't know that I went to visit your mom in Arizona? You must have made some mistakes, left your fingerprints in the apartment, or something of the sort."

"Of course, I've left my fingerprints almost everywhere. I don't care anymore. I just need to kill the bitch, and then they can do whatever they want with me."

"Well, isn't that lovely. They will catch you before you get to her."

"That's exactly why I made sure that she will be out of the country."

"*What*?"

"Yes, indeed. I have arranged a campaign for her overseas. In moments like this, it pays off to be the Editor in Chief."

You have to admit, when the loony puts effort into something, she goes all the way . . .

"Where is she?" Even moments before her death, Sharon felt she had to crack this case, to fully understand it.

"In Christchurch, New Zealand," Kelly smirked. "And do you know what this so-called campaign is about? Perfect Beauty! She had one last chance to save her life. She could have declined the offer, but, as predicted, she couldn't resist the temptation."

What model would decline a campaign like that? Kelly was obviously blinded by the manipulations that she used to justify her wrongdoings.

"Do you really think you can get on a flight before your name gets passed on to the authorities? After they see that you're not at home, or in the office, the first thing they'll do is head for the airport."

"That's why I'm driving to Canada with piles of money. There's an international airport in Vancouver that has direct flights to New Zealand. I have a fake passport and driver's license that I bought almost a year ago, and I'm sure that any car dealership would be willing to trade in my Mercedes without much fuss. And, by the way, for the last few months I've made high, but not unusual, withdrawals of money, enough to last me for a lifetime, not including my bank accounts overseas. Let the United States government enjoy what's left. It looks like they need it . . ."

"I guess you've truly thought of everything."

"Absolutely. The only thing I hadn't taken into consideration was a pesky, little cop that would dig too deep, but as you can see – that also worked itself out eventually." Kelly's fingers tightened on the trigger.

Sharon felt her heart pounding. She tried to exhale slowly, but her lungs felt drained and useless. She looked up at Kelly and forced herself to take a deep breath. She needed to stay focused. She had to stall Kelly until someone got here.

"But why Gloria McIntyre?" she asked again.

Kelly did not answer.

Sharon thought of the last few days that had led her to this moment. The meeting in Kelly's fancy office when Kelly had offered Sharon her full cooperation. Her own stubbornness to keep on digging deeper and deeper. The decision to visit Kelly's mother. Miranda's slip about the mysterious trauma her little girl had suffered. Looking at the old family photos . . .

Then she realized how Gloria was a part of the picture, literally.

"You knew Gloria as a kid, didn't you?" Sharon asked confidently, recalling the mysterious, yet familiar, character from the photos Miranda had shown her.

Kelly froze. *How could she know?*

"What happened back then? In 1990?"

Kelly was mortified. No one was supposed to know about her deep, dark secret. The secret that had eventually made her into the woman she was today – a murderess.

"How do you know?" Kelly gasped. She almost felt herself being sucked back into the miserable day that had changed her life, but she stayed strong. She managed to hold back the uncontrollable tears that appeared every time she thought about that day.

"What did she do to you?" Sharon took a leap. She wasn't really sure where she was going with this, but she noticed that it had an effect on Kelly. She could see it in her eyes.

"Stop! Enough! That's it! I need to get out of here!" Kelly screamed.

It seemed as if Sharon had struck a nerve. She'd finally figured out where all of this madness was coming from.

"What did she do to you that was so awful, that even twenty years later you're so desperate for revenge?"

Kelly gave her a lethal look. "It's time to say goodbye." She steadied her gun and aimed it at Sharon, her fingers still secured on the trigger.

"Kelly, if you think this is going to be easy, you're wrong. All this time you've been telling yourself that you're killing bad people. Sinners. What will you say to convince yourself that it's okay to kill *me*?"

"Sometimes the end justifies the means," Kelly tried to exude confidence, but deep inside she knew the cop was right. She knew Sharon Davis was a good person who did not deserve to die.

A person whose only mistake had been getting too close to the truth.

"Kelly, you know I'm innocent. Don't do this. You still have the chance to do the right thing," Sharon implored with glistening eyes, her voice not as steady as it had been earlier.

"No, this is the right thing to do." Kelly tried to keep her voice calm. "This is what has to be done."

"Please, don't . . ." Sharon's voice cracked. Tears glided down her cheek.

"I'm sorry. There's no other way," Kelly whispered. Her fingers tightened over the trigger.

Sharon kept staring straight at her. Hurt, agonized, defeated.

Kelly could not look at her anymore. She turned off the light, convincing herself that what happened in the dark was not real. The flickering city lights penetrated through the glass window and encircled Sharon's silhouette in a dim gleam. Kelly aimed her gun again and fired.

Sharon's shriek pierced the air and made Kelly twitch. She lowered her gun but her hands were still locked on the trigger and felt clammy. A deathly silence took over the room; all she could hear was her own rapid breathing. The stench of the gun powder, mixed with the smell of blood and charred skin, made her nauseous. She had to get out of there, and she needed to hurry. Someone must have heard the shot and the police would get here soon only to find the lifeless body of Detective Davis.

She carefully approached the slouched body, still seated upright in the chair. Imprisoned. Her shoulders slumped and head drooped down, suspended in a posture of eternal submission.

"You were a worthy opponent, but it seems as though the better woman won," she said. Kelly walked outside and closed the door behind her.

CHAPTER 27

The photo shoot would end in less than three days, Andy realized, after which he and Gloria would be on their way to meet Kelly Danes. He assumed Kelly would expect to see some of the photos, and wanted to guarantee that they would come out spectacular. Andy hoped to impress her. After all, she had given him a once-in-a-lifetime opportunity.

At the end of each grueling day of shooting, he would examine the photos he had taken that day and select the ones that caught his eye. Afterwards, he would print the photos on a special printing paper he had brought with him. Although Andy would have preferred developing the pictures in the old fashioned way, for enhancing the photographs' resolutions and shades, he felt that setting up a dark room in the middle of a secluded inn was a tad too zealous, even for him. So he settled for the printer instead. It would have spared him a lot of trouble if he had resolved to show Kelly the photos on the screen of his laptop, but he wanted her to have something tangible that could help her envision how they would look on the cover of her magazine.

His double role, photographer by day and a photo developer by night, had left him with very few hours of sleep. But despite that, he hadn't passed up a single chance to be with Gloria, even if he had to drink endless amounts of coffee to compensate. He wasn't afraid of hard work; on the contrary, it increased his drive to keep pushing harder - like a snowball rolling downhill, gaining momentum. And he loved every second of it.

He still found it hard to believe that he was on the other side of the planet, photographing the most famous model on earth; in short, every photographer's dream come true. The life he had lived just a few days ago, one that included a sloppy bachelor's pad in New York and late night outings to gloomy pubs with his best friend Bill, who always tried to convince him to "*forget these stupid artistic dreams and start focusing on making money*!" seemed so distant. He did not want to go back there. From here on out, he hoped that he would only move forward.

Andy stared at the screen, trying to decide which photos were worthy of printing. His eyes landed on a photo in which Gloria was not even looking at the camera. It seemed as if she were grinning at someone outside of the frame, not one of those camera-ready smiles, but an authentic, loving beam.

He found himself fascinated by the woman in the picture and wondered at heart who she was smiling at, what she was thinking, and how she was feeling. For a slight moment, he had even forgotten it was Gloria. He was simply curious to find out the story behind the photo; what was the tale of that candid moment that had been captured. Andy knew it might not have been the typical cover shot, but as far as he was concerned, it was, literally, picture perfect.

When Andy returned to his room, holding in his hand the printed photo, he saw Gloria sneaking out of her room and stopping in front of his door, fixing her hair a moment before knocking. She turned her head, and when she noticed him watching her, a broad grin embellished her face.

"Hey, what's that in your hand? Another photo from today?"

"Yes, my favorite one so far."

"Talk about high expectations. Let me see."

Andy passed her the picture. Gloria's face did not convey any expression of special admiration.

"Nice photo. Isn't it a little bit weird that I'm not looking at the camera?"

"That's my favorite thing about the picture."

"Really?"

"Yes. It's like a moment that was not supposed to be caught on camera had been captured. And we can only speculate but never truly know its true meaning. It's intriguing."

Gloria looked at the photo again, trying to apprehend what she had missed at first glance.

"Oh, I remember this!" Her thoughts went to Arthur when their eyes locked on the set.

"Come on, tell me! I'm still trying to unravel the mystery!"

"Not telling you!"

"Gloria, remember we talked about your teasing?"

"Remember we agreed there was nothing you can do about it?"

"Because you can't teach an *old* dog new tricks?"

"Watch it mister, or I'm going straight back to my room!"

"Oh, I'm sorry . . . My mother did always remind me that I needed to respect my elders."

"Andy!"

"Gloria . . ."

"Oh, wait. You've got some . . ." She reached a delicate hand and gently stroked his face.

"What?" Andy, distracted by her soft touch, looked into her eyes and smiled.

"Milk left on the corner of your lip," she said triumphantly and turned the other way, so she would have the upper hand.

"Gloria, wait," he ran after her, now used to the fact that she needed to be chased, and proved that she was worth the effort.

"I'm sorry, I can't hear you. I forgot my hearing aid in my room . . ."

Andy grabbed her and held her close to him.

"I wish that, at times, you chose not to hear all the nonsense coming out of my mouth," he whispered, "but I hope you can at least read my lips when I'm telling you I am madly in love with you."

Gloria looked at him, the combative expression in her eyes gone. She did not say a word, just let herself be embraced in his arms.

"Let's go inside," she said, taking Andy's hand and intertwining her fingers with his.

CHAPTER 28

The white light blinded her even before she opened her eyes. She felt as if her body had somehow loosened, a kind of floating sensation, that she could barely sense herself. Muffled voices whispered around her, although in her head there was utter silence. She felt as though she had reached the end of a long journey, and now had to face the finish line. Eventually she opened her eyes. A vague silhouette occupied the dazzling space.

"It's good to have you back with us, Sharon."

That voice was oddly familiar; a lot like her uncle Jack's, who had been killed on duty three years ago. He was also a cop.

"Where am I?" she asked in a raspy voice.

"Don't worry. It's alright. The most important thing right now is for you to get some rest. You've been through quite an ordeal."

Sharon didn't understand where she was. The last thing she remembered was the excruciating pain she had felt when the bullet from Kelly's gun had pierced her chest. She had been sure that she was about to die.

"What's going on here? I don't understand . . ."

"You're in Mount Sinai hospital. It's a miracle you're alive. It's important that you rest."

Sharon was so confused and overwhelmed. Who found her? How did she get here? Is she really going to be okay?

"You dodged a bullet." She heard that friendly voice again. "Well, not exactly, but you get my drift."

Sharon's eyes started to grow accustomed to the neon light. The vague silhouette began to look more and more familiar, from one moment to another.

"Rob . . . ?"

"You thought I wouldn't have my best detective's back?"

"What happened? How did I . . ."

"Survive?"

Sharon looked at him and nodded.

"It was close. When I found you, you were unconscious and had already lost a lot of blood, but I felt a pulse. It was weak but still there. You have always been a fighter."

Sharon glanced at the bruises the handcuffs had left on her wrists. She tried to recall what had happened after Kelly had shot her. She remembered hearing the sound of Kelly's footsteps approaching her after she had closed her eyes. In that moment she had known her only chance was to play dead. She hadn't dared to take even the weakest breath. Within minutes she had become trapped in her own doings, but it had worked.

"The paramedics who arrived at the apartment had a rough time keeping you stable due to all the blood you'd lost. It was only after they got you to the Hospital that I knew for sure I wasn't going to lose you."

Sharon smiled at him. It was one of those rare moments where Rob had taken off his cloak of authority.

"That's it. Twenty-four hours have passed since then. It's safe to say that you're out of the danger zone, but your body is filled with pain killers."

Oh, so that's why I feel like I'm hovering above a cloud or something . . .

"The doctor said you have to stay under observation for a couple of days and then take it easy." Rob stared at her. "Is that clear? You are not going back to work before the end of the month."

"Oh, no. Oh, no."

"Sharon. I don't want to hear one more word about this."

"No, Rob. It's not about that."

"Then what?"

Suddenly, it all came flooding back. Rob didn't know Kelly was the one who had shot her. Sharon hadn't had a chance to talk to him before she'd come back to New York.

"Kelly Danes . . . She was the one who . . ." Dryness overtook her mouth. It was harder than she'd thought, admitting that someone had shot her.

"I know," Rob said tenderly and held her hand.

"What are you saying?" She was certain Rob hadn't understood what she meant.

"I know she was the one who did this to you." He, too, could not bring the words to his lips.

"How do you know?"

"After I listened to the message you'd left me the night before, I decided to conduct an investigation of my own," Rob explained. "I realized Kelly Danes was probably hiding more than she's telling, so I decided to pay her a visit. But when I arrived at her office, I was told she had taken a sick leave, for the first time since she started working there. Already something seemed suspicious. I tried calling her cell, but there was no answer. I decided to check whether she was at home, even at the risk of the commissioner suspending me for misconduct.

"When I got there, nobody answered the doorbell, but I noticed the door was already slightly ajar. I entered and called Kelly's name while scanning the premises. The house looked squeaky clean, but when I got to the bedroom I noticed that in comparison to the other rooms, it was a total mess. Clothes on the floor, empty hangers in the closet, and the absence of a toothbrush in the bathroom ignited my suspicion. Something was odd, no doubt, but other than that it seemed as though I had reached a dead end. Kelly had disappeared.

"When I went back to the main floor I saw the staircase leading down to the basement and decided to take a look; down there I found an empty space surrounded by mirrors, which was a bit bizarre but nothing more."

He paused and cleared his throat. "As I was heading back up, I spotted a tiny stain on the wooden floor that looked like blood. I could no longer let Miss Kelly Danes enjoy the benefit of the doubt, so I called the forensic team. They confirmed what I already knew – it was blood. I realized that you had been right all along. I asked them to compare the new sample to the DNA samples of our victims, and this morning they called me from the lab to notify me that a match was made with Julie Tyfer, the last victim."

"Rob, you're awesome."

"No. You are awesome. I never should have doubted you. You have never failed me, and look at you now . . ." Rob shook his head.

"Don't you dare blame yourself, even for one second," Sharon implored.

But the look in his glistening eyes made it clear to her that he was taking full responsibility for what had happened.

"Anyway," said Rob, "right after I left Kelly's house I called you, but your cell went straight to voicemail. I figured your flight had already landed several hours ago, and, as well as I know you, it didn't make sense that you hadn't already bothered me with dozens of calls in order to find out if I had done what you'd asked," he smiled warmly. "I told myself that maybe you wanted to get some rest after the flight, but something just didn't feel right. After all the recent discoveries, I decided not to take a chance and went to check up on you, even if it turned out to be just a paranoid hunch."

Sharon suddenly remembered the flight back to New York. And Chris. It seemed like a lifetime ago.

"When I arrived at your apartment and saw the door was already open, I knew right away that something had happened. And then I found you there, bound to the chair. Bleeding . . ." The words choked in his throat.

"Rob. Don't worry. I'm okay."

"I know. If there's anyone who is able to decide they don't feel like dying and get out of it alive, it's you."

Sharon chuckled. It hurt. Especially in her ribs.

"That's it. I've already sent dozens of patrol cars after Kelly, but it seems as though she's vanished, without a trace."

I just need to kill the bitch, and then they can do whatever they want with me.

She had to stop her.

"I need to get out of here." Sharon carefully tried to push herself into a sitting position, but the pain pierced through her instantly.

"For God's sake, are you still trying to drive me over the edge, even now? You're not going anywhere."

"Oh, yes I am. I know where Kelly is."

CHAPTER 29

The drive was not as tedious as Kelly had expected it to be. Although she was used to the convenience of her luxury car, and didn't particularly care for the stale smell in that piece of junk she'd traded for at the used car dealership, she thanked God for the automatic transmission – otherwise she would have been arrested long ago. Her Jimmy Choos were not built for extensive clutch use.

She missed her Mercedes. She became nauseated just thinking about the greedy grin on the car salesman's greasy face. It made her sick to her stomach thinking that some lousy low-life would get to drive a car that had been intended for someone of the likes of her.

Oh, the sacrifices you have to make when you're a fugitive.

Kelly felt like one of those medieval women who'd been falsely accused of witchcraft just because they were too clever, too opinionated, too righteous. Why couldn't anyone understand that she was actually doing the right thing?

In a perfect world, not only would I not be accused of anything, I'd get a medal, too . . .

She watched the road with glinting eyes. Just like those wretched women, who were penalized despite their innocence, she, too, was being persecuted, a death sentence floating over her head; she was being unjustly portrayed as a witch. Now she would have to spend the rest of her life on the run. She may have dodged the death penalty, but she had lost her life and everything she held dear. She was condemned to a life of solitude; one without her prestigious job, without the glory and admiration that followed. She would probably have to undergo additional plastic surgeries to conceal her identity, after she had worked so hard to transform herself in the first place. And, worst of all, she could never kill again. Gloria's dying moment would become her peak, from which she could only descend. She would be left with nothing but sweet reminiscences, which would eventually dim as time passed.

Suddenly, the image of Sharon Davis, moments before she'd been shot, appeared before Kelly's eyes. She lost her concentration and swerved to the right. Kelly tried to shake the image of the stubborn cop out of her head. Even in death, Detective Davis would not give her peace.

The attempt to clear her conscience of the detective's murder hadn't worked very well. Sharon had been right. How could she justify killing a cop, whose only wrongdoing had been that she'd been doing her job too well? But there had been no other way. If Kelly hadn't stopped her in time, she would not be able to reach that one moment she had been looking forward to for all these years – the moment when she would finally get her vengeance.

Kelly tried to recall the loathing and hatred she had felt toward the cop in the last few days; emotions that further escalated the closer she got to her ultimate target. But now those feelings were almost completely gone. That night with the detective had changed something inside her, but Kelly knew it was her duty to forget about it and stick to the plan. The cop was already dead. *What's done is done.* She tried to remember if she had read about her death in the paper. It was strange that there had been no mention of an NYPD detective's murder in the news. She hadn't had time to dwell on it, but tomorrow morning she would search the paper to make sure her buds of guilt were not in vain.

Sharon Davis had to be dead. Kelly had felt her demise in every inch of her body: the dying shriek, followed by a deathly silence, stains of dark blood on her clothes, the tilted head. Kelly knew she had aimed that gun right at her heart. There was no way the cop could have survived it. Nevertheless, she would feel calmer after she verified it. Kelly could not face anymore obstacles, not when she had so carefully plotted every single detail of her perfect plan, not when she was so close to the end.

She noticed the gas light had turned red.

That son of a bitch didn't even bother to fill up the tank . . .

She stopped at a gas station by the side of the road, appalled by the possibility that people would think that this junky old car actually belonged to her. On the other hand, they weren't any better; just plain, insignificant people.

While a pimply faced man filled up the gas tank, Kelly entered the station's minimart. She had a long drive ahead of her, and she could not afford to stop every time her stomach grumbled.

The pickings were slim. Kelly was not used to greasy snacks and fast food, and the mere thought of having to eat it made her want to vomit. However, she didn't want to pass out behind the steering wheel due to an empty stomach either. She promised herself that she would compensate for the poor food choices later, once she crossed the border and had put the greatest danger behind her.

Kelly stood in front of the chocolate shelves and was appalled. Popular, cheap brands, considered delicious by the masses, repulsed her. Was this really some people's miserable substitute for dessert?

Who, for God's sake, buys this crap?

"Do you need some help?" A stock boy asked.

Kelly responded with a cold glare and walked away without saying a word.

The chocolate shelves always let you down.

CHAPTER 30

"**W**hat do you mean? How do you know where she is? The entire New York Police Department is looking for her!"

"I don't know exactly where she is now, but I can tell you where she wants to go, who she's looking for and when she will kill again. She told me everything."

"Are you serious?"

"Yes. She thought I was going to die anyway, and it seemed like she was looking for someone to brag to…" Sharon felt a slight tremor passing through her body when she recollected those last few minutes prior to what she had anticipated to be the moment of her death.

"I can't believe it. That bitch . . ." Rob trailed off.

"Finally made a mistake," Sharon completed.

"It's about freakin' time. Tell me everything you know, and I'll handle everything. In the meantime, I'll send someone to collect your official testimony."

"No way. I'm not telling you squat until we're in the car."

"Come on, Davis, you are in no condition to chase after a dangerous criminal, especially one that already tried to kill you!"

"Listen, she's about to kill again, and I know who.

I don't intend to lie down in bed like nothing's happening. I have to stop this murder. I have to stop *her*."

"Sharon, if someone's life is in danger, it is your duty to tell me everything you know right away. I understand you want to catch her yourself, but right now it's more important to prevent any additional bloodshed."

"Don't worry. We have about three days. That's more than enough time to get to New Zealand."

"What the hell are you talking about? What's New Zealand got to do with this?"

"That's where Kelly's headed. She figured we would be on to her, so she's going to Canada first. And don't bother trying to track her car by the license plate, because she has already replaced it, and her driver's license, too."

"Goddammit, that lunatic really did think of everything."

"Except for the possibility that I'd still be alive," Sharon smiled grimly.

Rob pressed her hand and she reciprocated with a determined squeeze.

"If you call the airport right away we may be able to book tickets for tonight. It's a long flight, but we can still arrive before Kelly. Until then, I promise to get some rest, but so help me God, I'm coming with you."

"Say, did you forget that you were shot less than twenty-four hours ago?" Rob chided.

"I'll get over it. Besides, you need me. I know what has to be done in order to put an end to this whole thing, once and for all."

* * *

As she continued driving west, the urban landscape transformed into green suburbs, and New York's famed skyscrapers were replaced by great mountains. Large raindrops began to cover the windshield, making it difficult to drive, but Kelly kept smiling.

All of this was so different from the wasteland where she'd grown up. As a child she could not stand the searing heat of summer, which in time had become an excuse for the revealing outfits of her classmates, leaving her behind, envious, trapped in her conservative clothes. During her youth she had so desired adulthood's independence, to be able to detach herself from her former life. She used to wander through the vast deserts surrounding her small town, longing to escape through the enormous fields, disappearing from the constant torment that had invariably surrounded her.

One of her favorite places to go had been the meteor crater – a gigantic, round cavity formed by an asteroid that had impacted the earth about fifty thousand years ago. Kelly used to sit there by herself, contemplating the emptiness all around her, finding comfort only in that special glow of the southern sun, moments before darkness arrived. At times she had continued sitting in the gloom, bursting with cries of frustration and anger, reenergized by the sounds echoing back to her.

That place had not remained her private asylum for long. The local teens discovered the great potential of the secluded sight, away from the observing eyes of their parents. Soon enough it had become their favorite spot for getting drunk and testing their boundaries. Obviously, she had not been welcomed.

Every time she had seen the beat-up cars heading over, and heard the rambunctious howls the lucky girls filled the quiet night with, she would hurry to make herself scarce. After a while, she had stopped going there completely. It was perhaps the only thing she missed about that awful town. She despised everything else that had anything to do with that rotten place, which was why she had never returned, not even once.

Kelly hadn't been the type of person who got along well with others. The social niches had been foreign and unnatural to her. She had always known she could only trust herself, and that was it. From a relatively young age, she had understood the massive gap between her and her parents. She did not belong there. She was better than all of them.

She had fantasized many times that she was actually adopted, hoping it would explain why she detested her parents so much. They were the cliché of small town, simpleminded people – rustic, friendly, and naive – everything she loathed about that place. Even as a teenage girl, she had dreamed of the day she would leave that godforsaken town and arrive in a big city, perhaps New York or Los Angeles, where she would make it big. There she would be appreciated for who she was and not be seen as a weirdo. There she would *fit in*.

Eventually, she had left. Ran away, to be exact; but it was nothing like she'd planned. Kelly *had* to leave. She couldn't bear the shocked, demeaning, pitying looks anymore. One might say that the shame had vanquished her. The stolidity with which her parents had supported her leaving also strengthened her feeling that she was doing everyone a favor.

Her life was never easy and probably never would be. For every single thing she had accomplished, she had shed blood, not like those girls she had grown up with, particularly one extremely beautiful girl.

Bottom line, she thought, what doesn't kill you makes you stronger. *However, those who don't get stronger should die*. Now it was Gloria's turn. Kelly tried to clear her head of these dark thoughts; she had to concentrate on the drive. She would have enough time to indulge in thoughts of sweet revenge during the long flight to New Zealand. She could not fall apart, not when she was so close to the end.

* * *

As always, Sharon ended up getting her way. Rob had agreed that she could join him, provided that once they got to New Zealand, she would stay at the hotel and get some rest. The doctor had explained that any form of strenuous activity would put pressure on the stitches and could easily reopen the wound, which was very dangerous considering the amount of blood she had already lost. Sharon had reluctantly agreed. She didn't *really* mean it, but she had agreed.

Before Rob left to finalize all the necessary arrangements for them to catch the earliest flight, Sharon had a special request.

"Don't you think it's too much?" he asked her, a hint of hesitation in his voice. "Your friends will read it . . . your family . . ."

"There's no other choice. This is war and sacrifices have to be made."

"But do you really think it's necessary to have a story in the newspaper about your murder?"

"Yes. I know Kelly. I'm sure that she'll look for proof of my death. If nothing is published by tomorrow, she will get suspicious."

"Okay, I'm on it."

If this were a game of chess, one might say that Sharon had gotten one step closer to taking Kelly's queen.

CHAPTER 31

"**S**he wants to kill *who*?"

Rob was shocked. Not simply because he had just found out that the world's most famous model was a potential murder victim, but also due to the fact that only yesterday her name had popped up on his search screen.

"You heard me right. Gloria McIntyre. The model," said Sharon, trying to adjust her pillow and sit up straight. Rob was sitting at her bedside and got up to help her. Their flight was scheduled to leave in a few hours, and the doctor had ordered Sharon to stay in the hospital until then.

"And how is Kelly planning to do that exactly? The woman must be surrounded by dozens of bodyguards!"

"As long as you're not exaggerating . . ." she dismissed him, although a similar thought had gone through her mind not so long ago.

"You know what I mean," he muttered.

"When will you finally realize that this woman is always two steps ahead? She has managed to pave her way to the murder of the world's most famous model."

With all of that ingenious tenacity, she could have been the first female president of the United States . . .

"So you're telling me that Gloria McIntyre is in New Zealand right now?"

"Exactly, and not by chance. Kelly organized the campaign for her to shoot over there."

"What campaign? How you can literally shoot a model to death?"

"Rob, don't forget we are dealing with the Editor in Chief of Inner Beauty magazine. She had at her disposal all the necessary means to orchestrate this whole thing."

"I guess you're right," he was compelled to agree.

Sharon laid out before him every detail that Kelly had told her that night, starting with the sophisticated way in which she had deceived Gloria into leaving the country, and ending with the confession that all of her previous murders had only been in preparation for this one.

"We have to contact Gloria. Call her agency. Her manager. Her grandmother. Her gynecologist. I don't care who. We have to find Gloria, before Kelly does."

By sunset they were on their way to J.F.K airport. Rob was driving and Sharon was sitting in the passenger seat, trying to make sure her bandages were properly secured. Bleeding to death was the last thing she needed right now; she simply had to get on that plane.

In the few hours remaining before the flight to Christchurch, Rob had been in a frenzy trying to find even a single scrap of information that could lead to Gloria's exact whereabouts. But he hadn't come across a single lead. She didn't have any close family beside her mother, who had passed away a few years back. Gloria's friends hadn't known exactly where she was, being used to her frequent travels. The only person that did know, her personal manager, Arthur Cohen, had gone along with her. They had a few phone numbers – Gloria's,

Arthur's, and Andy Swain's, the photographer – but when Rob and Sharon had tried calling, their calls had all gone straight to voicemail.

The relentless cops had tried calling repeatedly, but with no luck. They contacted the local police authorities in Christchurch, but they were clueless as well. The departure time was getting closer and they still had nothing.

"It will turn out to be that this entire trip was in vain," Rob grumbled and tightened his grip on the steering wheel.

"Perhaps we'll have a chance of finding them when we're actually on the same continent," Sharon noted wryly, trying to remain optimistic in her own cynical way. Rob was too tense to play along and just kept staring at the road.

"Hey, you know how much I want to catch her," Sharon turned to him. "We won't let anyone else die because of her."

"I hope so," his eyes lingered on a distant spot on the road.

"Do you know what I haven't figured out yet? I just don't know what has driven Kelly to wanting to kill Gloria so badly," Sharon wondered aloud.

Rob chanced a glance at her but quickly resumed his eyes on the road.

"I recognized Gloria from the old photos, so obviously they have known each other for quite some time," she continued. "But even before she shot me, Kelly refused to talk about it."

"I know why," Rob said in a frigid tone.

"You do?" Sharon looked at him, half surprised, half angry.

"Yes . . . I discovered the horrible thing that happened to Kelly all those years ago."

"And you've waited all this time to tell me?"

"If you haven't noticed, I've had other pressing matters to take care of."

"You're right. I'm sorry." Sharon turned her gaze toward the window, still upset.

They both were silent, lost in their own thoughts. Sharon didn't know if she should learn what had happened to the woman who had tried to kill her. All of the startling revelations she had uncovered in the last few days had almost cost Sharon her life.

But she would have to survive one last secret.

"Come on, will you tell me already?" she caved to her curiosity.

"Are you sure you want to hear this?"

"Absolutely."

CHAPTER 32

After driving continuously for nearly seven hours straight, Kelly decided to stop at a small diner located near a gas station. That way she could kill two birds with one stone.

She drank the terrible coffee that the waitress served her, reminiscing about New York's cafés, when she noticed that someone had left their morning newspaper on the table. Kelly picked up the paper and started browsing through it vigorously, knowing exactly what she was looking for. After a few minutes she found it:

Death of a Cop: Accidental or Malicious?
On Monday evening, February 24, the body of Sharon Davis, a homicide detective with the New York Police Department, was discovered lifeless in her Manhattan apartment. Initial observations of the ransacked apartment indicate an attempted robbery gone wrong. It appears that the cop entered her home and encountered the robber in the act. However, a source within the NYPD stated that the possibility of premeditated murder is also under investigation. No suspects are currently in custody. New York Police Department has no further comments at this time.

Kelly felt as if a huge burden had been lifted off her shoulders. Now I'm finally free, she sighed. She decided to celebrate by ordering the cherry pie she'd spied in the desserts display; she could afford to unwind for a few more minutes . . .

* * *

On Wednesday morning, February 26, Robert and Jillian Davis sat down for breakfast at their dining table. As usual, they smeared cream cheese across their hot Bialy bagels and divided the newspaper between them. The ritual of swapping sections occurred about twenty minutes later, and after an additional twenty minutes the couple would discuss the articles that they'd found interesting. Bobby always started with the sports section and Jill began with the news section. She started flipping casually through the pages when . . .

"Bobby . . ." Jill's voice trembled and she dropped her bagel on the floor.

Brandy, their beloved dog, eagerly pounced on the prize.

* * *

"*Shit!!!*"

Dozens of passengers turned their heads toward the loud and obviously ill-mannered woman. The man sitting next to her looked astonished.

"Shall I remind you that we are trying to keep a low profile?" Rob glared at Sharon.

"I forgot to tell them."

"Forgot to tell what to whom?"

"I forgot to tell my parents I'm not dead."

* * *

Chris Wallington had been in an exceptionally good mood for the last couple of days. He couldn't seem to forget the face of the beautiful detective who had sat next to him on the plane. He held in his hand the business card of *Sharon Davis, Homicide Detective, New York Police Department* and wondered when would be the right time to call. He had decided it would be better to wait another day or two; let her get some rest. She sure looked like she'd needed it. He had already realized from the few hours they'd spent on the plane that this one was not going to make his life any easier, but he did not mind. For the first time in his life he could understand why people believed in love at first sight. If he hadn't been such a cynic, he might have thought he was falling in love.

Chris glanced at his watch, grabbed the morning paper, and left for work with a broad smile stretched across his face.

CHAPTER 33

Kelly was only several hours away from the border. By the end of the day she would be on a plane to New Zealand, starting a new chapter in her life – the chapter in which she would fulfill her lifelong dream. Her mouth tasted sweeter than ever, the taste of impending revenge.

Her foot slammed down on the gas pedal. She began to accelerate, expediting her arrival to freedom, longing to leave all of her worries behind. She was sick and tired of hiding. She was sick and tired of waiting. After all, she had waited long enough; nearly two decades of her life had been spent waiting.

Her eyes did not stray from the route, but her mind drifted somewhere entirely different from the curved road ahead of her. She saw herself standing in front of Gloria while the model kneeled submissively at her feet. She saw herself releasing all the poison that had streamed through her blood for years, ever since that dreadful day. She saw herself . . .

Getting pulled over by a cop?

The siren abruptly snagged Kelly out of her delightful fantasy and brought her back to gloomy reality. The police car signaled her to stop.

How could everything I've worked for all these years go down the drain in a single moment?

She pulled up to the side of the road. A young, handsome officer in uniform approached her window.

"We both know why I pulled you over, don't we?"

Kelly sensed beads of perspiration starting to form along her temples. She tried to keep her breathing regular. It had never been this hard.

She tried smiling at the officer and maintaining her usual calm, composed facial expression, though she knew that this was it –she'd been caught.

"So . . . How are we going to solve our little problem?"

Kelly immediately thought about the piles of money she had stashed in the trunk of the car. Perhaps she could bribe him? No, that wouldn't help her this time; she had crossed an irreversible line.

She had killed a cop.

"You seem like a reasonable lady, so why were you driving above the speed limit? It's very dangerous."

Kelly was so relieved that she felt her heart almost fly into the sky. The oxygen came back to her lungs and she instantly felt revitalized.

"You are absolutely right, Officer. I don't know what I was thinking. I'm just in such a rush to get home," she flashed a flustered grin. "Dinner isn't going to make itself."

The young officer smiled back at the nice lady. She reminded him of his mom – always rushing to take care of everyone and, in the process of doing so, ending up forgetting herself.

"Still, I don't want to see you doing that again. Is that clear?"

"Of course, Officer, and again, I am so sorry."

"It's okay. Just show me your license and registration, please."

Kelly's heartbeat started racing again. She felt as if the bullet she had just managed to dodge had returned in a circular motion to snipe at her back.

She started searching nervously for the forged credentials in her purse. She had no idea where the registration of the lame car she'd bought just a couple of days ago was.

For God's sake, this is the last thing I need right now.

The officer looked at the anxious woman searching through her bag for the documents. He noticed the dark circles under her eyes and guessed that she'd had a rough day at work. He felt sorry for her. Maybe he didn't have to check her license; when he saw the papers falling out of her bag and scattering along the bottom of the car, he decided to cut the poor woman some slack.

He didn't notice the pile of bills that slipped out along with them.

"Okay, never mind. I'll let you off with a warning this time."

Kelly felt as if the treacherous bullet had suddenly lost its momentum and dropped to the ground.

"Thank you, Officer. Thank you so much," she smiled a broad smile – a real one for a change. What a break.

"Next time I won't be able to let it slide, so please pay attention."

There won't be a next time, you idiot . . .

"Of course, Officer, and again, thank you."

Kelly waited for a few moments in her car, letting the police car pass her. The stupid cop waved her goodbye.

Oh, honey, you have no idea what kind of mistake you've just made . . .

She was so glad that they let just anyone into the police academy these days.

Less than three hours later, Kelly had successfully crossed the United States-Canada border. It had not been an easy task since she'd had to rely on clumsy maps, roadside signage, and bystanders' faulty English. It all would have been much simpler had she just used the GPS on her smartphone, but she'd been afraid of being tracked.

Kelly stopped again to refuel and gave the guy an extra tip to polish the decrepit car. In the meantime, she took out the driving directions she had prepared in advance, looking how to get to the most luxurious hotel near Vancouver International Airport. She had a few hours to spare in this place and money was no obstacle.

After days and days of not being able to sit in a coffee shop for more than fifteen minutes or enjoy a decent meal, after the countless hours she'd spent in that reeking car, Kelly had to compensate. Fix the horrible injustices she had endured.

After her car had been polished and shined, she was ready to get behind the wheel for one last drive. Kelly had decided that the smartest thing to do would be to leave the car in the hotel's parking lot, so it would take some time to trace it. She would take a cab to the airport and from there fly first class. In New Zealand, the Porsche she had leased would be waiting to take her to the extravagant mansion she had rented, worthy of her status.

Kelly took the final turn on her direction sheet. She spotted the Marriott logo from a distance. She could hardly wait to slip into a big bubble bath, to scrub her body clean from all the filth of the last few days. She fantasized about the red, sweet strawberries, complementing the Dom Pérignon that she would order in her room. She could already taste the Champagne in her mouth and imagined how she would relish each and every drop.

When she arrived at the hotel, she approached the receptionist.

"Welcome to the Vancouver Airport Marriott hotel," the clerk greeted her. "Do you have a reservation?"

"No, but I would like to make one now. I need a room for today."

"I'm sorry, we are fully booked."

Kelly did not like this answer. She assumed that after three days in the same scruffy clothes and unwashed hair, she didn't look like someone who could afford a room in this kind of hotel.

"Are you telling me there isn't even one room available?" Kelly asked.

"Yes. All the single rooms are occupied."

"And the executive suites?"

The receptionist looked at her, surprised.

"The presidential suite is available," she answered condescendingly, "but . . ."

"I'll take it."

* * *

Sharon stared helplessly at the digital monitor imbedded in the seatback in front of her. There were sixteen hours left until they reached their destination, and she was feeling every minute of it. *And that's a whole lot of minutes.* She could handle the physical inconvenience but the actual waiting tormented her.

Sharon recalled her talk with Rob on their way to the airport, when he had revealed Kelly's secret to her.

"Are you sure you want to hear this?"

"Absolutely."

"Okay. On April twenty-fourth, 1990, sixteen-year-old Kelly Whitesporte was rushed to the hospital and then admitted to the psychiatric ward. She spent a month and a half there after what was presumed to be a suicide attempt."

Sharon's jaw dropped, just like in the movies.

Kelly tried to kill herself? Why?

She glared at Rob, waiting for him to fill in the blanks.

Rob continued: "She arrived at the hospital battered and covered with bruises, showing deep cuts in her wrists. The report said she had been found unconscious with an initial cut on her neck. Luckily, she most likely passed out before she could finish the job, so the paramedics were able to save her. After two days of medical surveillance, she was transferred for psychiatric observation and stayed there for quite some time. Due to medical confidentiality I couldn't get the reports from there. I don't know why she tried to kill herself. And I have no idea who released her and why."

"Only that the person who did that made a huge mistake . . ." Sharon muttered.

"Without a question," Rob agreed.

"We still don't know how Gloria McIntyre is linked to all of this and what happened there exactly, but I have no doubt she had a part in Kelly's suicide attempt, and a very crucial part, if Kelly's desire for revenge is still blazing after all these years," Sharon added.

"Kelly and Gloria went to the same high school. I wouldn't be surprised if we were to find out they were in the same class."

"How do you know that?"

"You'd be surprised to know how much you can learn with the help of Google," Rob smirked. "Gloria McIntyre has countless fan websites. And guess where she grew up?"

"Winslow, Arizona. Kelly's hometown."

"Exactly."

"We have to find out what the hell happened between them," Sharon asserted. "Damn it, Rob, don't you have any strings you could pull? We're trying to catch a killer! It's important for us to know Kelly's medical history," she insisted.

"Do you think I didn't act on it? It's just that with all the bureaucracy and those damned warrants the judge has to sign, it will take a few good days that we just don't have."

Sharon squinted into the distance. "Then I guess we'll have to figure it out some other way."

"How?"

"We'll just have to ask Kelly."

CHAPTER 34

Gloria looked out the window and watched the sunrise. The last day of shooting had arrived. She found it hard to believe that she would no longer wake up every morning to this incredible view; that Tom and Libby, the owners, would no longer welcome her with a gracious "good morning" at the start of each day; that Andy's door would no longer be a step away from hers, and that she would no longer be sneaking into his room every night and sneaking out of it every morning . . .

It may have only been ten days, but it was, without a doubt, a turning point in her life. She was not returning home as the same Gloria. She was a happier woman now, a woman in love.

Gloria hoped with all her heart that the connection that had formed between her and Andy was not just a passing fling. The thought of it might seem absurd right now, but she had never forgotten the words of Heraclitus, her favorite Greek philosopher: *"No man ever steps in the same river twice."* No one could ever truly know what would happen between them down the road; everything might change; it was just a matter of time.

She knew that in this beautiful place, heaven on earth, it was easy to be captured by love and let it blossom, but what would happen when they each went back to their normal lives? Would they be able to synchronize to a shared life? They may have had a few things working in their favor, like the fact that they both worked in the same field, but still, their lives were entirely different. And there was that age issue. Even though Gloria wasn't that much older than him, she knew there would always be people who were counting . . .

Secondly, Andy was just at the beginning of his career. He had many years ahead of investing himself in his work waiting before him, and as for her . . . well, she was already past all that. Gloria was well aware that she had already left her mark on the modeling world. She didn't jump on every campaign offered to her and she valued her freedom dearly. She could see that Andy was a workaholic and wondered how they would made things work outside of work.

And finally, even though she was a mature woman, Gloria still didn't really know what she wanted from a relationship. She had never been swept away by her previous flames, but now, for the first time, she was having trouble containing all of the intense emotions growing inside of her. She didn't know what Andy expected from her, or vice-versa, and the uncertainty arising within made her feel insecure.

If there was one thing life had taught her, Gloria reflected, it was that she couldn't plan everything – otherwise, she would still be serving people their coffee. She reached further than she had ever imagined life would take her. So why not jump in and see what happened? Perhaps instead of drowning she would find her safe haven. Therefore, Gloria decided that the smart thing to do would be to ignore all of her sudden doubts and go with her heart. She only wondered if Andy felt the same.

* * *

The last day of shooting was in full swing, and now it was already time for a lunch break. Andy found it hard to believe that by tomorrow they would already have left this special place. It was a bittersweet moment, since the end of the shooting would also symbolize the success of his first major project. He had managed to pull it off.

Before leaving, he had been filled with so many concerns that he could barely enjoy the fact that he had just landed his dream job. Andy had wondered why the editor of Inner Beauty magazine had chosen an inexperienced photographer such as himself. He had refused to believe that it was due to his raw talent alone. *Maybe she actually wants the project to fail?* Andy pondered, bitterly. No, that doesn't make sense; there's no apparent reason for that, he assured himself.

Only several hours before landing in New Zealand had he finally convinced himself that there was no one wishing for him to fail, and that he was perfectly capable of not just doing the job, but doing it well. And now, after the most amazing week of his life, he could say, without hesitation, that he'd nailed it.

However, the satisfaction he drew from his success was dwarfed by his feelings for Gloria.

Andy felt like a love-stricken man who didn't even know what had hit him. He felt a bit silly, perhaps because over the years he had come to believe that the one true love a person has is that first love experienced during youth, and that everything that follows is merely a cheap replacement. But Gloria did not replace anyone. She was everything he could ask for in a woman and so much more. He hadn't even included her dazzling beauty in the equation. She was smart and practical, yet spontaneous and adventurous. She was mature, but she also had a childlike side to her that he found charming. They could talk for hours without running out of things to say. Gloria was not afraid of challenging herself and that was why she had gotten as far as she had. And in addition to all of that, she also had a great sense of humor, which was pretty hard to find among her fellow models. What could he say? This woman had charmed his pants off.

But, most importantly, Andy had recognized Gloria's subtle vulnerability, which she had tried hiding beneath her tough exterior when they'd first met. That glimpse of sensitivity had left him feeling relieved, because he realized that she was not *too* perfect, that perhaps there was something he could do for her. Reach out and touch her heart, make her happy. From an unachievable ideal she had become a real person, flesh and blood, just like him – even if she did come close to approaching perfection.

Unfortunately, this pure love had been tainted by fears that had emerged as the return date had gotten closer. He was afraid that the euphoria they'd been immersed in would shatter in their faces the moment they landed back in New York. He did not care about their age difference or what people might say. He did not care that she was a famous model and that he was still a nobody with a long way to go. He did not even mind accompanying Gloria on her journeys while tracking his own photography projects. But he didn't know how she felt about all of this. Was she ready to let someone like him into her life? He knew that their relationship would require compromises, which he would be willing to make, but what about Gloria? What reason would she have for giving up so much just for him?

His thoughts were interrupted by the touch of soft hands covering his eyes.

"Guess who . . ."

"Patricia?"

"*Who?*" Gloria frowned. Luckily, Andy could not see her.

"My secret lover?"

Gloria's pout turned into a smile.

"Come here," he turned around and wrapped his arms around her.

"Aren't you afraid your girlfriend is going to catch us?" she teased.

"No, she's too old. She doesn't go anywhere without her walker anymore."

"Andy!" She gave him a playful smack.

"Ouch! I think I should call the domestic abuse hotline."

"I've got a feeling even they would hang up on you."

"Okay, you got me there. But don't gloat, it's not over yet," he said with a mischievous look in his eyes.

"Are you sure you want to lose again? Last time wasn't enough for you?" she smirked.

"What can I do, I'm a masochist."

"And what about me?"

"You're a sadist, of course."

"Andy!" She gaped at him.

"But that's why we get along so well!"

"Oh, really?"

"I like to suffer . . ."

Gloria stared at him, a bit confused.

"And you like to make me suffer!" he finished with a triumph note.

"Andy!" She smacked him again, this time a little harder.

"*You see*?"

"I guess you're right," she smiled. "But what will you say about this?"

Gloria put her arms around him and locked her hands behind his neck. He reciprocated with a warm embrace, securing his hands behind her back. She moved closer and let her lips brush against his cheek, reaching slowly to his lips yet denying them from a kiss. Andy could feel her breathing condensing on his skin and tightened his grip on her waist. Gloria let her lips flutter over his, touching yet not touching, until she finally united them together and swirled her tongue in his mouth.

Andy looked deep into her eyes and smiled. "I guess you won again, because I'm speechless."

CHAPTER 35

"**R**ob?"

"Yes, Sharon?"

"There's no way I'm staying back at the hotel."

* * *

Kelly Danes was already on the plane to New Zealand. She had adjusted her seatback to her absolute satisfaction and stretched in her spacious deluxe seat. There were just under fifteen hours left until they reached their destination. She felt freedom was closer than ever, but the fact that she was contained in a closed, cramped space, thirty thousand feet high above ground, didn't really help her claustrophobia.

"Champagne?"

"No, thank you, but I would love a glass of red wine. Dry please."

"Sure ma'am. I'll be back shortly."

Kelly could not understand how people were able to squeeze into the back of a plane like sardines for so many hours. The one and only time she had ever flown coach had been when she'd left her miserable home in Arizona in order to start a new life in New York and leave her past behind. She may have succeeded in the first mission, but the mere fact that she was on her way to kill the woman who had destroyed her youth seemed to indicate that the second mission was yet to be completed.

"Ma'am, here is the wine you ordered."

"Thank you." Kelly took a sip of the wine and swirled the intoxicating liquid in her mouth.

The mansion she had rented had already been prepared for her arrival. As per her request, it had been left empty, without the housekeeping staff that usually maintained it. She had paid a substantial amount of money to make sure the basement would be renovated with wall-to-wall mirrors, lighting, and, most importantly, a new door with a lock. Kelly had explained that her niece was a professional dancer and needed a space to use as a dance studio, but considering the amount of money she'd spent there, no one would have even cared if she had said that she needed it for committing a murder.

About three months ago, when she had not been accused of anything other than working too hard, Kelly had contacted a weapon shop in Christchurch that was located on the way to her new mansion. She had ordered a stylish silver-plated hand pistol that had cost a small fortune, and she had used one of her overseas accounts to make the payment in advance. Kelly had notified the shop when she would be arriving to collect her special purchase, and promised to add a generous tip if everything went well, without any unnecessary questions asked.

"Would you like anything else ma'am?" the flight attendant asked while clearing Kelly's empty glass.

"Actually I would. This wine is just splendid. I was wondering if I could purchase a bottle. I have very special guests coming over this evening."

* * *

The overnight flight from New York to Christchurch landed at 8:22 a.m., on schedule. Rob and Sharon hadn't bothered to bring additional luggage so they wouldn't lose even a moment of precious time. They marched in rapid steps to Passport Control, preparing in advance all the necessary documents. After the customs officer at the window had given up his poor attempt at flirting with Sharon and stamped her passport, they proceeded quickly to the exit doors.

The world outside was unaware of the race against time that Rob and Sharon faced. Around them, life progressed as usual. The airport was crowded with people: relatives welcoming their loved ones, chauffeurs holding signs with the names of their wealthy clients, and cab drivers searching for tired tourists.

Along the side of the road was an endless line of cabs waiting for the newly arrived passengers. Sharon hurried to the nearest taxi, letting Rob lag behind her. He was yelling something at her, but the adrenaline pumping through her body prevented her from hearing it. She slid right into the backseat, waiting for Rob to catch up. He opened the door, his face a bit reddish from the sudden run.

"Sharon–"

"There's no time!" she interrupted him. "Get in! We can rest later."

"But–"

"*Get in!*"

"Okay . . ."

"Driver, you can go!"

"Where to?"

Sharon froze. She had no idea what to tell him.

"Come on, Rob. Where do we need to go?"

"That's what I was trying to tell you. I don't know."

CHAPTER 36

It had been over an hour since they had landed and the situation remained unchanged. They were still stuck in the airport, helpless, exhausted, agitated, and mostly confused.

They had been so busy following Kelly's tracks that they had forgotten to confirm Gloria's whereabouts. While they were still in New York, Rob had instructed one of the officers to look for Gloria McIntyre's agency, but the search had yielded nothing. Apparently the world's most successful model did not belong to any modeling agency! The only person who could connect them to Gloria was her personal manager, Arthur Cohen, but he had left for New Zealand with her.

Rob had asked the young cop to track down anyone related to this Arthur Cohen since he was not available by phone, probably due to the poor signal in the area. With all this pressure, Rob had forgotten to call Arthur's wife, Evelyn Cohen. He felt like a rookie on his first day with the force. How could he have forgotten such a basic thing? Perhaps Rob could have tried to forgive himself in light of the fact that the young officer had obtained her phone number only a few hours before the sudden flight to New Zealand, which he'd had to account for in front of the budget committee.

Or due to the fact he'd had to explain to the police commissioner that his beloved friend, Kelly Danes, was a suspected serial killer who had also tried to kill a cop. Perhaps even because he had tried to explain, somehow, to his wife why he wouldn't be able to celebrate their seven year anniversary and mentioned casually that the reason was a trip overseas with another woman, a blonde nonetheless. Or trying to convince the airline to let them on the next available flight to Christchurch, even if it meant delaying it for another couple. Or since he had to explain to the doctor why someone who had just been shot needed to fly to the other side of the planet. Oh, Rob had almost forgotten, in addition to everything else, that he'd had to find Sharon's passport in her messy apartment and pack her a few essentials for their trip, because she wouldn't be released from the hospital until they left for the airport. So he definitely had justification for forgetting one detail.

But he would not forgive himself.

They had left the cab and called Arthur's wife, but she couldn't help them much. She had given them another phone number that they could use to reach Arthur, but repeated that he was in a low signal area. Evelyn did not even know where exactly the photo shoot was taking place. She offered them the number of the photographer, Andy Swain, but they already had it, and it still went straight to voicemail. Evelyn had promised to go through Arthur's documents and contact his lawyer for a copy of the contract. There might be more details there, she had explained, but it would take some time.

All they could do now was wait. None of them liked having the ball out of their court. Rob stared at his cell phone, as if he could make it ring by sending it a telepathic message; Sharon paced back and forth anxiously, her hand supporting the bandages that protected her wounded skin.

"You know, in your condition it's better if you don't exert yourself; you should sit down," Rob asserted.

"I can't. I'm too nervous. It's either I do this, or I'll shoot someone."

"Carry on then . . ." Rob knew it was pointless to argue with Sharon when she was feeling agitated. She acted like a lioness; the injury only kindled her tenacity.

"At least call your parents. I'm sure that the guys from the control tower have already delivered my message and your parents know by now that you are alive and well, but they would probably be glad to hear it from you in person . . ."

"Rob. Neither of us is touching this phone until Evelyn Cohen calls back and lets us know where the hell they are!"

The cell phone rang right as she completed the sentence.

* * *

The photo shoot had ended. The melancholy of parting was thick in the air. Tom and Libby seemed glum, Arthur was quieter than usual, and anyone could tell by the assistants' faces that they most certainly would have agreed to stay in this magical place for a few more days, even without additional pay.

Gloria and Andy were in an especially dismal mood. It was hard for them to leave all the surreal warmth that had surrounded them and return to the real world, filled with doubts and uncertainty.

The bags were already packed. The photos were taken. Breakfast was over. There was nothing left to do but leave.

"Andy?"

"Yes, Gloria?"

"What if we stayed a bit longer?"

"You've read my mind."

CHAPTER 37

Rob and Sharon were waiting in line at the Avis car rental agency located at the airport; no taxi would take them where they needed to go. In any case, it was better not to be at the mercy of a cab driver while they were in the middle of pursuing a killer.

Evelyn Cohen had called back. She'd gotten in touch with Arthur's lawyer and had found out where Gloria and her crew were staying. The information was not as helpful as they had hoped it would be, because it turned out that, unsurprisingly, the location was in an orientation equivalent to the Bermuda triangle: distant, wild, and obscure. In other words, a place where you could easily get yourself lost.

While Sharon went to buy a map and some snacks for the road, Rob waited in the seemingly endless line to rent a car. Sharon managed to return before he made it to the counter and grumbled about the lost time that could not be retrieved.

"Calm down, Davis, there are only two more people ahead of us."

"At this rate, more like ten. Why can't we explain that this is a police matter and cut ahead of them?"

Rob looked at Sharon with a frustrated gaze. "First of all, it's better that we don't attract undesired attention. We don't know if Kelly has already landed, so we shouldn't take the risk."

"Right," Sharon nodded agreeably.

"And secondly, it's because I hadn't thought of that sooner and I've already waited through this entire goddamned line!"

That was the first time Sharon had laughed since she'd been shot. "Well, don't worry about it," she smiled sympathetically. "Just ask for a car with GPS. I'm not very optimistic about my abilities to decipher these maps."

They reached the service counter and secured a gray, solid Toyota, making sure not to waive the geographic navigation system. There was quite a long drive ahead of them, about four hours, assuming that all went well.

When they got to the car, they both naturally approached the driver's door.

"Sharon, what do you think you're doing?"

"Driving."

"Why?"

"Because I always drive. Besides, you drove last time."

"Because you've been shot! And if I'm not mistaken, that still hasn't changed."

"Lame excuse. You just don't want me to drive because I'm a woman . . ."

"Say, could it be that while you were in the ICU the doctor operated on your brain as well? 'Cause it seems to me that you've lost your mind!"

"That still doesn't mean that I can't drive, so hand over the keys," Sharon insisted.

"Sharon, we've been working together for quite some time. Do you really think I'm a chauvinist who doesn't want to let you drive because you're a woman?"

"No . . ." Sharon answered reluctantly.

"And do you understand that you can't strain yourself? Therefore, I can't let you drive while we are on our way to catch a murderess. You need to save every ounce of strength you have."

"Well . . . okay. But damn it, I just really wanted to drive!"

That was the first time in his life that Rob Jackie had ever managed to beat Sharon Davis in an argument. He would not forget about it for years to come. So what if she happened to be on three different types of pain killers . . . ?

* * *

The last hours Andy and Gloria had spent at the inn were magical. It was one of those days that made you wonder whether you were dreaming or not and eventually became a treasured memory. Even though Andy was sad about leaving, he was equally excited for what was yet to come. Finally, he could present his work to Kelly Danes, an important persona in the media world, who not only had given him a golden opportunity for his big breakthrough, but also a once-in-a-lifetime chance at love. And for this love, he was willing to postpone this long-awaited moment for a bit longer.

Tom and Libby were thrilled that the young couple had decided to extend their stay. They quickly fixed them a marvelous picnic basket filled with scrumptious treats and urged them to hike around and further explore the beautiful surroundings. Andy and Gloria jumped at the opportunity.

After all, it was their first date.

The exquisite scenery enveloped them in a fairy tale of their own. Gloria felt like a little girl again and took off her shoes to feel the crisp grass beneath her feet. She was amazed at the realization that what made her feel sheer bliss did not even cost a single dime.

Gloria looked up and let the sunrays caress her; a great beam illuminated her face. She started skipping and hopping like she used to when she was a kid, when life was much simpler.

"Hey! What's going on with you?" Andy called after her. "I can't run with this basket without dropping everything, it's too heavy!"

"Too bad, Grandpa . . . Catch me if you can!"

Andy placed the well-stocked basket on the ground and raced after her. Gloria tried to pick up the pace, but he caught up with her in mere seconds and wrapped his arms around her to keep her from moving.

"Nooo, let me go!" Gloria commanded him with giggles, while trying to free herself from his strong grasp. She would not let some *kid* beat her.

"No way. I want to make sure you stay by my side," Andy answered, fastening his arms around her.

Gloria's slender physique allowed her to squeeze through his arms and face him. "Don't worry, I'm not going anywhere."

She stood on her tiptoes and kissed him. Andy's grip relaxed, but Gloria stayed close to him.

After they found the abandoned picnic basket, they continued their journey, searching for their own piece of heaven. Finally, they found it under the shade of an old oak tree. There was something special about this place, where there was no value assigned to any title or status they had obtained in their lives, where they were nothing more than man and woman.

Andy could not restrain himself, nor wanted to; his hands began exploring Gloria's body. His palms embraced her flawless outline, stroking her from top to bottom, forming the coveted shape of an hourglass. He laid Gloria on the ground with him on top of her, his hands still caressing her. Even though nothing concealed them, they were far removed from any prying eyes. The wilderness kept their secret.

Coral-colored sand grains began covering Gloria's milky skin, as if they were tainting it; but she didn't even mind that her body was rubbing into the soft earth. Andy began to pull off her dress, but she stopped him from doing so. Now it was her turn to be in charge, to touch him with every bit of intent, like she had fantasized when they were sitting next to each other on the drive over here. Her shyness was gone, but her desires remained.

She climbed on top of him, pressing his back against the ground. Those same coral grains that were slowly falling off Gloria's back began sticking to his body. He lifted his arms to hold her, but she did not let him. Instead, she leaned toward him and began to kiss him, her lips following along his body, until she had reached the zipper of his pants. Andy tried to sit up, but she pushed him gently back down toward the reddish sand.

She guided her hand slowly under her dress, ensuring his gaze was following her, and pulled her panties aside. Gloria took pleasure in beholding his breathing increase excitedly, wanting to burst out of his wide torso and making her slim body move up and down accordingly. She climbed on top of him, feeling the connection that was formed between them, and began to ride. Gloria's back remained straight, but between her thighs she felt this certain warmth that made her experience a comforting weakness. She arched her back and felt lost in pleasure, but then Andy held her by the waist and began to steer her into the ultimate climax. The heat she felt inside almost blazed through her; the cool wind that stroked their exposed bodies only enhanced her blistering passion. Gloria felt all of her inhibitions slipping away like a needless shell. She allowed herself to scream like she had never screamed before, Andy's moaning swallowed in hers. Their voices echoed in the open field, but they were lost in the wind, lost in the wild.

Gloria rolled over and lay beside Andy. He took her hand and intertwined his fingers with hers. They remained alone in the world, embracing under the open sky.

It seemed as though the sunrays had touched them, but only for a minute, and their time had now ended. They had to leave.

"Perhaps we should postpone this whole thing until tomorrow?" Gloria asked in a seductive voice.

"I know, I'd like that, too. But there is no way to let Kelly know that we'd be late. There's no cellular signal in this area."

"So what?" she replied.

"What do you mean 'so what'? The woman has flown half way around the world to meet us, and you want to blow her off?"

"Who said I want to blow her off? I just want to postpone the meeting for a few hours. Or days . . ."

"Gloria, this is my first serious job in this industry. This incredible woman gave me the opportunity of a lifetime."

He paused for a moment, trying to think of a way to soften Gloria; her piercing stare made it clear to him that she did not intend to give up so easily.

"Thanks to her, I met you. I think the least I can do is arrive to our meeting on time."

Gloria smiled. Frankly, she, too, owed this woman quite a lot.

"Okay, but you're buying me a Snickers. There's no way I'm spending the next five hours locked in the car without chocolate."

CHAPTER 38

Kelly glanced at her watch. Beforehand, when the pilot had announced the approximate landing time, she had changed it to the local time. Now it was almost 1:30 p.m. She was right on schedule. After collecting her luggage and passing through passport control, she would be out of the airport and on her way in less than an hour. She just hoped her guests wouldn't be early . . .

"Is there a problem with your seatbelt, ma'am?"

Kelly looked at the stewardess, compelled to detach herself from her sweet thoughts.

"Oh, no, sweetheart. I just didn't notice the sign." She tightened the seatbelt to her body until it clicked.

"Ladies and gentlemen, we will be landing shortly." The pilot's voice sounded over the speaker. "Thank you for flying with us."

Kelly could feel the plane gradually descending. The pressure in her ears increased. That was her least favorite part of the flight – besides take off, of course.

"We would like to remind you to please remain seated while the red seatbelt sign is on." The flight attendant's voice echoed throughout the plane.

As the wheels of the plane kissed the ground, a few passengers clapped their hands. Kelly was mortified by the stupid, folksy custom, but tried to ignore it. She closed her eyes and took a deep breath.

Finally, she had reached her safe haven.

A short hour later, Kelly was already on her way to her new home, at least for the next few days. She knew that after she executed her plan, once again she would have to leave in haste. This time she hadn't planned ahead where she would flee. She decided it would be safer to decide on the spot which flight to catch, and then disappear without leaving a trace. She toyed with the idea of Tahiti, Crete, or even Japan, but she would have more time to think about this later; right now she needed to stay focused on her plan. Tomorrow, at the exact same time, she could put this whole thing behind her.

The navigation system calculated the shortest route to the mansion, but first she had to make one stop. She typed in the address of the weapon shop. Twenty minutes later she was there. In the parking lot next to the store, there was one spot left – just for her.

A sign from above, she smiled at her reflection in the rear-view mirror.

Kelly entered the store, letting her eyes adjust to the dim light. The owner stood behind the counter and sharpened an ancient sword.

"Hello there, are you looking for something in particular?"

"Actually, I am. I came to pick up a special order. I arranged it with you several months ago."

An intrigued grin appeared on his face. "Yes, of course. I was expecting you. I'm always curious about special orders. They happen, but not very often. That's why I always keep tabs on them."

Kelly felt a little bit anxious in light of the fact that someone had engraved in his memory the details of her murder weapon.

"Here, take a look. What a beautiful piece." He showed her the silver gun with admiring hands.

Kelly approached it, her eyes sparkling with anticipation.

"I'll just verify we have all the details in place, Miss . . . ?"

"That's not relevant," she answered hastily while sliding a stack of bills toward his side of the counter.

The vendor looked at the money and then turned his gaze to Kelly, as if trying to arbitrate between his curiosity and his greed.

"You're absolutely right."

Kelly was still amazed to see the amount of influence a small pile of bills possessed.

Like a puppet on a string . . .

She put the silver weapon in her pocketbook, along with a pack of bullets, and headed toward the exit.

"Pleasure doing business with you," he called.

She didn't bother to reply.

CHAPTER 39

They had been driving for over three hours and still had plenty of time left together in the confined metal box.

"So what did your mom say?" Rob asked Sharon.

"That she's going to kill me and that my dad almost had a heart attack."

"Ouch. I wouldn't want to be in their shoes. Or yours, for that matter."

"Well, it's not like I had a choice. It's better that my murderess thinks I'm dead rather than planning to kill me again!"

Rob arched an eyebrow. "There's a sentence you don't hear every day."

Sharon chuckled. "Anyway, she was mostly just upset because I had neglected to fill her in on our little plan." Her mother's scolding voice still echoed in her head.

"Sharon Elaine Davis. Do you know what a parent's worst nightmare is? Hearing that their child is dead. And do you know what's even worse? Reading about it in the newspaper! Do you have any idea how many phone calls I got? People were asking me when the funeral is, while I hadn't even realized what happened. I'd already called Reverend Rayner to discuss burial

arrangements, and you couldn't even find one spare minute to let me know that you're still alive? And not even that, I had to hear it from some airport representative? And then trying to explain to people why the funeral was being postponed, because I can't tell anyone that you're actually alive? What the **hell** *were you thinking, young lady?"*

That was the first and only time Sharon had ever heard her mother use that word.

"Say, what about that guy you met on the plane?" Rob's voice drew her back to reality, thank God.

"Who, Chris?" Sharon could feel the blush creeping along her cheeks.

Rob smiled. In all the years they had worked together, he had never seen her so perplexed, and because of a guy, nonetheless.

"In case you haven't noticed, I've had a lot on my plate for the last few days. I haven't had a chance to talk to him yet," she said briskly.

Rob had foreseen that response. Sharon had so many defense mechanisms that he wouldn't be surprised to find out she was wearing copper armor under her clothes.

"And in case you haven't noticed," Rob emphasized, "we have spent the last three hours counting red cars on the road."

"I still can't believe we've only seen seven. I would have expected a lot more."

"Sharon, you're changing the subject."

"Could be," she glanced out the window.

"So how about you call him now? At least let him know you're still among the living."

Only then Sharon realized that Chris might also read the New York Times.

* * *

The number that appeared on the telephone screen was clearly international. He tried to remember if any of his friends had gone overseas recently, but he couldn't think of anyone.

"Hello?"

"Hi, Chris?"

He wasn't sure it was her. After all, he had only talked to her once, and since then she hadn't answered any of his calls.

"Yes . . . ? Speaking."

"It's Sharon. The cop. From the plane."

"You'd have to be more specific."

"Very funny." Although she tried to sound cynical, she couldn't keep from smiling.

"So, you're not dead?"

"Oh, no. We had to print that article as part of a big case I'm working on. I'm sorry I couldn't fill you in earlier."

"What are you talking about?"

"The article in the New York Times about my murder. I assume that's why you asked me if I'm not dead."

"Actually, I asked you that because you never returned my calls . . ."

* * *

Rob glanced at Sharon while she was on the phone with Chris. She was acting like a seventeen-year-old girl. While talking to him, she toyed with her golden hair, and Rob could see the subtle blush appearing on her cheeks.

She managed to explain to Chris very briefly – keeping full discretion one might add – about all the insanity she had been through in the last few days, starting with the fact she'd been shot and ending with the chase that had brought her all the way to New Zealand. After passing this hurdle, they proceeded to talk about other things. Rob was glad that someone had managed to get Sharon interested in something other than work.

The closer they got to their destination, the more the cellular reception weakened, and Sharon was forced to end the conversation.

"You're cute," Rob teased.

"No, I'm not."

"I can't help it. It's a fact."

"Why?"

"Because you really like this guy."

"You're wrong. I was just being polite."

"Sharon, it's not a shame to admit at your age that you like someone."

"Okay, I do. Are you happy now?"

"Actually, I am," he smirked.

She rolled her eyes. "Well, I'm trying again to get a hold of Arthur or Gloria or that photographer, Andy. Perhaps now that we're closer . . ."

She tried calling, but still no answer.

"Don't worry, Davis. We'll be there in less than an hour."

She leaned back. "Finally, things are starting to move along."

Right as Sharon settled back in her seat, Rob's cell phone rang. She answered. It was a short conversation, but by the time it ended her face had already gone pale.

"What the hell happened?" Rob demanded.

Sharon sighed. "While we were on the plane, the forensics team finished sweeping Kelly's house. They found another body."

CHAPTER 40

Kelly passed through the heavy, wooden door into the spacious and extravagant lounge. The sound of her footsteps echoed with each stride she took across the pristine marble floor. She looked up and noticed the twinkle of the crystal chandelier hanging from the ceiling. She strolled through the house, admiring the expensive carpets and the art work that adorned the walls. The entire place had been tastefully decorated and looked really impressive. *Worth every penny.*

Kelly walked into the kitchen and opened the refrigerator. As per her request, it had been stocked in advance with delectable foods. Hunger began badgering her, but she decided to ignore it. More than anything, she craved a visit to the most important place in the house: the basement.

Kelly marched rapidly toward the staircase. She stood in front of a closed door and gripped the handle firmly, eventually shoving it forward. She headed down the stairs, her heart racing more and more with each step down.

The room was completely dark and it took her a few moments to locate the light switch. The space that was revealed to her was almost identical to the one in her own home. Kelly stood in the middle of the room, surrounded by the reflections that appeared in the newly-installed mirrors on the wide wall in front of her. She looked at the woman gazing back at her from the mirror. She could see the wickedness in her eyes. Kelly wondered how she had become the person staring back at her, why had she chosen such a gory path when anyone else, who possessed the same power and influence she had achieved, would have just moved on? Was the heavy cost that she had paid really worth this single moment, when she would finally lay her hands on Gloria McIntyre?

Kelly wondered what she would do the next morning, after she had attained the revenge she had been dreaming about for years. What would she yearn for then? She'd always thought that there was something bittersweet about a dream come true, as if fulfilling the dream entailed shattering it. Kelly had been so engulfed in planning every little detail leading to this moment that she hadn't thought about what she would do after it. What would be next? What aspirations did she have left? She tried to recall her former self, before the dreadful event that had changed her forever, but her mind went completely blank.

Kelly knew that she could never go back to being *"Kelly Danes – Editor in Chief of Inner Beauty magazine,"* and her heart ached. The last few years had been the only ones in which she had felt appreciated and prosperous, and now they were lost for good. The only pleasure that remained was plundering the beauty and lives of those corrupted girls. Would she continue doing that? Kelly had always told herself that although they'd each had it coming, they had merely been practice for the *grand finale*; but what was the point of training after she had already won the final act?

After the first time, Kelly had known that she could never stop, even if she had tried to tell herself otherwise. Even killing the cop had been exhilarating, despite her guilty conscience.

Kelly looked into the eyes of the woman staring back at her from the mirror. It was a moment of awakening; she had no choice but to accept her destiny, the path that she would follow for the rest of her life.

I, Kelly Danes, am a murderess.

CHAPTER 41

"**W**hat?!"

"You heard me correctly, another body."

Rob narrowed his eyes at the road. "What do we know about it?" he asked crisply.

"Not much. It was found buried under the basement floor, wrapped in a white blanket. One of the floorboards was slightly loose and the cops noticed there was something under the surface. They still don't know how long it's been buried there, but at first glance the coroner believes that we're looking at several years."

"So it's possible that Mandy Sheldon wasn't the first victim?"

"Exactly."

"Goddammit."

"You read my mind."

* * *

When Andy noticed the sign of the gas station, he slowed down the vehicle and turned down the path leading to it. The familiar yet dreary scenery reminded him of a surprisingly romantic moment.

"Why are you pulling over?" Gloria asked in a drowsy voice, too lazy to open her eyes.

"I promised you chocolate, didn't I?" he smiled at her.

Gloria's eyes opened slightly. A subtle smile crept to her lips.

"What a joy that the photo shoot is over. Now I can indulge without feeling guilty."

"In that case, should I get you both a Snickers *and* a Twix?"

"Don't push it."

Andy stifled a laugh. "Which one do you want?"

"Do I have to decide right now?"

"Yeah, unless you want us to arrive at Kelly's tomorrow."

"Actually, it wouldn't be so bad spending another night alone with you . . ." She flashed a seductive smile.

"Are you trying to distract me from the fact that you can't decide what you want?"

Gloria tilted her head down and chuckled. "You know me too well."

"If you can't make up your mind right now, then I'll just have to choose myself," Andy threatened.

"No!" she exclaimed.

"Why don't you let me surprise you?" he implored.

"And if you make the wrong choice?"

"And if, God forbid, you'll actually be pleased?"

Gloria looked at him with a contemplative look on her face, as if she were seriously considering what to do.

"You know you're seriously disturbed, right?" he teased.

"Why?"

"Do you understand how much energy you're wasting over a little chocolate bar?"

"Oh. When you become a model, you will understand."

Andy gave her a sidelong glance. "I don't think that's going to happen anytime soon."

"Then surprise me."

Gloria had been waiting in the car for a few long minutes, staring at the minimart's front door. It was not a trivial matter for her, letting Andy make the decision for her. She had to make sure that he made the right choice. But how can he do that when I don't even know what I want? she asked herself, anxiously. Gloria couldn't take it anymore. She stepped out of the car and entered the store, hoping to catch Andy in time. She saw him standing in front of the chocolate shelves, at the same spot where they had shared their first kiss.

"I was wondering how long it would take you before you came in here." His smile revealed a pair of tantalizing dimples. "Nearly four whole minutes. Congratulations."

"I see that you're still debating, too."

"No. Actually, I already chose."

Gloria's heart skipped a beat. "So what did you choose?" she asked nervously.

"Both of them. We'll eat one half of each, and that way you won't eat more than the quantity of one chocolate bar!" he declared triumphantly.

Gloria looked at him with glistening eyes. She did not say a word.

"You're not happy?" A crease of disappointment formed between his eyes.

Gloria threw herself at him with a long, passionate kiss. "I couldn't have made a better choice myself." Her arms remained around him.

On their way to the register, Andy thought to himself that he would never understand what the deal was with chicks and chocolate.

* * *

The two cops had run out of whatever remaining patience they'd had.

Rob and Sharon were just a few miles away from the elusive inn where the famous model was staying, but they couldn't find it. It seemed as though the navigation system refused to acknowledge the existence of the small guesthouse and kept instructing them to drive in circles. They realized that only after they had passed by the same crossroad for the third time. Needless to say, they were not happy.

After they had cursed and sworn at the inventor of the GPS, they decided to forgo their dignity and asked one of the locals for directions. The man told them they were about fifteen minutes away. They drove in silence for the last stretch, resenting the bad cell reception in the area that had deprived them of obtaining additional information on the latest – or, to be exact, the first – victim of Kelly Danes.

The frustrated Sharon tried to recollect all the information they had so far. The primary data suggested that the victim was a grown woman, but there were no identifiable details on the body that could reveal her identity. The forensic investigator promised to call Sharon and let her know as soon as the postmortem autopsy results were in, but she figured they wouldn't hear anything until they would be back in New York. In any case, as much as her curiosity tormented her, there were more pressing matters at stake: the reason they had come to New Zealand in the first place was to stop Kelly Danes from achieving her final goal – now they were running out of time. The clock hands refused to slow down. She just hoped they were not too late.

CHAPTER 42

The clock hands refused to move any faster. In a few short hours it would finally happen. She would stand face to face with Gloria McIntyre.

Kelly was sitting in an antique velvet armchair. She placed her coffee mug on the table and reached for a pack of cigarettes. She hadn't smoked in years and missed it tremendously. Today, she decided, was a special day; she could allow herself to indulge, relax, light up a cigarette, and wait ...

While the warm smoke spread down her throat, she couldn't help but think about that dark day, one that had started like any other day, but its ending had changed her life forever. She had tried to repress it for years, but now, so close to the long-awaited end, the memory threatened to possess her.

Kelly gazed at the clouds of smoke she exhaled, slowly fading into nothing, and took another long breath in the hope that what would go in could drive away her memories.

Too late.

The course of events from the darkest day of her life, April 24, 1990, started to unfold in her mind.

The opening day of the Spring Carnival.

* * *

Usually, Kelly did not attend social events that were crowded with people, such as Winslow's annual Spring Carnival, but this time was different. At the beginning of the school year, she had gotten to know the person who would later become her one and only friend, Vicky Hermont. Vicky's family had moved to Winslow after her parents had stumbled into financial difficulties; they'd had to sell their old home and move in with Vicky's grandmother. Like Kelly, Vicky also was ostracized by her schoolmates, and the two had no trouble finding comfort in one another; loneliness had brought them together. That was the first time they each had gained a true friend.

Both of them were good students, even exceptional, but that was where any resemblance ended. While Kelly was often pushed aside due to her quiet nature and bashfulness, Vicky lashed out at her classmates and acted in a patronizing way that often aroused hostility. She was a misunderstood girl. If Kelly's name was one that not many could remember, Vicky's name was the object of ridicule. But no matter what, Vicky always stood beside Kelly, even at her own expense. When Kelly recalled the torment her young friend had faced, her heart ached as if it were her own. In all of her life, Vicky was the one person that Kelly had truly loved. *My guardian angel.*

The grand opening of the carnival had been scheduled for that day, and Vicky had suggested they go.

"I don't think it's a good idea," Kelly hesitated.

"Why not? It will be my first time at the carnival!" Vicky used an imploring tone that revealed her disappointment.

"Yes, but everyone is going to be there, including *you know who*."

The two girls may have been social outcasts, but one group of boys had taken things a step too far. They were one year older and notorious as the town troublemakers. Practical jokes and harmless pranks were just not enough for them, and their gags many times bordered on cruelty. The two girls were not the only victims of their antics, but Vicky, who always proclaimed that she was too good for this place, was their favorite target of abuse. Kelly, as far as they were concerned, was just collateral damage. In their eyes, no one was off limits, except for one girl.

Gloria McIntyre.

Gloria was a year younger than Kelly and Vicky, and she was the perfect, beautiful girl, loved by the entire town. Gloria's mother was a nurse at the local hospital and had helped deliver many of the town's children. That year she had become ill and Gloria, whose father had abandoned the family when she was only a child, had to carry the burden on her own. Ever since, as if admiring the little bitch hadn't been enough, her status had been elevated to that of an angel. The neighbors, who knew that Gloria's mother could no longer work, made sure to send over casseroles and food. Even Kelly's mother had sent over a few trays of her famous oatmeal cookies every now and then.

God, how she hated oatmeal cookies.

Even the troublemakers treated Gloria's mom with respect, mostly because the gang's leader, Jerry Dunwood, was hopelessly in love with Gloria. He pranced around her and tried to impress her with his pranks, but she seemed rather appalled by them. However, her best friends back then were actually attracted to the bad boy's image and had managed to persuade Gloria to hang out with them, knowing she was their entry ticket into the group.

Vicky couldn't stand Gloria. She had seen right through her for who she really was, beyond her phony façade. Vicky had always suspected that Gloria was the one who had turned Jerry against her, since they had never liked each other. Kelly remembered how she used to dismiss Vicky's conspiracies. It was true that Vicky and Gloria weren't friends, but Kelly did not believe that Gloria could be so malicious.

Boy, was she wrong.

* * *

She remembered that awful day as an out-of-body experience, as if she had been watching from afar all the wrong that had been done to her. On that bitter day, Kelly had been nervous about going to the carnival. She didn't want to run into Jerry and his friends, but Vicky had convinced her that the boys would be too busy pursuing the town girls and getting drunk, so they wouldn't have time to hassle them. With that in mind, Kelly and Vicky had decided to go to the carnival.

This was the worst decision Kelly had ever made.

Kelly and Vicky had been walking around the carnival booths, enjoying the liveliness that had been brought into their small town. Suddenly, they'd noticed Jerry's gang and decided to take precautions. A mere glance was enough to plan their escape route. They decided to split up, knowing that Jerry would rather look for girls in pairs. Afterwards, they would meet at the entrance and go to the meteor crater, which would be empty for the two of them while everyone else was at the carnival. They had parted in silence, stepping away from each other.

If only I had stayed with Vicky, nothing bad would have happened, she sadly thought to herself.

Kelly could not remember what exactly she had been doing when she wandered off alone; probably just walking around, enjoying the nonsense around her, attempting to stretch out time like a chewed piece of gum between her fingers until it was time to meet her friend at the entrance. But then, only God knows why, she went into the house of mirrors.

The most horrific place on earth.

She remembered the course of events as if they were a part of an old movie she had watched years ago, each time remembering the same scene in a slightly different way.

Kelly had walked between the bizarre mirrors, which sometimes deformed her and at times reflected her exactly as she was. She couldn't tell them apart. Kelly had hated her unmemorable features and mousy figure. Vicky had tried to talk her into giving her a makeover so she could transform into the beauty Vicky knew Kelly could be, but she always refused.

Oh, how proud would you be, Vicky, if you could see me today.

However, back then, in the gloomy hall of mirrors, Kelly had only been the ugly duckling trying to hide from its own reflection. She could not stand to look at herself, to be reminded of what a failure she was. She would be nothing more than a Plain Jane. She would never be admired or revered; most of the people she knew could barely remember her name. Her fate was to be forgotten, she sadly realized. Kelly's eyes glistened brighter than the shining mirrors that surrounded her.

"Oh, I'm sorry. I didn't mean to intrude. I'll come back later." It seemed as though Gloria felt embarrassed witnessing this intimate moment of self-reflection. She headed toward the exit.

"It's okay, you can stay. I have to leave anyway," Kelly assured her.

So why didn't you? she yelled at herself in her mind, as if she were a character in a horror film that was bound to die, no matter what.

"Okay." Gloria did not seem entirely at ease, but she stayed.

They stood on opposite sides of the room, hesitating, fearing they might somehow invade the other's territory.

After a few silent minutes, they finally broke the ice.

"My mom asked me to thank your mom for the oatmeal cookies. They always cheer her up," said Gloria.

"You're welcome." Kelly was surprised by Gloria's kind words, even if she was only being polite. "I'll be sure to let her know."

Kelly thought for a moment she had noticed movement in the shadows, but when she looked again she didn't see anything; probably just a figment of her imagination.

Gloria looked at her, confused, trying to find something to talk about. "So . . . Where's Vicky?" she eventually asked.

"Where's Jerry?" Kelly countered.

"You caught me. You're not the only one who's trying to avoid him." The confusion on her face turned into a smirk.

"Oh, you guys aren't a couple?"

"Absolutely not."

Kelly arched an eyebrow. "So you wouldn't be offended if I told you he's a real jerk?"

"I might agree with you." A subtle smile stretched across her face.

Kelly chuckled. She glanced at her watch; it had been fifteen minutes since she'd left Vicky. She might be waiting for her at the entrance. Alone. One of the boys might find her.

"Why do you look so worried?" Gloria asked.

Perhaps because your boyfriend is on the loose?

"I was supposed to meet Vicky."

"Here?"

"Yes." Kelly didn't know why she lied.

"Well, she will probably be here any minute now. You girls are practically inseparable," she declared decisively.

Kelly flashed an awkward smile.

Gloria stared at the floor for a few seconds, but then she looked up at Kelly and their eyes met. "By the way," she added, "I want to apologize on behalf of Jerry and his friends for treating you guys the way they do. I know it may seem that way because Vicky and I don't get along, but I've never encouraged those jerks' disgusting behavior. Quite the opposite." She seemed sincere.

Kelly looked at Gloria in awe, like a little girl waking up on Christmas morning to a tree filled with presents.

"Thanks. You have no idea how nice it is to hear that."

Oh, Kelly, why were you so naive?

After a few minutes, their reticent talk changed to a candid conversation. The two girls sat on the wooden floor, their backs pressed against opposite mirrors, while they faced one another.

"Ugh, I look so fat!" Gloria cried.

"Are you kidding me? Even like this you still look beautiful." Kelly stared into Gloria's eyes through the mirror. An awkward silence took over.

"Say," Kelly broke the silence. "Do you think that in a different world we could have been . . . ?"

"Friends? I think so," Gloria said thoughtfully.

Kelly did not take her eyes off of Gloria.

"But in this world you're Vicky's friend, and my best friends hang out with Jerry and his gang, whether I like it or not. I'm afraid we're on opposite sides of the fence," Gloria pointed out.

"Like Romeo and Juliet," Kelly's voice softened.

"Perhaps," Gloria smiled, trying to figure out if Kelly was trying to imply something. "It's weird that Vicky hasn't shown up yet."

Kelly chanced a glance at the exit sign, but quickly shifted her gaze back to Gloria. "Yeah, never mind, I'll see her some other time," she muttered.

How could I abandon a true friend for this fake doll?

"Well, it's getting late. I should head home," Gloria got up.

Kelly stood up and caught up with her. "Once you leave everything will go back to the way it was, won't it? You'll go back to being a part of Jerry's clique." She enunciated the last two words with a hint of aversion.

"And you'll be back with Vicky," Gloria stated.

"I guess we have no choice," Kelly sighed.

"It appears so."

"Well, goodbye, Gloria McIntyre."

Kelly leaned toward Gloria and kissed her on the cheek. Gloria froze in her place.

Kelly did not want to part from Gloria's soft skin. She tried to reach her lips.

Gloria turned her face away from her. "Kelly, stop," she said gently.

"You traitor! How could you do this to me?" Vicky's enraged voice jarred on Kelly's ears right before her image appeared from behind the mirrors. She marched angrily toward them.

"*Vicky*?" Kelly gasped. "I don't understand . . ." her voice trailed off.

"I don't understand either how you could throw me to the wolves for . . ." She turned her head and cast a hateful glance at Gloria. "For *her*!"

"Vicky, you need to calm down. Nobody has done anything against you," said Gloria.

"You stay out of it, you arrogant little princess!" Vicky snapped. "Why are you trying to steal Kelly away from me? Do you hate me that much? Seducing my only friend in this damned place just to make me suffer? What have I ever done to you to deserve that?"

"I don't know what you're talking about. I just–"

"Don't say another word!" Vicky screamed. "I saw you just now. I saw the way you looked at her," she turned to Kelly.

"Vicky, I'm so sorry," Kelly tried to placate her.

"Spare me."

"I think this is all a big misunderstanding," Gloria intervened in an attempt to calm Vicky.

"And I think I finally realize what's really going on here." Vicky narrowed her eyes at them. "I will *never* forgive you!" She ran toward the exit and slammed the door shut.

* * *

After a few awkward moments Kelly broke the silence once again.

"Listen, I'm sorry you had to . . ." She stopped, looking for the right words.

"Forget about it. It's not your fault the girl is *nuts*." Gloria contorted her face with distain.

Kelly felt a pinch at her heart. *Why did Gloria have to talk about Vicky that way?*

"In any case, I'd better get going," Gloria turned toward the exit.

"Do you really have to?"

"I think so," she said without looking at Kelly. "It's better for the both of us," Gloria added right before she disappeared behind the door. That was the last time Kelly had ever seen her.

Kelly had plummeted down and leaned against one of the mirrors. She had remained alone in the empty space, too exhausted to get up, not knowing how to fix the damage that she had caused. She was deep in thought when she'd suddenly heard the unsettling sound of a squeaky door.

Three large, dark figures walked in, Jerry Dunwood and two of his bully friends.

"Hey, Whitesporte! What the hell did you do to Gloria, you pathetic little lesbian?!"

"What are you talking about?" Kelly was completely taken aback.

"We heard you tried to rape her and that it was pure luck she got away from you." Jerry got closer and stood right in front of Kelly, his bulky build casting its shadow over her. "Did you really think you could pull off something like this and get away with it?"

Kelly was aghast. Fear consumed her entire body. She remained fossilized at Jerry's feet, staring at his large, muddy shoes, just inches away from her. She felt cold perspiration beginning to drip down her nape. "Listen, you're wrong. It's just a big misunderstanding," she tried to explain.

"No, you listen, bitch," he spat out the words. "I don't give a fuck about your sick fantasies, but if you ever come near Gloria again, you're dead. Sawed into pieces and scattered in the sand. Is that *clear*?"

Kelly felt her body beginning to shiver involuntarily, though it wasn't even the least bit cold. She could not utter a word. She was absolutely petrified.

Jerry didn't wait for an answer. "You're going to pay. Big time."

"That's a lie!" Kelly mustered enough courage to reply, her voice choked with horror.

"Don't even try. I know it's true, *first hand*."

I can't believe Gloria sold me out like this. How could she do this to me?

The three boys started closing in on her and she cringed away from them. Kelly's heart was pounding out of her chest. Her skin was glistening with beads of cold sweat exuding from her pores. And then came the first punch, followed by so many others. Kelly flinched when she relived the attack, the heavy beating she endured while her ears picked out the curses and insults slung at her from the incessant flow of words spewing from their mouths. It all happened so fast and painfully slow at the same time, somewhere between an endless nightmare and a sudden awakening to her tragic reality. Her body was sprawled out on the filthy floor, waiting to be punished. For a moment, the torment stopped. Was it finally over?

Jerry picked Kelly up by the shirt collar. "Do you really think you have the right to even go near her?" She felt his intoxicated breath condensing on her skin. "You're so disgusting, ugly, repulsive! It's obvious why you've given up on men." He kicked her hard in the crotch.

Kelly screamed in agony. Streams of pain gushed out of her. Jerry kept kicking her, ignoring her cries, and invited his friends to join him. They were merciless. As the barrage of blows renewed, her head spun from the overwhelming pain. The blows became stronger and stronger. She was lost in a swirl of torment.

After what felt like eternity, she was left discarded on the floor like a useless trash bag. Kelly's body was covered with a mix of mud and blood. Her mouth tasted like spew. She heard the sounds of laughter drifting further away from her.

She remained all alone.

Kelly barely got up. She could hardly breathe. Each breath of air ached.

She limped slowly, trying to avoid the mirrors enveloping her. She did not want to look at them. She had been mutated into a monster, a freak; no wonder everyone had abandoned her, even Vicky.

She just wanted this feeling to end, for all of this to be over.

She could not take it anymore. The distorted figure looked at her from every angle, from every corner. She felt her throat constrict.

She had to do something.

She slammed her body up against the walls, spinning around in ecstasy, smashing the mirrors around her, feeling fresh cuts form on her skin and drops of blood begin to spill. The pain was cathartic.

She struck her head a third time. She could no longer stand up. She fell to the floor and her eyes closed. A sense of relief washed over her, a victorious smile spreading across her face. Now she was ready to open her eyes and enjoy the sweet darkness that encompassed her. No one would ridicule her anymore. No one could see her.

CHAPTER 43

Kelly did not know how long she had been lying on the floor in the house of mirrors, perhaps a minute, perhaps an hour.

She had heard steps running toward her, but could not open her eyes to see who it was. Kelly felt the mirror shards being brushed away from her hand and the bandages being wrapped around her wrists. Later on she had recognized the muffled sound of the siren blare as she'd been rushed to the hospital, and then she had been dazzled by the bright lights hanging above her as she'd been whisked down the hall to Intensive Care.

Her next memory occurred a few days afterwards. Although she was physically stable, Kelly wasn't being released from the hospital because she had been recommended to stay in the psychiatric ward for further observation. That day she had been granted a visit by someone special.

When she opened her eyes, she immediately noticed the familiar face sitting by her bed.

"Vicky?" she asked in a weak voice, still dazed from the sedatives.

"Yes, honey. It's me."

"I thought that . . ." Kelly felt the dryness in her mouth impeding her words. "I thought that you'd never want to see me ever again," she eventually completed the sentence.

"Do you really think I would abandon my best friend?" She squeezed Kelly's hand.

Kelly smiled faintly. The last few days had depleted her of all her strength.

"I can't believe they did this to you, those bastards." Vicky muttered the last two words angrily.

The already frail smile vanished from Kelly's face instantly.

"And to think it was all because of that spoiled bitch . . ."

Kelly wheezed heavily. "What do you mean?" She felt short of breath. "Who?"

Vicky's lips puckered as if they'd let slip something that was not supposed to be told.

"Forget about it, honey. The most important thing now is for you to get better."

But she knew Kelly would not drop it.

"No. I want to know what you're talking about." Kelly elevated herself to a sitting position.

Vicky helped her adjust the pillow behind her back. "Okay," she caved. "I'm talking about Gloria McIntyre."

"What does she have to do with this?" she insisted. Kelly's last memory of Gloria was the image of her graceful figure heading out the door.

"You really don't get it, do you?" Vicky stared at her.

Kelly gazed back at Vicky, trying to decipher her expression. It couldn't be that all of this had happened because of *Gloria*. Why would she do that to her? After they'd had a heart to heart talk for the first time? Maybe Gloria wanted to get back at her for trying to kiss her? No, that was way too brutal. Only a heartless person would have done something like this in order to make a point.

"Well," Vicky took a deep breath. "After I left the house of mirrors, I didn't go straight home. I was waiting for you, because I wanted us to patch things up. After a few minutes, I saw Gloria storming out the door looking for something. *Or someone.* I saw her running to Jerry, shouting and waving her hands. When I got closer, I heard her telling him that you'd told her that he and his friends were a bunch of jerks and that you'd tried to turn her against them."

"Are you sure?" Kelly may have expressed her reservations about the shady gang, but it was nothing compared to what Gloria had said about them. How could she tell them that, after she'd confided in her? She thought she could trust her!

"Yes, and that's not all." Vicky gave her a meaningful look.

Kelly listened attentively.

"I heard Gloria blaming you for trying to hit on her, saying that you forced her to stay and wouldn't let her leave."

Kelly felt as if all the oxygen had rushed out of her body in a split second, leaving her as a limp, lifeless sack.

"Jerry was mad like I'd never seen him before and said he'd take care of you. Gloria thanked him and gave him a kiss on the cheek."

*She **thanked** him?*

"That's not true," Kelly sobbed. It seemed as

though all that was left in her body were thousands of tears.

"I'm sorry, honey. I really didn't want to have to tell you this. But I saw it with my own eyes."

"No. No. No." Kelly felt as if she were yelling with all her might, but what actually came out of her throat was a weak shriek.

"Yes. Yes. Yes. I really am sorry for you. But don't you worry, I'll take care of her," Vicky assured her. Kelly thought she'd spotted a glimpse of wickedness in her eyes when she said that. She started to get worried.

"What are you going to do?" she asked hesitantly.

"I've made it clear to her that she won't get away with it," Vicky asserted. "She even had the audacity to come visit you here, but I told your parents that this was all her fault and they made sure to keep her away from you."

Maybe she came to apologize? Perhaps this was all a big misunderstanding?

"She probably came here to threaten you not to tell anyone about this," Vicky commented, as if she could hear Kelly's thoughts, bursting her little bubble of hope.

"Yeah, I guess . . ." The oxygen still was not reaching her entire body. She struggled to breath.

The elegant woman sitting on the velvet sofa in her splendid home still got goose bumps when she remembered that moment. The horrifying discovery of Gloria's betrayal had extinguished the little remaining hope left in her sixteen-year-old self. That stage in her life was left vague in her memory. The only thing that had helped her hold on was Vicky's frequent visits.

Gloria hadn't come back to see her at the hospital, not even once. Actually, even after Kelly had returned home, the two acted as strangers. Kelly's mother had never again asked her to deliver her famous oatmeal cookies to Gloria's house.

After she'd moved to the East Coast, Kelly thought she would be able to put the past behind her. She'd risen to the top using her talent and tenacity, but Gloria had soared even higher, and received infinite fame and admiration thanks to her looks alone. *Some things never change*, Kelly thought bitterly. She had been so naive as to think that if she would only ignore Gloria's existence, then she could overcome what that bitch had done to her – but twenty years had passed and she still had not forgotten. She couldn't, nor wouldn't, let her get away with it.

If only Vicky knew what she was about to do today, she would be so proud.

CHAPTER 44

Rob and Sharon could finally see the little lodge at a distance. Sharon was fiddling with the car window, raising and lowering it, up and down, over and over.

Soon this whole nightmare will be over . . .

"You're driving me nuts!" Rob exclaimed.

"Welcome to the club. If you spent one minute inside my head, not only would you open the window, you'd jump through it, too!"

Rob did not attempt to argue. He could not imagine what it would feel like to be chasing after the person who had nearly shot you dead.

Well, almost.

"Hang in there, we're getting closer."

A few minutes later, they'd already parked on the dirt road behind the decorated wooden structure. They crossed the front porch that looked out over the green landscape, heading straight to the doorway.

"After you," Rob gestured with his hand.

Sharon knocked firmly on the door. Her patience was about to run out.

The door was opened by a young, amiable woman who welcomed them inside.

"Hello, how may I help you?"

"Where is Gloria McIntyre?" Sharon demanded.

"Excuse me? Who are you?" she asked in a slightly agitated tone.

Sharon had officially run out of patience. "Listen to me, it's a matter of life and death–"

"New York Police Department," Rob intervened and presented the woman with his badge. "It's an urgent matter. We would appreciate your cooperation."

Libby's face turned pale. "Tom, get over here! It's urgent!" she called to her husband.

"So where's Gloria?" Sharon repeated, this time a bit louder.

"I'm sorry. She's already left."

* * *

How many hours can you be stuck in a car? Gloria wondered. Luckily for her, Andy was with her, and even better, he was the one driving.

"I know that my preference not to drive is fulfilling every chauvinistic expectation out there, but I really don't understand what's so fun about it."

"That's why opposites attract," he laughed. Andy, unlike Gloria, loved the feeling of the wheel in his hands.

"Really? What else are we opposites at?"

"I like being behind the camera and you love being in front of it," he suggested.

"Is that all you've got? Lame!"

"I'm a glutton and you're always watching your weight. You're an exercise freak and I'm a PlayStation addict. I love hiking and you're a city girl."

Gloria turned to Andy and smiled.

"I'm young and you're . . ."

"Don't you dare finish that sentence!" she exclaimed.

"You wanted me to tell you what else we're opposites at, no?"

Gloria turned away from Andy and gazed out the window. "Okay, fine, you win," she surrendered. "I'll just have to take your word for it."

* * *

"What do you mean she's already left? Where to?" Sharon demanded.

"She and Andy left a while ago for a meeting with their editor. I think her name is Kelly."

Sharon fists clenched. *We're too late.*

"Do you have, by any chance, a phone number where we can reach them, or the address where they're headed? Anything will help." Rob took command as he noticed that the stress from the last few days had started to take its toll on Sharon.

Tom entered the room. "What is going on in here?"

"It's the police. They are looking for Gloria. They say it's a matter of life and death!"

"Do you happen to have the address where Gloria and Andy are headed?" Rob asked again.

"No. But maybe Arthur, her agent, does. Could you please explain to us what's going on here?"

"I can't specify, but we have reason to believe that Gloria McIntyre's life is in danger."

"I'll go get Arthur," Tom said as he ran upstairs.

* * *

In less than an hour they would arrive at Kelly Danes' house. Gloria was thirsty for a nice glass of wine and some news from the outer world. This had been the longest period of time she had spent without her cell phone. Somehow, Andy made it look insignificant.

Too bad she hadn't met him sooner; her phone bill could have been dramatically reduced.

"Hey, you're up?" Andy asked, stroking Gloria's hair with one hand, while the other one remained steady on the wheel.

"Yes. I was just daydreaming," she smiled.

"Are you hungry? We can stop somewhere and grab a bite to eat."

"No, never mind. We'll probably have dinner with Kelly after we finish reviewing the pictures."

"Are you sure you can last until then? It will take a few good hours."

"I'm good at delaying gratification," Gloria boasted.

"Oh really? I wouldn't brag about it, if I were you."

"You would have already stuffed your head into an extra-large bucket of fried chicken if you were me."

"Probably," Andy flashed his dimpled smile.

"God forbid. You are so unhealthy. I'll have to teach you how to eat right," Gloria chided.

"My mom has been trying to do the same thing for the last twenty-five years. I still won't touch Brussels sprouts."

"They're not that bad."

When you have to maintain flat abs, you can't afford to dismiss low-calorie food.

"Come on, it's just us now. They're absolutely *terrible*," Andy complained.

"Well, perhaps." A tiny smile slipped out of her lips.

"Could it be that I'm winning twice in a row? Watch out, Miss McIntyre."

"One more word and I'll make sure that we eat

Brussels sprouts with every meal!"

"I don't think that gourmet restaurants serve Brussels sprouts," he teased.

"They do when your name is Gloria McIntyre, so perhaps *you* better watch out."

". . . And what a knockout! The crowd is going wild for Raging McIntyre!"

"You can be such a fool sometimes!" Gloria laughed.

"A fool in love."

The butterflies in Gloria's stomach were fluttering.

"Then I guess I'm quite the fool as well," she smiled.

* * *

Fifteen minutes after they had arrived, they turned back to their car and started over.

The phone numbers Arthur had were the same ones they'd already tried calling and were still unreachable, but he had managed to provide them with priceless information: the current address of Miss Kelly Danes' summer home.

Ironically, Rob and Sharon had to drive back almost the entire route they'd already driven in order to get to their new destination. Sharon would have burst into laughter if she hadn't already been on the verge of tears. It turned out that Gloria McIntyre, along with the photographer, Andy Swain, had left about an hour before Sharon and Rob arrived.

We must have passed by them along the way, Sharon realized as she watched the curvy road leading them through the familiar view.

They had to pick up the pace. Rob slammed his foot down on the gas pedal in an effort to minimize the gap between them, but it still wasn't enough to catch up with them.

Sharon just hoped that it wouldn't be too late.

CHAPTER 45

The red dot on the GPS display flickered as a constant reminder of where they were destined. As if they could forget.

Once again, they had to be caged inside their rental car on their way to Kelly's summer home. Rob may have transformed their small Toyota into a speedy race car, but time was against them, and they still faced another hour of driving.

At least Rob can focus on driving, Sharon thought bitterly. She felt helpless, and she hadn't felt that way since . . .

Well, since Kelly had shot her and left her bleeding to death.

I have to do something. I can't go on like this.

She took out her cell phone and dialed.

"Who are you calling?" Rob asked.

Sharon ignored him. "Hello. Can I get Miranda Whitesporte's number in Winslow, Arizona?"

* * *

The smooth wine slid down Kelly's throat while she listened to classical music. She closed her eyes and gave in to the marvelous melodies that filled the room, and pictured herself at Carnegie Hall.

Kelly felt as if she were on top of the world. Soon enough any remnant of her former loser self would be erased, and she would finally get her big win.

Kelly looked around her. All of this splendor was nothing compared to what would transpire here in just a matter of time. She glanced at her expensive, custom-designed watch. The princess was running late, of course. She had not expected that the novice photographer would allow her to do so, but unfortunately she was well aware of the strong influence Gloria McIntyre possessed over others, especially if they belonged to the opposite sex.

In the meantime, she could use the opportunity to unwind. She took another sip of wine and closed her eyes, relishing its rich flavor, when suddenly the doorbell interrupted her enjoyment. Now her eyes were wide open.

You always had such perfect timing, Gloria . . .

* * *

Sharon was staring at her cell phone, unaware of Rob's demanding looks. They were supposed to arrive in about half an hour, but she felt trapped in another time zone. Sharon could not believe how meaningful a twenty minute conversation could be. She was still trying to absorb all the details. Sharon felt as though after months of working to put together all the missing puzzle pieces, they had finally come together to form   a clear picture.

It had not been easy telling Miranda that her daughter was a murder suspect, and in order to clear her doubts, Sharon had told her about Kelly's attempt to kill her. She had also revealed Kelly's plan to go after none other than the international model Gloria McIntyre. She'd needed to make Miranda understand

and cooperate as quickly as possible, and it worked. Rob, who had only heard bits and pieces of the conversation, did not understand what it was about.

"Sharon, what's going on?" he demanded.

She finally put the phone down and looked at him. "You are not going to believe this."

* * *

"Hi, Kelly! I'm so sorry we're a little late. It was a long drive and we got a bit lost along the way." Andy thought that in this case a little white lie would benefit everyone.

"It's not a big deal, really. It gave me a little more time to relax after my flight," Kelly smiled, giving off a fake warmth.

"Hello, I'm Gloria McIn–"

"Of course I know who you are, dear. Come in."

The couple followed Kelly into the lavish house.

"You have a magnificent home," Andy gushed.

"Thank you. Unfortunately, I don't get to stay here very often. Working for the magazine doesn't leave me much time for long vacations," Kelly smirked.

Gloria felt herself detaching from the conversation for a moment. Although she had never met Kelly Danes before, there was something strangely familiar about her . . .

The look in her eyes.

"Excuse me, Kelly, have we met before?"

Kelly froze. She was certain that the litany of plastic surgeries that she had suffered through had completely erased any resemblance of her former self.

She forced a laugh and looked away, waving her hand nonchalantly. "I doubt it, darling, but you know how it is. You've probably seen me at one media event or another."

"Yes, perhaps." Gloria had the feeling that the renowned editor was trying to avoid a straight answer.

Kelly kept smiling at her.

It's probably all in my head . . . she told herself and kept following Kelly through the house in slow steps.

* * *

Sharon told Rob everything she had just heard from Miranda Whitesporte, and in the process she tried to digest the astounding information herself.

Kelly had found out that Gloria had sent her shady friends to mess with her at the carnival. She blamed Gloria for being admitted. After nearly two months in the psychiatric ward, Kelly had refused to stay in Winslow and decided to take off and start a new chapter in her life. Her parents ached for her so they hadn't stopped her from leaving. Kelly's best friend at the time, Vicky Hermont, was the only one who had visited her during those dark couple of months. She had even followed Kelly to New York in hopes of finding her, but Miranda had never heard from her daughter if they ever had met.

Ever since her departure, Kelly had never returned to her hometown, not to visit her parents, not even when her father passed away a couple years ago. She had explained to her mother that she could not deal with the trauma. Actually, in the last few years, she hadn't even bothered calling, but every now and then she would send letters or New York postcards describing her various successes in The Big Apple. It was like her past never existed. Kelly had refused to talk about what had happened and her mother had decided to respect her wishes. Miranda couldn't tell what exactly had transpired in that house of mirrors, the place where her daughter had been found bleeding, beaten, and covered in lacerations.

Sharon wondered if Vicky Hermont could shed some light on this dark turn of events. If she and Kelly were close, she might be able to fill in the blanks where Miranda couldn't. But it would take time to track her down, a luxury they did not have. The GPS alert informing they had arrived to their destination confirmed that.

They had just arrived to the upscale neighborhood where Kelly's mansion was located. There was a security guard standing at the entry gate, checking the entering vehicles.

"Hello, where to?"

"New York Police Department. Could you point us to Kelly Danes' house? And hurry, please."

CHAPTER 46

"Would you like something to drink? I bet you've had a long drive. I just opened an excellent bottle of wine that I picked up on my way here."

"Yes, we would love to," Andy replied, oblivious to Gloria's cautious behavior.

Kelly disappeared into the kitchen and returned after a few moments with two wine glasses. The bottle was already on the coffee table, along with her glass.

"Thank you," Gloria said politely when Kelly poured the wine into her glass.

"You're welcome, dear," Kelly answered sweetly, staring at her.

As their eyes locked, Gloria felt a sudden flinch.

I'm positive I know her from somewhere, but from where?

"Well, perhaps until the food gets here we can look at the photos?" Kelly proposed.

"Yeah, of course!" Andy opened his laptop enthusiastically. "They aren't fully processed yet; some of them were only taken yesterday. But they sure came out great." He looked at Gloria with adoring eyes. Kelly wanted to puke. She immediately recognized the lovesick puppy look in the photographer's eyes. This loathsome woman did not deserve to be loved.

Andy faced the laptop toward Kelly and browsed through the pictures slowly. They were breathtaking. Kelly wanted to smash the damn screen over Gloria's head and kill two birds with one stone.

"Absolutely wonderful," she forced a smile. "I definitely see some photos with cover quality about them. I can almost picture it . . ."

The last and final photo of Gloria McIntyre, who would never be beautiful ever again.

"I'm so glad you like them. We all worked very hard for it. I also have printed copies that I can leave for you in the meantime."

"That would be great," Kelly tried to appear enthusiastic.

"Of course I'll have to edit the photos when I get back to New York, but even now, without any touch ups, you can see the potential. It was an amazing experience working with a professional like Gloria, you were right to insist on her."

Kelly nodded quietly. She felt she couldn't let her lips fabricate yet another compliment.

It's time.

". . . And again, thank you so much for having us over," Andy continued.

"Actually, I had another reason for inviting you here. Especially you, *Gloria*." Kelly savored every syllable of her name, letting it roll off her tongue.

Gloria stared at her with a surprised look.

"After more than a decade in the journalism world, I have decided to return to my first passion, sculpting." Her lips finally pronounced the words she had practiced repeatedly in her mind, her cover story. "My work focuses mainly on sculpting the human body," she explained. "In fact, my last work was a statue of your image," Kelly turned to Gloria. "An old friend of mine who works at the Metropolitan Museum was very impressed with it and offered to present it this spring as part of a special exhibition examining the relationship between mass media and modern art."

"*Really?* Are you serious?" Gloria was truly stunned, flattered, and bewildered all at once.

"Absolutely," Kelly nodded. "He asked me to try to convince you to attend the grand opening, so that the inspiration can be presented along with the actual piece, and thus illustrate the exhibition's motif. Besides that, there is no doubt that your presence would spark interest among the public and attract a crowd."

Gloria was speechless. She tried to appear calm but she could feel the warmth of color invading her cheeks.

"I have to give him an answer as soon as possible. Obviously, I wouldn't ask for your consent without you seeing the piece first. The statue is in my private studio downstairs."

Gloria couldn't believe what she had just heard. If there was one place in New York where her image had not yet appeared, it was the Metropolitan.

"So if you're not ruling out my request on the spot . . ."

And I know you won't, you're too vain.

". . . I would love to escort you down to the basement so you can see it with your own eyes. It will only take a few minutes. You can give me your final answer after you return to New York."

In a coffin . . .

"I would absolutely love to see it!" Gloria was thrilled. She had been photographed thousands of times and even had her portrait painted once or twice, but she had never been sculpted.

"Great." The smile that spread across Kelly's face was entirely real this time.

"Absolutely," Andy agreed. "Let's go." He eagerly pushed himself up from the antique couch.

Kelly did not intend to let the idiot photographer ruin the most important moment of her life.

Keep on dreaming.

"Actually, the food I ordered should arrive any minute now, and I'm afraid that if we don't answer the door, they'll leave. Would you mind waiting here so we don't miss them? I'm sure you're starving. I would feel terrible if the food were to be delayed for yet another hour."

It seemed as though the dilemma of whether to soothe his empty stomach or see his beloved model immortalized in stone really troubled him.

"Don't worry, it won't take more than a few minutes. And after we eat, we can go back downstairs and I'll show you my other sculptures as well."

"Well, okay," Andy reluctantly agreed. He returned to his seat and poured himself another glass of wine.

As she left the room Kelly swiftly turned up the volume of the classical music playing in the background.

It's show time . . .

CHAPTER 47

On their way to the "studio," Kelly pondered the ironic situation she had created in order to end the model's life. The same vanity that caused Gloria to glow from the thought that her image would be perpetuated in stone was currently leading her straight to her death. Fate just had a sense of humor *to die for*.

The two women faced the heavy, wooden door that Kelly had requested to be installed at the top of the stairs. Kelly's hands fingered the iron key in her trouser pocket – it was the only copy.

Two went into the basement, but only one would come out of there alive.

"After you," Kelly smiled at Gloria, gesturing with her hand toward the dark flight of stairs.

* * *

The two detectives drove around the dark suburb, which was remarkably quiet. Kelly's mansion was at the other side of the neighborhood, facing the Pacific Ocean.

"Drive faster!" Sharon implored. She was as tense as a bowstring.

"Sharon, if you don't want to miss the place, let me drive in peace!"

"Now you see why *I* wanted to drive?" she chided.

"Shall I remind you that the only thing that's preventing you from bleeding to death is an elastic band?"

"And still, I would get there faster than you!"

Rob couldn't stop himself from sneaking a little smile. This woman was undefeatable.

They passed by the impressive villas. The classic brick houses, painted in soft shades of ivory and mahogany, were encircled by the vivid hues of their tended gardens. If she hadn't been up to her elbows chasing after a killer, Sharon might have been able to admire the stunning architecture that surrounded her.

But that wasn't the case.

Enjoy your last few minutes of freedom, Kelly, because this time you won't get away.

* * *

Gloria descended slowly down the stairs. Kelly had yet to turn on the light.

I guess the light switch is downstairs, she figured.

The studio was pitch black and Gloria couldn't spot the sculpture. She heard the wooden door slam shut and the lock click, but she hadn't yet suspected that anything was amiss.

Suddenly she felt a hand clutching her shoulder, preventing her from continuing any further. Gloria turned around, startled, and noticed Kelly standing a step above her. Even though it was completely dark, she spotted a spark of madness glinting in Kelly's eyes. Only then she realized something was wrong, but it was too late. Kelly pushed her down the stairs.

Gloria tumbled down and fell flat against the rough wooden floor. The few moments she required to recover were all the time Kelly needed. She picked up the pistol she had stashed ahead of time on the shelf by the stairs, along with the roll of duct tape she had bought at the hardware store. Then she flipped the switch.

Let there be light.

Gloria's eyes were blinded by the sudden glare and she covered them with her hands. After her eyes had adjusted, she looked up and saw Kelly standing over her, grasping the pistol tightly; it was aimed directly at her.

"Are you insane? What the hell is going on here?" Gloria asked, completely astonished.

"I would keep my mouth shut if I were you. You don't know what might make me pull the trigger," Kelly said in a low, frozen voice.

Gloria paused. She had known from the moment she'd met her that there was something strange about this woman.

"Andy! Help!" she called in vain.

"Shut up!" Kelly commanded. "It's not going to help you anyway. There's no chance he can hear you from upstairs. And by the time your *Romeo* realizes what is going on, it will already be too late." An evil grin spread across her face.

"What do you want from me? What did I ever do to you?" Gloria struggled to understand.

Kelly's face grimaced involuntarily. "What did you *do* to me? Do you really want to know? You ruined my life!" she shouted.

Gloria scrolled the name "Kelly Danes" through her mind; it didn't sound familiar, not even slightly.

But she knew for sure that she recognized this woman from somewhere.

"Now move," Kelly commanded.

Gloria stumbled forward as she lifted herself off the floor.

"Catch," Kelly threw the roll of duct tape at her aggressively.

Fear, anger, and total shock overtook Gloria. She caught the duct tape with trembling hands.

"Walk to the chair."

Only then Gloria turned around to face the room. The vast space, surrounded by mirrors, was almost entirely empty besides a wooden chair stationed in the center of the room next to a small table.

"Are you disappointed that your beautiful sculpture isn't here?" Kelly taunted her. She felt almighty with the gun in her hands.

Gloria stepped slowly toward the chair, trying to stall so she could maybe figure out what the hell was going on here.

"Hurry up!" Kelly ordered.

Gloria reluctantly picked up the pace and got to the chair.

"Now, sit down. Tighten your legs against the chair and then wrap the duct tape around each leg separately, five times around each."

"What? No way!" she exclaimed.

"Do it, or I'll punch you from here to Mississippi."

Gloria unwillingly did as she'd been told. Kelly oversaw her actions and forced Gloria to bind the duct tape even tighter, until the skin above the tape strip turned red. After making certain that Gloria was helpless from the waist down, Kelly carefully approached and tied Gloria's hands behind the chair. An overwhelming sense of déjà vu flooded her. She recalled her last encounter with Detective Davis; but this time, however, Kelly knew there would be no remorse.

"Well done, now we can proceed," Kelly said, pleased with the way things were going so far.

"Who are you?" Gloria demanded. "And just what do you think I've done to you?"

"You didn't even bother to remember me? After everything you've put me through? Well, what *can* you expect from a model . . ."

"Who are you?" she raised her voice.

"If you really want to know . . ." Kelly put the pistol aside and picked up a knife from a line of various knives and blades that were spread across the table. She approached Gloria and pressed the knife to her neck.

"April twenty-fourth. 1990."

"I don't understand . . ."

"April twenty-fourth. 1990. The spring carnival."

Gloria's face was frozen in thought. The harsh realization of what had happened that day, almost twenty years ago, began to appear on her delicate features.

"Do you recognize me now?" Kelly whispered in a venomous tone.

Gloria took a long, hard stare at the woman standing before her. Her eyes were vicious.

"It's me, *Kelly*."

"*Who*?"

"Kelly Whitesporte."

Gloria froze. "No. It can't be. You're not her!" she shouted at her.

"I have undergone a number of plastic surgeries to look like this, so it may not be easy to recognize me, but I assure you, it's really me."

"That's not true! I knew Kelly Whitesporte. You're not–"

"Shut up!" Kelly snarled. "I've heard enough out of you!" She crudely tore off a thick piece of duct tape and fixed it across Gloria's mouth.

"Now it's *my turn* to talk."

CHAPTER 48

The gray Toyota slowed down when they arrived at Kelly's street. Its headlights illuminated a spectacular mansion. Sharon rolled down the window as they got closer and tried to listen carefully. It was quiet outside and she could hear the crickets chirping. Nothing out of the ordinary, so far.

"I think we're here," Rob said.

"Great! Now, let me out." Sharon reached for the door.

"Hold on a second, let me park and we'll go in together."

"Rob, there's no time, we might already be too late."

"Sharon," Rob turned to face her. "I'm worried about you. Do you really think you can face Kelly on your own?"

"But I won't be alone. You'll be there in a few minutes. Call for backup. I'm heading out."

"Shouldn't we–"

There was no point in completing the sentence. Sharon had already slammed the car door behind her.

* * *

As much as Andy enjoyed listening to Chopin's piano concerto, which was further enhanced by the beautiful acoustics of the room, he was getting impatient.

Perhaps I should go downstairs and check out what's going on?

The doorbell rang. Luckily, he heard it over the crescendo of the orchestra. Andy walked to the door and opened it. In front of him stood a young woman with a determined look in her eyes, but without any bags of takeout food. Instead, she held a gun and presented him with a police badge.

"Detective Davis. New York Police Department," she whispered.

"What's going on here?" Andy asked. Instinctively he lowered his voice as well.

"I need you to tell me, right now, where Gloria and Kelly are."

"They went down to the basement studio about ten minutes ago. Why? What's happening?" he asked again.

"Gloria's in great danger. Now, I need you to cooperate and do exactly as I say."

* * *

While Kelly passed the knife back and forth along Gloria's bare skin, she told her about all of her previous victims. Every now and then, when she got excited, she jabbed the knife into the model's flesh, covering Gloria's fair skin with tiny red stains. Kelly enjoyed the sight of Gloria's dripping blood, but she stopped herself from going too far. She would not let Gloria be stabbed to death; she could not let her die in such a mundane way. Oh, no, she had planned something far more cruel and excruciating for her . . .

* * *

"I need you to show me where the basement is," Sharon ordered in a hushed voice.

The stunned Andy pointed to his left, toward the large, wooden door.

"Alright. Now I need you to stay here. Another detective named Rob will be here shortly. Ask him to call for backup and point him to the basement. And please," she looked into his eyes, "don't try to be a hero and follow me."

"But you said Gloria is in danger!" The fear in his voice was reflected in his eyes.

He couldn't lose Gloria; after all, he had just found her.

"And I will do everything in my power to make sure she comes back up those stairs safe and sound. But it will happen only if you do exactly as I say."

Andy nodded his head in agreement.

Sharon entered the elegant foyer. She crept in utter silence toward the basement door and tried to open it.

As she suspected, it was locked.

* * *

The knife continued piercing Gloria's body. Kelly reminded Gloria why she deserved to die. Her eyes glistened as she recreated those dark moments in the house of mirrors. When Kelly blamed Gloria for sending the three savage boys after her, Gloria shook her head vigorously in opposition and her eyes widened in shock.

"Even now you still won't admit the truth?" Kelly snapped. "You won't let me have peace of mind? I think you need an immediate attitude adjustment."

Kelly placed the knife under Gloria's eye.

"If you can't see the truth, then I guess you'll no longer need these." She smiled an evil grin.

But then a smashing sound interrupted her cathartic, torturous ritual.

That idiot photographer.

She pulled away from Gloria and picked up her pistol, pointing it at the gloomy flight of stairs.

"Prepare to see your boyfriend die," she whispered fiendishly.

Kelly heard the sharp sound of the door breaking and deduced that someone had shot the lock. She barely heard the quiet steps descending down the stairs, but she was more alert than ever.

No one would prevent her from executing Gloria McIntyre.

CHAPTER 49

Kelly intended to shoot the moment she spotted a human silhouette, but the vision that appeared before her eyes momentarily paralyzed her. That was exactly what Sharon needed.

They faced each other; the gun of one aimed toward the other. They were equals.

"What are you doing here?" a bewildered Kelly asked, quickly adding, "I thought that I'd already gotten rid of you."

"I guess it's not as simple as you thought," Sharon kept her composure.

"Trust me, this time I won't leave any room for doubt."

"Just try me." Sharon's fingers locked on the trigger.

If I'm going down, you're going with me.

"I'm not done yet," Kelly smiled an evil grin and placed her hand on Gloria's shoulder.

"Let her go," Sharon commanded.

"Keep dreaming."

"Listen, you've got no choice. The house is surrounded. Backup will be here any minute," Sharon lied, halfway hoping it really was true. "And then all it takes is just one wrong look from you and one of the snipers fixed on you will take the shot, without even thinking twice."

Kelly didn't know if Sharon was lying or not, but fear began to take root within her. She took a slow step back.

"I am giving you the opportunity to end this peacefully. Put the gun on the ground!"

"Now you listen to me. You're in no position to haggle with me; I've got a hostage." Kelly did not even bat an eye toward Gloria, who seemed flushed and frightened. Sharon noticed the blood stains on her skin. ". . . And if you don't want me to blow her head off, then *you* put the gun down, Detective."

Sharon hesitated. She had to stall until Rob got there. "Kelly, if you don't put the gun down in the next thirty seconds, I will have to shoot you. And believe me, it won't be especially hard for me to do so. Save yourself and put the gun down!"

Kelly acknowledged the bitter truth. The odds were stacked against her. If she aimed the gun at Gloria, Sharon would shoot her; and if backup really was on its way, she might not even get the chance to fulfill her dark desire.

And she had to try.

"Okay," Kelly said coolly.

"Okay," replied Sharon, somewhat relieved by Kelly's decision.

Kelly took advantage of that spilt second when Sharon momentarily let her guard down and turned the pistol back to Gloria. Sharon detected Kelly's sudden movement and instantly responded by pulling the trigger three times, but it was too late; Kelly's pistol had already fired.

Kelly's body hit the same chair that Gloria was bound to before collapsing on the floor. A large puddle of blood began to encircle the two.

Sharon couldn't believe her eyes, which were bombarded by intense shades of blazing red. She had focused every ounce of her being into stopping Kelly in time, but had failed at the last minute. She could not tear her eyes away from the growing crimson pond.

Having uncovered step by step the painful tale of the two women, she simply could not shake off the tragic ending of their lives; even in death the two were intertwined.

"Sharon!" she heard Rob's voice calling from upstairs.

"I'm okay, Rob," she called, and then took a deep breath. "It's all over."

CHAPTER 50

Sharon advanced cautiously toward the bodies. Kelly's pistol was lying at a safe distance, probably blown out of her hands from the impact of the shot.

"Gloria? Are you okay?" The echo of Andy's quick steps seared through Sharon's heart. She'd promised him that she wouldn't let Gloria die.

"Wait," she heard Rob's voice stopping Andy from getting any closer.

"Nooooooo!" Andy's scream pierced through the air. "No . . . it can't be . . . Please, let me see her."

"Stop," said Rob. "Sharon? What's going on there?"

Sharon moved Kelly's lifeless body aside. The blood stained her hands. She looked at Gloria, all covered in blood. Her eyes were closed.

Even in death she was breathtaking.

Sharon suddenly thought she noticed breathing. It was faint, but Gloria was breathing. She gently placed two fingers on her neck.

"There's a pulse! Call for an ambulance!"

Andy sprang back upstairs.

Sharon untied the knots that confined Gloria to the chair and placed the wounded body in her lap, gently stroking Gloria's hair and whispering: "You'll be okay, you'll be okay."

Rob approached and checked Kelly's pulse. "She's dead."

Sharon knew she shouldn't be glad, but that was exactly how she felt.

As she stroked Gloria's hair, she noticed that Kelly had missed her heart only by an inch, probably because Sharon's shots had caused her hands to swerve.

Suddenly Gloria's eyes squinted open; she seemed hazy.

"It's okay. It's all over. Kelly is dead," Sharon told her.

"No . . ." Gloria whispered.

"Yes, I promise you. Kelly Danes, or Whitesporte, or whatever her name is, she's gone."

"No . . ." Gloria struggled to finish the sentence. "I know that woman, and she wasn't Kelly."

CHAPTER 51

Detective Davis sat beside the most famous model in the world, who was lying motionless in the hospital bed. Andy sat on the opposite side of the bed, slumped over and fast asleep.

The doctors had made it clear that even though Gloria's condition was stable, the painkillers would keep her sedated for the most part of the day; but that didn't matter to Sharon. She had to know who that woman was, the one who had claimed to be Kelly Danes.

She recollected what had transpired in the past twenty-four hours. It seemed as though a lifetime of events had been compressed into one day. Thoughts on top of thoughts ran through her mind, but what was the point in agonizing over it when the key witness was unconscious?

Her gaze caressed the frozen features of the global icon. They radiated beauty even against the dull background of the hospital bed.

Sharon realized that she wasn't going to solve the mystery in the next few hours; she felt so useless. The realization did not improve her already bleak mood. She took a deep breath: she would have to be patient since it didn't look like Gloria was going to wake up anytime soon. She leaned back in her chair and sighed.

Now here's a model I really do want to see get back on her feet...

* * *

Kelly Danes' estate, the previous day

"I know that woman, and she wasn't Kelly."

"*What?* Are you sure? Then who the hell did I just shoot?"

But Gloria had already closed her eyes. For a moment, Sharon feared that Kelly had completed her mission.

The medical crew made their way to the basement and moved Sharon aside. After a few long minutes of resuscitation attempts, the paramedic announced, "She'll pull through. We need to get her to the hospital immediately, but she'll be okay."

Sharon heaved a sigh of relief.

Finally, there's a happy ending to this story...

And yet, she could not shake off Gloria's striking revelation. Should she believe it?

The studio began to fill with local police officers and Sharon felt she could use the rest. Her eyes were looking for Rob when she spotted him standing in the corner of the room, talking on his cell phone and looking distressed.

She approached him, trying to figure out what the heck could be making him worry so much, when only ten minutes ago a deadly gunfight had taken place in here.

Rob turned around, his face was pale. "There was a match to the body they found at Kelly Danes' house in New York," he said grimly. "It's Kelly Whitesporte."

Sharon looked at him without saying a word, trying to form the pieces of information into something coherent. She was only further confused.

"For heaven's sake, they're supposed to be the same woman . . ." he murmured to himself, trying to figure out how this was possible.

"I heard the same thing from Gloria. She told me she knew the woman I shot, and that it wasn't Kelly Whitesporte. She knows who it is."

"Who? Tell me!" The color began returning to his face.

"She passed out before she could answer."

"Damn it," Rob blurted. "So what are we supposed to do now?" he asked bitterly.

"We go to the hospital, and we wait."

* * *

"I thought you could use this."

Sharon was surprised to find herself at the hospital. Rob was standing in front of her, holding a cup of coffee and a butter croissant. She'd somehow fallen asleep without even realizing.

"Thanks." She bit hungrily into the croissant and finished the coffee in one gulp.

"Need a break? I can take the next shift," he offered.

Sharon glanced at her watch. Gloria was supposed to wake up in the next few hours. She could not afford to miss it.

"No thanks, I'm good."

Rob looked at her despairingly and sighed. By now he could tell when he was facing a losing battle.

"I'll go get more coffee."

CHAPTER 52

When three different types of painkillers are coursing through your veins, after nearly bleeding to death, you feel as though you are floating on air, far away from your hospital bed.

But then you open your eyes and have to face the harsh reality.

Sharon observed Gloria as she finally regained consciousness. For someone who'd had a near death experience herself, she knew exactly how Gloria was feeling; therefore, even though dozens of questions were running through her mind, she waited to give her a chance to recover.

Gloria, who was still drowsy from the medication, smiled when she noticed Andy sitting beside her. To his credit, Sharon noted, he hadn't left her side for even a minute, and not because he had to solve a serial murder case that had been agonizing him for years.

Little by little, as Gloria started to remember what had happened to her, the smile disappeared from her face and her eyes landed on the bandages covering her chest.

Sharon was at the end of her rope. Gloria hadn't even noticed her presence. She decided it would be better to wait a little longer and let the exhausted model get some more rest before presenting her with some tough questions. She got up quietly and turned to the door.

"Detective Davis?"

Sharon turned back to Gloria.

"I wanted to say thank you. You saved my life. I will never forget that."

Sharon shook her head humbly. "No need to thank me. I was just doing my job."

"Still, if there's any way I can ever return the favor . . ."

"Actually, you can." Sharon returned to the same spot she'd hardly moved from for the last twenty-four hours.

"Whatever you need."

"Do you remember what you told me right after . . ." her words trailed away.

"I got shot?"

Sharon looked at her and nodded.

"Not really. The last thing I remember was that lunatic's gun pointing at me."

Sharon paused for a moment before she continued. "You told me that it wasn't Kelly Danes who shot you."

Gloria gazed into the distance, as if she were trying to remember.

"Can't you do this later?" Andy asked in a concerned voice, tenderly holding his loved one's hand.

"No, it's fine," Gloria turned to him. "I want to help."

"I'll go look for the doctor, so he can come and see you now that you're awake," he offered meekly.

After Andy had left the room, Sharon continued. "So if that wasn't Kelly, then who the hell was she?"

"Vicky Hermont."

Vicky Hermont?

"She was one of Kelly's friends."

Of course! Vicky had been the only person, outside of Kelly's parents, who had come to visit Kelly after she'd been hospitalized. Miranda Whitesporte had told Sharon about her.

"But why was she posing as Kelly?" Sharon wondered aloud.

"I have no idea," Gloria admitted. "It's not like we stayed in touch. We'd never gotten along with each other."

"What can you tell me about April twenty-fourth, 1990?"

Gloria looked at Sharon with a surprised expression. Her face turned pale.

"It's okay," Sharon calmed her. "I already know that you'd sent your friends to get back at Kelly and that it got out of hand, but it wasn't your fault; you were just kids back then."

"*Excuse me?*" Gloria asked furiously. "Do you really think I would be capable of something like that?"

Sharon looked at her, completely confused. "That's what Miranda Whitesporte told me. That was the reason why Kelly, er, I mean, Vicky, hated you so much."

"Well, Detective Davis, everything you were told is bullshit."

CHAPTER 53

April 24, 1990. Winslow, Arizona. The Spring Carnival

Vicky could not believe that her pathetic friend had dared to betray her like that. She had always known she couldn't be trusted.

After they had decided to split in order to avoid Jerry and his friends, Vicky had changed her mind and had decided to follow Kelly instead to make sure nothing bad happened to her. She loved Kelly too much to just leave her there, all alone. Vicky could not forgive herself if Jerry ever got his hands on Kelly.

She noticed Kelly entering the house of mirrors and felt relieved. There was no way that those idiots would go in there. Vicky was watching the booth, making sure that no one from Jerry's gang was around. She was just about to leave and wait for Kelly at their meeting point when suddenly she saw . . .

Gloria McIntyre stepping inside.

Vicky rushed over and sneaked in quietly on the tip of her toes. She wanted to make sure that the little bitch wouldn't make fun of Kelly, or even worse, might have been followed by one of her awful friends.

Vicky stood there, in between the shadows, hidden by mirrors of all shapes and sizes, which all reflected the same image: Gloria and Kelly talking to each other.

Vicky became furious. Kelly was an innocent girl who could easily be fooled by Gloria's devious charm. Vicky had never been able to stand Gloria; she seemed too perfect and, therefore, almost certainly had some kind of hidden flaw. She just hadn't found it yet. And it was pretty obvious that Gloria didn't really like her either.

She kept watching the two girls, who were still talking to each other.

She was *jealous.*

"Say, do you think that in a different world we could have been . . ."

"Friends? I think so."

Those words seared through Vicky's heart like the mark of Cain that would never fade. She wanted to burst in and cease the heinous betrayal going on in there, but her calculating side, which had always been more dominant, forced her to stay put for now and spy on the two in silence.

"But in this world you're Vicky's friend, and my best friends hang out with Jerry and his gang, whether I like it or not. I'm afraid we're on opposite sides of the fence."

"Like Romeo and Juliet . . ."

The mention of the purest love story of all time, as an allegory for the relationship between Kelly and Gloria, broke Vicky's heart.

You were supposed to feel this way about me.

". . . It's weird that Vicky hasn't shown up yet."

"Yeah, never mind, I'll see her some other time."

How could you abandon a true friend for this fake doll?

Vicky thrust her nails into her skin, aching in the shadows, listening painstakingly to the rest of the conversation.

"Well, goodbye, Gloria McIntyre." Kelly leaned toward Gloria and kissed her on the cheek.

Vicky watched the horrific scene, completely fossilized. She noticed Kelly's lips trying to approach Gloria's. She watched Gloria's frozen figure, not resisting, as if she were welcoming Kelly's innocent intimacy. Every bit of wrath in Vicky's body gathered into a burst of hatred. She thrust her nails even deeper into her skin, until she was bleeding. Vicky noticed Gloria whispering quiet words to her lover, but could not hear them.

That's it. She had to stop it.

"You traitor! How could you do this to me?" Vicky appeared from behind the mirrors. She marched, enraged, toward them. Kelly's shameful expression was a feast for her eyes.

"Vicky? I don't understand . . ."

"I don't understand either how you could throw me to the wolves for . . ." She turned her head and hurled a hateful look at Gloria. "For *her*!"

"Vicky, you need to calm down. Nobody has done anything against you."

"You stay out of it, you arrogant little princess!" Vicky snapped. Even Kelly's attempts to make amends hadn't gotten through to her.

". . . I will *never* forgive you!" she swore aloud and ran toward the exit door.

But she didn't leave. Vicky slammed the door shut so Kelly and Gloria would think that she'd left, when actually she had stayed hidden in the dark room, eavesdropping. Her heart pinched when she realized that Kelly wasn't coming after her; she didn't even care what could happen to her out there, all by herself. *Some friend she is.* It seemed like Kelly had forgotten all about her. Instead of running after her and apologizing, Kelly had tried to convince that insufferable Gloria to stay.

Kelly had made an awful mistake choosing Gloria over her, and for mistakes one had to pay.

* * *

"So you're saying that you and Kelly were ... friends?"

"Not exactly, but we were getting there. Maybe if all of this hadn't happened ..."

Sharon gave Gloria a sympathetic look, but then a crease of confusion formed between her eyes. "Wait a minute. So if you didn't send Jerry and his friends after Kelly, then who did?"

"Well, Detective, what other option do you have?"

CHAPTER 54

The beautiful girl stood outside the wooden booth, wondering to what extent the disfigured images reflected in the mirrors inside had been different from the reality she lived in.

Gloria looked around her. Although there were so many people surrounding her, she still felt lonely. To her surprise, she kind of missed the girl who had stayed inside the house of mirrors.

Maybe it's the beginning of a wonderful friendship after all...

Gloria started walking slowly by the flashy carnival stands toward the exit, when she noticed the group of cocky guys headed her way.

Not now...

Gloria quickly stepped aside in the hope that she wouldn't be spotted. She waited a few moments but no one followed her. It seemed as if she had managed to avoid their searching eyes. She began to retrace her steps when suddenly she heard familiar voices. She stopped and listened.

"There's no way she did that."

"Believe me, she did. I was there. She was lucky to get away from her."

"I don't believe you."

"What reason do I possibly have for lying? Kelly is my friend. I'm just feeling sorry for your poor friend."

Gloria froze. Were they talking about *her*?

"Think carefully about what you're saying, because if it's true . . ."

"I couldn't believe it myself. I walked in there by accident. I saw it with my own eyes."

"Your friend is nuts!" Jerry snapped.

"I was flabbergasted. I tried to stop her. I really hope Gloria is okay."

What, for heaven's sake, is Vicky telling them? Why is she trying to get Kelly in trouble?

"I'm going to kill that bitch. I can't believe she tried to mess with Gloria. Doesn't she know that whoever lays a hand on Gloria has to answer to *me*?"

"I don't think she really cared," Vicky tried to spur Jerry's anger.

"Come on, let's go. We need to catch her before she gets out of there."

Gloria heard footsteps quickly moving away. She tried to process what had just happened, but couldn't comprehend it. She sneaked a peek. Vicky was still standing there, an evil grin smeared across her face. Gloria stepped out of her hiding spot and faced Vicky. Vicky looked at Gloria, completely surprised.

"What the hell did you just tell them?" Gloria demanded.

"What are you talking about?" Vicky answered with fake innocence.

"Do you realize how much trouble you're getting Kelly into?" she asked in a concerned voice.

"I didn't get her into anything. If *your* friends are mad at her for some reason, it's not my fault."

"Are you playing dumb on purpose, or what?" Gloria exclaimed. "I heard you! You told them something that made them want to hurt her. Something about me. What have you done?"

"You shouldn't have messed with me," Vicky hissed.

"What are you talking about?" she asked, confused.

"You're the reason she doesn't care about me anymore; you've basically forced me to do this." Vicky narrowed her eyes at Gloria.

Gloria didn't understand what Vicky was talking about. All she had done was talk to Kelly. But she didn't have time to dwell on this right now. She was the only one who could stop Jerry and his friends. She needed to find them before it was too late.

"You're crazy," Gloria asserted brusquely and turned her back to Vicky. She started running back toward the hall of mirrors.

"Hey! Where do you think you're going?" Vicky ran after her, eventually catching up with her. She thrust her nails into Gloria's back and stopped her.

"Don't touch me, you maniac!" Gloria tried to shake off Vicky's grip.

"You are not going over there," Vicky insisted, her hands clutching Gloria's arm.

"Don't you understand that something really bad could happen to Kelly? You know how those boys are."

If Gloria had been trying to raise some kind of empathy or mercy or even plain rationality out of Vicky – it hadn't work.

"Don't worry, I'll save her . . . eventually. But before that, she must pay."

Gloria shook herself away from Vicky in blunt aversion. "You're completely insane. Stay away from me!" As she turned to run again, Vicky shoved her from behind with unexpected force, and she fell to the ground. Gloria could barely get up; a deep cut had formed on her thigh, and the blood slowly trickled down her leg.

Not the best time to be wearing a mini dress . . .

"I swear that if you take one more step, your slim leg won't be the only body part bleeding." Vicky enunciated each threatening word in a peaceful voice, surprisingly calm, which scared Gloria even more.

"Okay, you won." Gloria brushed off the dirt from her dress and started limping away in the opposite direction. After a few steps she looked behind her. Vicky was standing in the exact same spot, staring at her, making sure she wasn't coming back.

Gloria knew she had no one to turn to. If Jerry were to find out she'd ratted him out, God only knew what he would do to her. Her only option was to get home as soon as possible and call in an anonymous tip to the police hotline. She tried to walk faster, but her wounded leg slowed her down.

She just hoped it wouldn't be too late.

CHAPTER 55

"So you're saying that Vicky was the one who provoked your friends into hurting Kelly?" Sharon stared at Gloria, completely surprised.

Gloria felt revulsion when Detective Davis referred to that group of Neanderthals as her friends. Even after all these years, it still bothered her.

"Yes. I would never do something so heinous," she proclaimed.

Sharon felt like the puzzle she'd been working so hard to assemble had revealed an entirely different picture than the one she'd imagined. Now she had to try and rearrange the pieces once again.

"But I thought that Kelly and Vicky were friends…"

"Does that seem to you like something a *friend* would do?"

Absolutely not…

"How did they end up staying friends after everything that had happened?" Sharon asked.

"Simple," Gloria answered. "Vicky blamed the whole thing on me."

"What are you talking about?"

Gloria took a deep breath. "When the police finally arrived at the house of mirrors, they found Vicky sobbing miserably over Kelly's unconscious body, while trying to stop the massive hemorrhaging from the cuts on her skin. Vicky waited with Kelly until the paramedics got there. She claimed she'd found Kelly unconscious, and that she didn't know who had done this to her. On the other hand, she told Kelly's parents that Jerry and his friends were responsible and made sure my connection to them was clear. She convinced them not to press charges, so Jerry and his friends wouldn't have any excuse to hurt Kelly again, but the real reason was to erase her own connection to the whole incident.

"When I tried to visit Kelly, Vicky was waiting there and stopped me from seeing her. She yelled at me, saying that she knew I was the reason Jerry and his friends had assaulted Kelly, and that I wasn't welcome there. I noticed Kelly's parents watching us from the side, Miranda Whitesporte wiping her tears. I decided I wouldn't come back and cause them anymore grief," she explained in a sad voice.

"So you just let everyone think you did this?" Sharon didn't understand how Gloria could have let that manipulative bitch get away with it.

"Not exactly. Vicky made sure that Kelly's parents wouldn't discuss the details of the case with anyone. She knew that if the whole town got suspicious, I wouldn't take it anymore, and Jerry might come forward and tell the truth."

"But didn't it bother you that Kelly's parents believed Vicky's lie?" Sharon insisted.

"It ate me up inside," Gloria admitted. "But I had a sick mother I needed to take care of, and I couldn't take the chance of Kelly's parents approaching my mother and telling her what *they* thought had happened to their daughter." Gloria gave Sharon a meaningful look. "It would have broken my mother's heart. Besides, back then Vicky never budged an inch from the Whitesportes, so I could never get a moment alone with them." She pursed her lips and shook her head. "That girl was nearly as smart as she was cruel."

"Without a doubt." Sharon replayed in her mind the recent events.

"I had no choice but to stay away," Gloria sighed.

"And Kelly never discovered the truth?" Sharon inquired. She found it difficult to think of Kelly Whitesporte as a victim rather than the cold blooded murderess she had gotten to know.

"Not for nearly two decades. But about three years ago, the truth finally came out."

"How?"

"I told her."

CHAPTER 56

Sharon was blown away. Every time she thought she got a step closer, she realized the finish line was even further away.

"What do you mean, you told her?" Sharon glared at Gloria. "Had you stayed in touch all those years?"

"Not at all. We bumped into each other at Washington Square Park near NYU."

"Of all places . . ." Sharon wondered aloud.

"You don't have to tell me. At first, I thought I was just mixing her up with someone else. It took me a moment to recognize her, because she looked nothing like herself," Gloria explained. "Actually, Kelly was the one who had spotted me."

"Are you saying she had undergone plastic surgery?"

"Absolutely, and more than one. Actually, she looked a lot like Vicky, who'd also had quite the makeover since she'd left Winslow." Gloria squinted her eyes in an attempt to recall. "Come to think of it – they looked almost like twins."

Sharon was yet to transform all these bits and fragments of information into a discernible image, but she was most certainly trying.

"So what were you doing at Washington Square Park?" She decided to take it one step at a time.

"I was spending my day off at the village, walking around one of my favorite areas in the city," Gloria smiled with reminiscence.

"And Kelly?"

"Kelly was a student at NYU. She was in her second year of med school."

"*Really?*" Medicine and journalism didn't have much in common, Sharon thought. The connection between Kelly and Vicky started to seem more and more peculiar.

"Yes," Gloria confirmed. "She'd been a bright student when we were in high school."

"How come she started school so late?" Sharon did the math; Kelly was probably in her early thirties when she'd started med school.

Gloria was silent for a moment. Sharon recognized a spark of sadness in her eyes.

Gloria took a deep breath. "Kelly had never recovered after what had happened. I had hoped that moving to New York would be a fresh start for her, as it had been for me, but years later it became clear that my hopes had turned out to be far from reality. Even after turning a new leaf, supposedly, the events of that day had continued to haunt her.

"When we met that day, Kelly confided to me she still had nightmares at times, although they had decreased substantially ever since she'd gone back to school. For years she'd barely left the house, fearing the outside world. She couldn't hold down a job or sustain a social life, let alone fly back to Winslow and see her parents; she was just terrified of dealing with those dreadful memories." Gloria's voice became brittle. "Kelly may not have been readmitted to the psychiatric ward, but it was obvious that she hadn't lived a normal or happy life." Gloria's eyes glistened.

"But still, she started med school and got back on track. That was a good sign, right?" Sharon tried to cheer her up.

"Yes, but it was only after seventeen years of endless torment, which I could have prevented had I been strong enough to stand up to Vicky." Tears glided down her cheek, leaving her eyes bluer than ever.

"It's not your fault," Sharon said softly and held Gloria's hand in a supportive gesture.

"Maybe not entirely, but I will never stop wondering how things could have been different, if only I had . . ." her voice trailed away.

"Listen to me." Sharon pressed her hand. "This is not your fault in any way. This was all the act of a girl with a sick mind and a heart made of stone."

Gloria looked at Sharon with sparkling eyes. How true was the saying, "*Don't judge a book by its cover*," Sharon pondered. She never would have imagined the amount of sadness that was stashed within a woman who, from the outside, looked so happy and majestic.

But Sharon's philosophical judgments quickly switched back to the practical line that always characterized her.

"Wait a second. If Kelly couldn't hold on to a job, then how could she afford the tuition?" Sharon figured the amount had to be tens of thousands of dollars per year.

Gloria's face contorted in a way that completely clashed with her delicate features.

"Vicky paid for everything."

CHAPTER 57

When Andy returned to the hospital room, he saw that Gloria and Sharon were so immersed in conversation that they even failed to notice him. He decided, therefore, it would be a good idea to get a cup of coffee and give them some privacy. He turned around and walked away.

"So let me get this straight. Kelly and Vicky had remained in touch for all those years?" Sharon was astonished by yet another new revelation.

"I can't be sure. During our conversation she hadn't mentioned Vicky at all, so I assumed she was no longer a part of her life. But when I asked her how she could afford to go to NYU, she muttered that Vicky had loaned her the money."

Perhaps that was how the two got back in touch, Sharon guessed. Miranda had told her that Vicky had left to New York in search for Kelly.

"She seemed pretty embarrassed when she told me about it," Gloria continued. "It was important for her to emphasize that it was merely a loan and that she intended to pay Vicky back the full amount as soon as possible."

With this much money involved – it had to be more than just a loan, Sharon concluded.

"So how did Kelly react when you told her about Vicky?" she cut right to the chase.

"It wasn't easy," Gloria admitted. "Toward the end of our conversation, Kelly had looked at me with little girl's eyes and asked me why I'd done it. Her expression didn't show anger or accusation, just deep sorrow. I couldn't take it anymore and disclosed to her the truth I'd wanted to tell her years ago."

"How did she take it?" Sharon asked gently. She could not imagine what it would have been like to hear such crucial information nearly two decades later.

"Very strangely." Gloria stared at a distant point, trying to remember. "At first, she was quiet for a few long moments, just staring at me. She didn't try to argue or doubt what I was saying, but it was obvious that she was in a state of complete shock."

"She didn't get mad or even cry?" Sharon couldn't decipher the meaning of Kelly's odd reaction.

"No. She just looked troubled and murmured something about having to go and fix something, that she had a big assignment due and needed to hurry back to campus."

Gloria remembered the last thing Kelly had said to her that day: *"I wish you would have told me sooner. Perhaps we really could have been friends."* Then she had smiled a sad, remorseful smile and left. Gloria chose to keep this memory to herself. There was no point sharing her feelings of loss with the rest of the world, because then they would become more real; and that was the last thing she needed right now.

"That's it? She just ignored what you'd told her and returned to her books?" Sharon wondered.

"I don't think so," said Gloria.

"What do you mean?"

"When Kelly left, she didn't head in the direction of the campus, rather she went the opposite way, toward the park exit."

CHAPTER 58

The flight back home was supposed to be heavenly compared to the hell Sharon had been through on her way over. The murderess she'd been chasing after had finished her duty on this planet, Gloria McIntyre was alive and well and was supposed to be discharged from the hospital by the end of the week, and she had finally solved the case that had been haunting her day and night for the past three years.

But even at thirty thousand feet, she wasn't on cloud nine.

Something still bothered her. Sharon felt that the story of her and Kelly Danes, or Vicky Hermont, or whoever she was, was not over yet. Why, for God's sake, hadn't Kelly admitted that she was, in fact, Vicky Hermont? Had Vicky actually believed that she was the real Kelly Whitesporte? And had she killed Kelly in order to live out her fantasy? To Sharon's disappointment, Gloria hadn't known the answers either when she had asked her those same questions. Besides, the autopsy results regarding the circumstances of the real Kelly Whitesporte's death hadn't come back yet. The coroner stated that the primary cause of death was a severe skull fracture as a result of blunt force trauma, but it was not yet clear if it had been sustained as a result of an accident, suicide, or murder. Sharon leaned toward the third option, but she could not dismiss any of the possibilities in light of recent discoveries.

Did Kelly's mother really not know anything? And what exactly had happened between the two women that had merged their lives together so tragically? Sharon could not let it go just yet; she had to find out.

Only fourteen hours to go, and then she'd be home.

The pursuit of time began once more.

* * *

Home sweet home . . .

Sharon was happy to see that the door leading to her apartment was locked, and for once was glad to linger for a minute searching for her keys.

When she entered, Sharon turned on all the lights and scanned the rooms. Suddenly, she realized that the horrifying ordeal she had experienced in her apartment just a few days ago would not be forgotten from her mind anytime soon.

Great, now I finally have time to process the fact that I've been traumatized.

Sharon dropped her bags near the door; she would deal with them later. She took off the clothes she'd been wearing for nearly twenty-five hours straight and lay down exhausted on the couch. She snuggled with the woolen blanket that was on top of the pillows, a souvenir from the many nights she'd fallen asleep between piles of papers, not being able to carry herself to bed. Then she picked up the phone from the charger. She had three calls to make that could not wait until morning.

The first call was to let her mother know that everything was okay. She'd left Sharon about nineteen messages on her voicemail.

The second call was to NYU. At this hour there was probably no one there to answer, but at least she could leave a message and ask them to call her back ASAP. She wanted to take a look at Kelly's registration documents. Perhaps she could find something there that would catch her eyes, which by now were draped with dark circles of fatigue.

The third call was to the Chinese restaurant down the block. She was starving.

CHAPTER 59

Two hours later, Sharon was still sitting on her couch, surrounded by small takeout cartons filled with fragrant oriental delicacies. She'd finished four eggrolls within the first five minutes and consumed all the dumplings in the wonton soup (she never bothered to drink the broth). Now she'd gotten to the real deal: spicy beef with broccoli; Kung Pao chicken; fried rice with sautéed vegetables; and, of course, roasted duck in garlic sauce, her absolute favorite.

Normally she wouldn't have ordered all of her favorite dishes at once, but she figured that sometimes you just have to give yourself a break and say *to hell with it.* After everything she'd been through, she deserved a treat. Besides, if there was anything she loved more than Chinese takeout food, it was Chinese takeout leftovers.

The microwave is just the most ingenious invention.

After devouring the contents of the cartons she had ordered, Sharon felt the jet lag running its course. She had just gotten back from twenty-four hours of travel and had a long day ahead of her tomorrow. The hands on her watch pointed out that it was after midnight.

Yet she could not fall asleep.

The television channels aired reruns of old sitcoms – Sharon's favorite kind – but she couldn't focus. She closed her eyes and tried to relax, listening to the comforting sound of familiar jokes. Suddenly, her cell phone vibrated. Sharon was startled. At this hour, it couldn't be good news.

You can meet the love of your life this week!
Just reply with a text
and we will send you the number of your soul mate.
So what are you waiting for? Press Send right now!

Sharon despised those types of messages. She didn't understand why it was other people's business that she was still single. Wasn't the disappointed look in her mother's eyes enough?

At least nobody died, she tried to cheer herself up.

Sharon kept staring at the message on the screen.

So what *are you* waiting for?

No one had ever accused her of having too much patience.

* * *

It was ridiculous to call him now; it was almost 1 a.m. But when had she ever listened to the voice of reason?

The dial tone sounded from the other end of the line. There was no way he would answer at this time of night.

"Hello?"

"Hey, Chris?"

"Sharon, is that you? What time is it?" he asked in a slightly drowsy voice.

"Almost one."

"You can't do things the normal way, huh?"

"What's so abnormal about a late phone call?"

"Well, considering the last time we talked you were calling from New Zealand, informing me that you hadn't really been murdered . . . Maybe you're right, after *that*, nothing seems too crazy."

A smile crept to her lips. "I never promised you a rose garden."

He chuckled. Even after waking him up in the middle of the night, she'd managed to captivate him. He couldn't wait any longer.

"So when will I finally get to see you? To verify that you really are alive and well?"

Sharon looked around her. Her apartment was a total mess.

There's no way you're coming over here anytime soon . . .

"I have just one last thing to wrap up with the case I've been working on, and then I'll be free."

"So I'll see you this weekend?"

I always work better with a deadline . . .

"Absolutely."

"Oh, Sharon, one last thing."

"Yes?"

"The next time you decide to fly off to another continent, please, just let me know."

CHAPTER 60

By eight o'clock in the morning Sharon was already on her way to NYU. She had talked to the university secretary and after presenting herself as a detective with the NYPD, she hadn't encountered any problems getting access to the registration file of a former student. The documents were waiting for her there. She was a short subway ride away from finding out the truth, or at least part of it, and she couldn't resist the temptation. Sharon texted Rob that she was taking the day off. She figured he would be happy that she was finally taking some time to recover.

But how can you stop yourself from completing a crossword puzzle when you only have one word left?

She took the train to West Fourth Street. On her way she passed by Washington Square Park, the same place Gloria and Kelly had met years ago. She admired the impressive marble arch from the other side of a large fountain, and the perfect harmony that formed between them. It looked so peaceful at this time of day. But she knew that by lunchtime the park would be crowded and no bench would be left unseated. A saxophone player was standing in a strategic location, waiting for people to pass by. Sharon looked for some change and tossed the coins into his instrument case on her way out of the park.

When she arrived, Glenda Milton, the university secretary, handed Sharon a thin file that was marked in black: *Kelly Whitesporte*. It didn't contain many papers, and Sharon guessed she would finish going through it within the hour. Most of the documents contained technical details needed for administrative purposes and didn't tell her much.

Sharon brushed through the papers, acknowledging the fact that she probably wouldn't find anything there that she had hoped to reveal. But then, toward the end, she noticed something strange. On the receipt for the tuition payment, which showed the student's information as well as the payer's details, the fields of home phone number and address were identical.

At first, Sharon thought that maybe someone had gotten confused. After all, they were both named Kelly. But then it clicked.

They were roommates.

CHAPTER 61

"I need to you to meet me at Kelly Danes' house in thirty minutes."

"Davis, weren't you taking the day off?"

"What happened? We're back in New York so you stopped calling me Sharon?"

"Don't you get it? When you get on my nerves, you're Davis."

"Then you won't be calling me Sharon anytime soon . . . Meet me there?"

"Do I have a choice?"

Half an hour later, Sharon was standing outside of the house that had formerly been occupied by "Kelly Danes," and was currently surrounded by the NYPD yellow stripes. A few minutes later Rob showed up, wearing dark sunglasses and taking fierce steps.

"What the hell are we doing here?" he asked impatiently.

"That's Kelly's house."

"I know."

"Not Kelly Danes' house, Kelly Whitesporte's."

"What are you talking about?"

"They were living together."

* * *

Rob Jackie did not want to spend his first morning after an exhausting flight at a crime scene that happened to be the home of a murderess who was no longer among the living. He couldn't understand why Sharon wanted to pursue this any further; there was no one left to save.

In spite of it, he couldn't leave her alone. They'd started this whole thing together and he sure wasn't going to back off now. The question, though, was whether Sharon would ever be able to put this whole affair behind her.

As Rob had expected, they didn't find anything revealing among the various objects in the house, nothing that could uncover the story that would otherwise remain forever untold by the two deceased women. Sharon looked desperate. She had hoped that the new information would lead to the solution of the remaining enigma; but it just wasn't happening. She turned her head away and let out a long sigh.

Why can't I let it go?

"It's in your blood," Rob said, as if he could hear Sharon's thoughts. "You can't drop something if you don't feel like all the loose ends are tied. That's what makes you so damn good at your job."

Sharon cracked a smile. Maybe she wasn't so crazy after all.

"*However,*" he continued, "sometimes you need to accept the fact that some things will always remain a mystery."

"I know you're right, but do you understand why it's so hard for me to throw away something that has been a part of my life for so long? That almost cost me my *life*?" she implored him.

"Yes, I understand, *Sharon.*" Rob put his hand on her shoulder in a fatherly manner. "But don't let this story suck you in; otherwise, you might miss out on your own tale."

Sharon's thoughts wandered to Chris and the fact that she had been putting off their date because she'd felt like she had to solve this case once and for all.

"Listen, as far as I'm concerned, this case is closed," Rob determined. "Tomorrow it will be officially sealed and moved to the archives."

"But Rob—"

"No buts," he interrupted her. "As your boss, I'm telling you that there is no reason to keep wasting the NYPD's workforce on this case."

Sharon crossed her arms and looked aside. She felt betrayed.

"And as a person who deeply cares about you," he continued, "I think this case has put you through enough hell and you should get some rest. Goddammit, your stitches haven't even healed yet!"

Sharon chuckled. "Are you implying that I should take another day off?"

"A sabbatical is more like it."

"Let's settle for the rest of the week."

"I couldn't hope for more. It's a deal."

* * *

After Rob had left hastily in order to meet his wife for lunch, Sharon remained alone in the empty house. She decided to take one last look around before she left this place for good. Sharon didn't know how to explain it, but she could somehow feel the eerie presence of the souls that had ended their existence here.

When she got to the second floor she felt cold chills breathing down her neck and came to a resolution it was time to leave. But then she noticed the half open closet door in Vicky's bedroom. It had probably been left that way ever since the forensics team had scanned the house after finding Kelly Whitesporte's body in the basement.

Sharon walked over to the closet and opened the door. Dozens of suits were hanging, densely packed and in meticulous order, not leaving room for anything else. She ran her hands along them, letting her fingers glide over the fine fabrics. She opened the bottom drawer and looked through the expensive-looking lingerie, but there was nothing there. Stacks of sweaters were color coded on the top shelf, perhaps concealing something behind them, but Sharon could not reach that high without a ladder.

In a burst of despair, before she could drop the whole thing forever, Sharon slid an antique chair in front of the closet and stood on it. She moved the neatly organized sweaters aside, letting a few of them tumble to the closet floor, revealing an old cardboard box pushed up against the wall.

"Ha!" Sharon called out triumphantly, though no one else was in the room.

The box was filled with yellowing papers, and among them she found a golden necklace and some old photos. The pictures showed Kelly Whitesporte's mousy figure, only she was no longer a teenager but in her late twenties. She was wearing the same golden necklace that Sharon found in the box. Vicky stood beside her with her new and improved looks as Kelly Danes.

Perhaps this was some kind of memory box, where Vicky had kept all of her souvenirs from Kelly, Sharon presumed. A box that just might contain the answers she was so desperately looking for.

Sharon decided to take the box home with her. Now that the case was closed, it wouldn't bother anyone if she borrowed it; it was no longer protected evidence.

Sharon just hoped she wouldn't run into Rob on her way out. Breaking the rules was one thing; an angry boss was a whole different issue.

CHAPTER 62

The sun hid behind the clouds and the sky dimmed. A few drops trickled from above, heralding the upcoming rain. Sharon was glad she didn't have to leave her apartment anytime soon. Now she could focus all her attention on the dusty box that had been forsaken for so long.

While she took out the contents and arranged them on the table, she thought about her talk with Miranda Whitesporte, just moments ago. It did not make sense for a mother not to know her own child. Maybe she'd been cooperating with Vicky all along? If so, she was one hell of an actress, because Sharon had completely believed her when she had mourned the loss of her only daughter.

* * *

"Are you saying my Kelly is dead?"

"Yes, for three years now."

"No! It can't be! I used to get letters from her. She told me things, about the magazine and her job as Editor in Chief."

"I am really sorry, Mrs. Whitesporte, but it wasn't Kelly writing you those letters. It was Vicky Hermont."

"What?"

* * *

Sharon had almost finished emptying out the box and had begun organizing the scattered pages in a way that she could read them. There were a lot of papers, so she decided to pour herself a glass of white wine – just enough to get in a nostalgic mood, but not enough to cloud her judgment.

* * *

"So what made you think that 'Kelly Danes' was actually your daughter?"

"What do you mean 'what'?" Miranda asked, slightly irritated. "She told me."

"You mean, wrote you?" Sharon corrected her.

"No, she told me over the phone. Shortly after she'd moved to New York she called to let me know that she was intending to have plastic surgery and change her name, so she could have a fresh start," Miranda sighed. "And believe me when I say that I know my own daughter's voice."

Sharon's eyes widened in surprise. "That means she told you about becoming Kelly Danes . . ."

"Over a decade ago," Miranda completed the sentence for her.

"Had she come to visit you since she'd moved to New York?"

"No," Miranda answered in a grim voice. "She said she couldn't deal with coming back to this place – too many painful memories. She didn't want anything to do with reminders of her former life. Not even me." Her voice cracked. "But still, she sent photos of herself after she'd gone through the surgeries and articles that mentioned her name."

"As Kelly Danes?"

"Yes."

"And she told you she was working for Inner Beauty magazine?"

"Of course. Ever since she'd told me she was going to study journalism."

Considering the fact that Kelly had started med school only four years ago, Sharon realized that the deception had been going on for quite some time.

But why?

"Excuse me, Sharon, but I really don't want to deal with all this right now. I still can't process what you've told me about Kelly. And, frankly, I don't understand how digging into this does any good." The grieving mother put in simple words what Rob had tried to get through to her earlier that same day.

"Yes, you're right. I'm very sorry for you loss. I won't bother you again."

* * *

Sharon felt a tad guilty when she finally sat down with her glass of wine, looking at the stack of papers on the table. She knew that once she started reading those yellowing papers, she might be a step closer on her quest for the elusive truth, but in the process she would be letting down the people dearest to her heart.

She picked up one of the papers, but then the doorbell rang, preventing her from completing her act of betrayal.

Please, just don't let it be Rob. If he took one glance at the table, he would know exactly what she was up to.

"Hey, Sharon, it's Chris. Open up."

Sharon instinctively let her golden hair down, that beforehand had been pulled up in a messy ponytail, and brushed her hands over her clothes, making sure she looked alright. She tried to keep a slightly tough expression; after all, the guy had barged in without any notice. But as soon as she opened the door a silly grin popped onto her face.

As much as Sharon wanted to stop smiling, she couldn't.

"Hey, what are you doing here?" she asked. Sharon tried to look upset, but her damned facial muscles did not allow her to do so.

"Your boss called me. He told me I'd better keep you close, or you might run away . . ." Chris looked into her eyes and smiled.

Sharon could feel the blush invading her cheeks. "How did Rob get your number?"

"I was wondering the same thing. I guess being an NYPD Captain has it perks."

Sharon laughed and brushed a strand of blonde hair behind her ear.

"So . . . Are you going to invite me in?"

Sharon turned and looked behind her. The wine glass and the pile of yellowing papers were still covering her table.

"Actually–"

"Actually," Chris interrupted her, "I wasn't asking. Your boss asked me to tell you that it's an official order."

Sharon arched an eyebrow. "What do you mean *an order*?"

"You have to spend the evening with me or he'll force you take another week off."

"What? He can't do that!" Sharon began to protest but then her eyes met his. She paused for a moment and then let out a gleeful chuckle.

"Well, I have to do what the boss says."

"In that case, I'll be sure to send him a dozen roses first thing in the morning."

The guy just kept making her laugh.

"Well, I know you were supposed to take me out to do a little sightseeing in the city, but I was thinking that after everything you've been through, that I don't even presume to realize, we can just stay in and watch a movie."

He took out from the pocket of his jacket a DVD case with the title of Sharon's favorite movie of all time, *Breakfast at Tiffany's*.

"How did you know?" she asked excitedly. Sharon was thrilled. After all the horror she had been exposed to lately, she'd kind of forgotten that life also had a lovely side to it.

"A little birdie told me?" Chris tried to keep the mystery.

"Rob?"

"Yes," he admitted.

They laughed again.

"By the way, on my way over here I passed by this cute Chinese restaurant, really close by. I thought maybe we could order some takeout, if you're hungry."

Wow, I think I've found the love of my life.

"Sure, if you're in the mood for Chinese." Sharon tried to conceal her enthusiasm. It was better that he found out about her culinary obsession as late as possible.

She opened the door wide and Chris walked inside.

"Sorry for the mess."

"It's okay. You have a perfectly good excuse; you only got back home less than two days ago."

"So I won't tell you that it always looks like this."

He smiled at her. "Where's your phone? I brought the takeout menu so we can order."

Should I tell him that I already know it by heart?

"It's on the table."

Suddenly, Sharon remembered that she'd had an entirely different plan for the evening. It seemed that Chris noticed, too.

"Oh, I'm sorry. It looks like I really came at a bad time. Work stuff?"

Sharon gave the pile of papers a prolonged look.

"Nothing important," she said, and in the blink of an eye raked everything back into the box.

EPILOGUE

March 18, 2007

She felt as if her entire world were crumbling down on her. Things she had believed in wholeheartedly had turned upside down and crushed her soul.

She marched quickly in the hopes of getting home as soon as possible; maybe she could still catch her before she left.

She inserted the key into the lock with trembling hands but turned the doorknob with a firm grip. When she entered, she didn't see anyone. She was all alone, just her and her thoughts.

Kelly went up the stairs of the lavish house and entered the room of her best friend, her mortal enemy, her greatest savior, the one who had betrayed her and lied to her for years.

"Hi, honey, you're back from school early. Is everything okay?"

And there she stood, applying with grand gestures, red lipstick across her lips. Her platinum blonde hair was brushed back. Sparkling diamond earrings adorned her earlobes.

"My class was canceled," Kelly muttered.

"Well, some free time never killed anyone." Vicky smirked as she surveyed her reflection in the mirror.

"Yes . . ." Kelly felt sick to her stomach. She wanted to throw up everything that was inside of her. The tremendous rage for the wrongful act that had been done to her all those years ago; her heartache after that awful betrayal; the frustration of having been denied the truth all this time; the regret for all of the things that could have been different . . .

Gloria.

"Hey, are you sure everything is okay?" Vicky turned around and looked at Kelly, but she only stared back with a vacant expression. Kelly's skin was pale and grayish, and it looked like she could barely stand on her feet. "Maybe you should sit down, get some rest." She gestured with her hand toward the canopy bed. Then she turned her back to face the mirror and applied mascara on her eyelashes.

"Yeah . . ." Kelly stumbled over to the bed. She was exactly behind Vicky, who was absorbed with her own reflection in the mirror. She wanted to jump at her from behind and end this whole thing, here and now.

Kelly clenched her fists and took a deep breath. For the first time since that dark day, in fact for the first time in her life, she decided not to stay silent while others trampled over her.

"I know," she said quietly.

"Know what?" Vicky asked.

"I know," Kelly raised her voice.

"What do you know, honey?" Vicky turned from the mirror and faced her. Kelly's stare stung her like a whip. It was cold, hostile, and disgusted. Vicky became engulfed with a horrifying feeling.

Does she know the truth?

I'm panicking about nothing, she tried to reassure herself. No one but her really knew what had happened that day almost seventeen years ago.

"I met with Gloria McIntyre today," Kelly dropped a bomb.

Any hope that Vicky had managed to gather crashed in a split second.

"*What?*" she gasped. "How? You've kept in touch with her?" Vicky didn't even try to conceal her anxiety.

"No. We just happened to run into each other today."

"Oh . . ." Vicky mumbled. "Well, isn't that nice," she tried to crack a smile.

"I *know*."

"What are you talking about?" Vicky decided not to show her hand before she absolutely had to. Perhaps this was all a big misunderstanding.

"I want to hear you say it." Kelly rose from the bed and approached her. "I want to hear you say that it was *you* who wrecked my life. That it was you who made *them* come after me." Even after all this time, Kelly still couldn't bring their names to her lips. Tears flooded her eyes. "That it was you who wanted to hurt me so badly. That it's you who has lied to me for all these years without even batting an eyelash!" She picked up the mascara tube Vicky used beforehand and chucked it at the floor.

Vicky looked at her in stunned silence. Her lips quivered, but no voice emerged from them.

"How could you do this to me?" Kelly asked in a broken voice.

"I'm sorry. I'm *so* sorry."

"I don't think that two lousy apologies really compensate for an eternity of betrayal," she hissed at her. Kelly almost didn't recognize herself. She had never spoken like that to anyone, let alone her best friend.

"Don't you know how much I love you?" Vicky sobbed. "You mean the world to me! Haven't I proven that in all our years of friendship?" she demanded. "I changed my name to feel closer to you. I was the one who suggested that we tell your parents that *'Kelly Danes'* is actually you, so they wouldn't be worried, and in the process of doing that I had to give up the relationship with my own parents," she reminded her. "I haven't spoken to them since I left to find you in New York. They probably think I ended up in some drug den." Her face contorted with disgust. "They will never learn about my accomplishments." She narrowed her eyes at Kelly. "They will never be proud of *me*."

"I didn't ask for all that! You were the one who wanted to get a fresh start. You were the one who wanted to run away from your family, your town, and everything you had ever known. So don't you dare blame me," Kelly slammed at her.

"I gave up my identity, everything I was, *for you*. Everything I've done has been for you," Vicky insisted.

"Even what happened at the house of mirrors was *for me*?"

Vicky looked at Kelly through a curtain of tears; the image in front of her became blurry.

For the first time in a long time, she was lost for words.

"If you hated me that much, why did you look me up in New York?" Kelly continued. "Why did you offer to let me stay with you? Why did you help me get back on my feet?" Tears were gliding down her cheeks. "Why did you pay for med school? Why didn't you just let me die in some godforsaken alley and put an end to the agony

I've felt every single day, all because of what you did to me?" At this point Kelly was screaming at Vicky, though she was only a few inches away from her.

"Because I love you, Kelly, with all my heart. Can't you see that I'd do anything for you?"

Kelly shook her head vigorously. "Maybe because you're so full of guilt. If you truly loved me, you wouldn't have done this to me." She gave her an empty look and left the room.

"Kelly, wait. Don't do this." Vicky followed her.

"I never want to see you again!" Kelly picked up her pace and headed to the staircase.

"No, don't go." Vicky grabbed her arm, preventing her from going down the stairs.

"Don't touch me!" Kelly tried to shake her off, but her mousy body structure had never been useful in physical conflicts.

"Enough! Don't let something that happened seventeen years ago ruin what we have now!" Vicky implored.

"What we *have*?" Kelly looked at her in astonishment. "What we have is a pack of lies. Total deception."

Vicky felt as if a knife had stabbed her right in the heart.

"What if I hadn't happened to meet Gloria today?" Kelly continued. "Would you have ever bothered to tell me the truth?"

That name caused currents of the strongest hatred Vicky had ever felt to pass through her body. The bitch had ruined her life. After all these years, she had finally done it. Gloria had gotten what she'd wanted all along; she had taken Kelly away from her.

"Don't say that name," she commanded.

"What name?" Kelly got confused for a split second. "Gloria? You want to tell me that this was all about *her*?"

"I was about to lose you!" Vicky cried. "She tried to snatch you away from me. I saw the way you looked at her."

"Wait, you did this to me because you were *jealous*?"

"Girls like her get what they want, when they want it; and when they're bored with it, they simply throw it away like yesterday's newspaper." Loathing dripped from Vicky's voice.

"I don't know about girls like her, but *she* is the loveliest person I've ever met," Kelly declared defiantly and sent her an icy glare.

Vicky could feel the exact same sparks of jealousy and rage that had surfaced on that dreadful day all of those years ago once again surging within her.

"Take it back," she strengthened her grip around Kelly's arm.

"Let go! You're hurting me!" Kelly tried to release from her clutch. "No matter what you do, I won't say anything bad about Gloria. One thing is for sure, though; she was a better friend than *you*."

"Take it back! Tell the truth! What has she done to you? You're not Kelly!" Vicky shook Kelly as if she were trying to exorcise a demon from her body.

"Let me go, you maniac! Let me run far away and never come back!" she cried.

"No!" Vicky exclaimed.

The two were fighting an ancient battle: one was trying to escape, while the other one was not ready to set her free.

"**Let – me – go!!!**" Kelly roared, and with a sudden twist, with a force that she didn't know she possessed, she managed to shake off Vicky's grip.

But in doing so, Kelly lost her balance and tripped, falling down the stairs, tumbling like an old rag dull.

"**No. No. Nooo. Nooooo!!!**" Vicky screamed.

It took Kelly a few seconds to hit the ground, producing the most horrendous smashing sound against the hardwood floor. A puddle of blood encircled her head like a halo, staining the polished floor.

Vicky ran down the stairs, almost tripping herself, and leaned over her body.

"Kelly? Can you hear me? Please, say something. Please?"

Kelly didn't answer. The vermillion circle surrounding her head gradually grew.

All of a sudden, Vicky noticed she was dripping with the blood of her beloved friend. *The purest blood there could ever be.* She gazed down at her bloody hands and smeared them across her face.

"You're not dead, Kelly. *You are not dead.*"

The blood was still warm. She stared at the lifeless corpse and realized that this was it.

Kelly Whitesporte was gone.

But Kelly Danes was still here.

ACKNOWLEDGEMENTS

I would like to thank three special people, who with outstanding amounts of patience, acted as my trusty advisors. To Lyndsey Senet, Sonny Cohen and Leron Cohen, I will be forever grateful.

I would also like to thank the rest of the Cohen clan, Uncle Moshe, Laurie and Edan, my dear family residing in New York City. Your warm hospitality allowed my frequent visits to The Big Apple. This amazing city has become an inseparable part of me and of this book.

A special thank you goes to my dear friend, Nir Vidas, who believed in my vision for the cover and helped me design it to perfection. You are exceptional in taking mere ideas and turning them into reality.

Jacky Lowell, I was incredibly lucky to have you as my editor. Thank you from the bottom of my heart. Carol Kay, thank you so much for your outstanding precision and delicate touch in proofing this Novel.

Last, but not least, is my mother, Galia Cohen. I am dedicating this book to you. Without your insightful remarks and never-ending support, my book would have ended up as just another Word file on my laptop. Thank you for helping me pursue my dream. You are the best mother a daughter could ask for.

WHEN THE

ILLUSION

GETS

DARKER

. . .

Made in the USA
Middletown, DE
02 November 2015